CACHE A PREDATOR

A Geocaching Mystery

M. Weidenbenner

Cache a Predator, a Geocaching Mystery

Copyright 2013 by M. Weidenbenner

Cover design by Cathy Helms, http://www.avalongraphics.org

Photographers for the cover are: Elena Elisseeva (Dark Forest) and Miroslava Lipa (Girl Crying) and Scott M. Liddell from Morguefile.com (Girl on the Bridge), www.scottliddell.net.

Published by Random Publishing, LLC
Printed in the United States of America

ISBN: 978-1-9894049-7-6

Acknowledgements

This book wouldn't have been possible without the support of my number one fan, my dad. He bounced edits back and forth about the plot, cheered me on, listened to my frustrations, and brainstormed titles.

Mom, on the other hand, gave me the imagination gene. Without that I wouldn't be the dreamer, creator, and emotionally caring person I am today. Mom taught me that anything is possible in America if you want it badly enough.

A huge thanks to Susanne Lakin, my developmental editor and encourager. Even when she critiqued the bare bones of this manuscript she saw the possibilities, knew how to draw the critical elements out, and pushed me to write the best story I could.

Thank you to my beta readers: Paul, Steve, and Tom St.Germain, Brenda Mangan, Benji Ganz, Jim Seibold, Marty Baker, Mary Clemens, Tracy Helms, and my blog partner, Robin McClure.

Thank you to Paul St.Germain, my brother, for being the best word-of-mouth marketer a writer could have. Without his enthusiasm for this project the doubt devil sitting on my shoulder would have talked me out of publishing this beast.

Thank you Tom St.Germain, my youngest brother, for giving me the best compliment a reader could give—that the story brought tears to his eyes. When a writer can move a reader to tears, we celebrate.

To Steve St.Germain, my other brother, (I have five) thank you for your edits and confidence in keeping the story as-is.

Thank you to Dan St.Germain, my first subscriber to my blog, RANDOM WRITING RANTS, for your support in seeing the big picture of what an author must do in this ever-changing industry.

Thank you to Mark St.Germain, my oldest brother, for believing in me.

Thanks also to the following team: Sergeant Chad Hill of the Kosciusko County Sheriff's office for discussing crime scenes with me; John Sadler, Kosciusko Deputy Coroner, for describing a #22 scalpel, rosette key, an H-loader, a mausoleum, and what happens to an embalmed body; Michael Trobec, MD, who taught me about tourniquets, chloroform, and Ketamine, and how to slice a body part; Araceli Grant for giving me the insight to our CPS, Dr. Denise Fraser-Vaselakos, Illinois licensed clinical psychologist and writer, who helped me understand the foster care system.

For my writer's group: Robin McClure, Monica Caples, Karrah Creamer, and Tanya Satoski. Thank you for sharing your talent and your enthusiasm over this project, for brainstorming, critiquing, editing, and creating never-ending pseudo-names. You give me an outlet for my craziness, a place where I feel free to be me, where I can imagine colorful stories and heroic characters.

Thank you to my children and grandchildren who refrain from rolling their eyes when I talk about my stories.

Finally, thank you to my number one encourager—my husband and best friend, for reminding me, "It's only fiction, Michelle," when I cry for my characters.

"Child abuse casts a shadow the length of a lifetime." Herbert Ward

Chapter One

Death was like a low-pressure system. It could occur in any season, causing storms in people so great it changed them. I saw it happen to Father when Mom died years ago.

It happened to me several weeks ago. Death caused a tornado that swirled in my head, making me braver than I'd ever been. It scared me because I had to leave my house to do something, in the dark. I didn't want to, but I needed to prove that I was not a coward or a freak.

I clamped my teeth together and stomped my foot. I would not be called a sissy anymore. I'd show everyone. People would finally like me. And maybe they would thank me.

I dressed for the first job in black pants, a hoodie, and latex gloves, then paced in my doorway. Did I forget anything? No. I tapped my backpack and closed my eyes, picturing my supplies. The scalpel, syringes, needles, rubber bands, and baggies were in place. I counted, one, two, three, four. Yep, they were all there, each in their spot. I glanced across the room. Yes, I'd put the surgical books back on the shelf in alphabetical order.

The video played in my head, over and over again. Slice, mutilate.

Go, just go!

My heart beat fast like the train rolling on the tracks in the distance. It was just before midnight. I climbed into my truck and headed for Sheridan Street across town, past the sign "Welcome to Hursey Lake, Indiana." After parking, I entered the graveyard exactly where I'd planned. Streetlights threw shadows onto the tombstones.

Hurry and get it done. Then you can play hide-the-cache.

My heart jumped like a ball in a gaming machine. It was the storm.

I kept my head down and hitched over the short iron fence, summer's humidity following me in rivulets of perspiration down my back. The sky's moon hid behind thick clouds, making it dark, but I'd memorized the map.

My feet shuffled in rhythm on the pavement, past the markers for Sarah Jane Miller, Jerome Streeter, Mabel Hudson, and so many others. I counted their stones as I passed them. There were 989 dead people present.

A dim light illuminated the mausoleum at the east end of the park, guiding me, like a spotlight on a stage. I moved toward the light.

Large tombstone shadows hovered over the smaller ones. Some stones were made of marble, but others were smaller, chipped, and decorated with flowers that had faded from the sun. The way they were lined in rows, with husbands and wives side by side and children lying near their parents, made it look like a village, like shadows of square people hiding and watching without emotion. Like me.

They were my audience. They wouldn't make me look them in the eye.

Overgrown red petunias crept over the edges of the sidewalk, and the smell of cut grass lingered in the air.

The windowed door to the mausoleum was locked. I dropped my shoulder and slid the bag off my back. After unzipping it, I reached in for the picklock. It dangled from its circular key chain, clinking as the metal brushed against the other keys. I picked at the lock. The first one was too big. My breathing quickened, and I could feel the blood pumping in my neck. I tried the next. And the next. Finally, the fourth one fit. *Open, open.* I twisted and turned the lock.

Score. Dr. Spear had taught me that word.

I slipped inside. My adrenaline raced. The body was so close. After closing the door, I clicked on my headband flashlight. Shadows danced across the tile floor and the granite-faced crypts as I moved my head from side to side.

I paused, rocking back and forth, remembering that night. I was eight and hiding in the toolshed. It had been dark, and the dirt floor smelled like cat pee. He was after me. My legs ached from being cramped for so long. He waved a flashlight back and forth across the floor behind old boards and tools. The light stopped on my foot. "I see you! Get the hell out of there, or I'm coming in after you, you chicken shit."

Stop rocking! Take deep breaths like Doc Spear showed you. Concentrate on the job. That was another time. You're in control now.

Yes, I was in control.

The room was clean and smelled of floor wax. Square-faced crypts lined two walls. The one in the center, two drawers from the top, was the one I needed. It was him.

After setting the backpack on the floor, I hurried to the closet at the far end of the room and wheeled out the hydraulic lift. Its wheels squeaked and rattled across the floor like they had when they'd put him in.

Kneeling in front of the crypt, I dug through my backpack until I found the rolled towel. Inside was the rosette key, the #22 retractable scalpel, a plastic bag for the body part, and the casket key. I reached for the rosette key first and poked the tool into the holes of the granite face until they clicked. One by one, I unlocked all four bolts and placed the supplies on the towel in front of the crypt.

Gripping the edges of the granite, I pulled the heavy stone out, sweat beads creeping down my temples. After maneuvering the block onto the towel, I slid it across the floor and out of the way.

As I positioned the lift, I rehearsed my steps: slice and save. No need to tourniquet this one, no vascular pressure. The movie played in my head over and over again. Fast forward, Rewind. Slice and save.

This would be better than when I put dog poo in his dinner, and spat in his coffee thermos. Taking a hold of the casket's end, I rolled the wooden coffin toward me, out of the chute, and onto the lift. As it rolled toward me, my heartbeat drummed louder in my ears. The box slid over the scattered BBs rolling in the bottom of the drawer, clattering.

A car's horn honked far in the distance. I glanced out into the cemetery, skimming the grounds. The dead slept. The voice in my head shouted.

Do it!

Moving back to the towel, I gathered the casket key, the scalpel, and the bag and faced the front of the coffin, placing the tools at my feet. I was ready to open the lid. I paused. What would he look like?

What did it matter? What was I waiting for?

One square hole was positioned at each end. I reached for the casket crank and inserted it into the left hole and turned, then the right.

Hopefully his eyes would be closed. If they were open I'd stare at his forehead—like I had before.

I lifted the top half first. The lid squeaked. My heart thumped tight. Holding my breath, I took one quick look, and dropped the lid.

Thud!

My stomach lurched. A white furry mold had grown over his graying skin. He was uglier than before. He wore a dark suit with a white shirt and a red striped tie. His hands rested on his middle, holding a rosary. What a joke.

Too bad he couldn't watch me now.

Don't look at his face.

My eyelid twitched as I lifted the lid again and set the corner hinge to a locked position. Then I lifted the bottom half of the casket, avoiding his eyes, and set the lock there too.

When I unfastened the belt around his trousers, the belt buckle clinked and my fingers trembled. Clumsily, I undid the button at the top. Stooping over him, I yanked his pants down to his thighs, exposing his nakedness. I bounced on my toes and laughed. Loud. My heart thumped in my ears, keeping rhythm. He was shriveled. I clapped and laughed again, the deep sound muffling off the room's walls.

I reached for the scalpel and the bag and deployed the blade, lifted his dick, and sliced with one quick movement. *Aaaargh.*

In one fluid motion it was gone and in my gloved hand. My head spun like when I twirled in circles. I felt light, almost numb.

All he had left was a stub.

I giggled like a child and held the flesh up for the tombstone people to see. "Look!"

With a smile, I placed it in the bag and pinched my fingers along the top, sealing it shut.

After retracting the blade, I set it on the towel, opened the backpack, and took out the sealed container. I placed the plastic bag inside, secured the lid, and placed it in the backpack.

Laughing, I moved back to the body, pulled up his pants, buttoned the top, and fastened his belt. The laugh started low in my belly and escalated into a high-pitched wail as memories of him touching me, damaging me, came flooding back. Years of pent up anger boiled inside me. He'd dragged me out of the toolshed and into the house. I'd kicked and curled into a ball, but still he came at me.

Now, grunting, I balled my hands into fists and beat his chest.

Thud.

Again.

Thud. Again and again until my fists burned. I inhaled and exhaled deeply, then released the hinges of the casket and dropped each lid with a bang, suddenly in a hurry.

Who's the big man now?

After locking the coffin, I rolled it back into place, slid the granite face across the floor and lifted it to the opening. The anger gave me strength.

The casket clanked and clattered back into place. I scooped the rosette key from the towel and refastened the hardware. An opera sang in my head, the singers' voices getting louder and louder, keeping rhythm with my heartbeat.

Gathering my supplies, I put everything back into their place in the backpack, wheeled the lift back into the closet, took out the antibacterial wipes in my bag, and wiped down the floor. I flung the pack over my shoulder and onto my back, then glanced around the room. No mess.

Once outside, I shone the flashlight on the lock and left it the same way I found it.

When that was complete, I flipped my flashlight off and began my trek to the cache site, counting the rows and stones. The drums of the concert played their final beats, and my mind went quiet. I glanced at my watch. I was on time.

There was much to do. I needed to keep to my schedule. I shuffled out of the cemetery, mumbling in rhythm. Find. The. Cache. Box. Bury. The. Stub. Find the cache box. Bury the stub. Find the cache box. Bury the stub.

#

The night's darkness surrounded Jake as he stumbled up the porch stairs of his rented bungalow on Ditch Road in Hursey Lake. He mumbled under his breath. "Damn broken boards. Shit-ass landlord doesn't fix a pissant thing."

He reached out in front of him, waving his hand in the air, searching for the door handle. "Should have left the blasted light on." His fingernail clinked on the metal knob. He turned it, murmuring under his breath, "At least I left the sucker unlocked."

He pushed the door open, practically falling into the living room. After he flipped on the lights, he headed to the bathroom, relieved himself, then crossed the hall to his bedroom—a small room with one window. Beer bottles cluttered the dresser. Dirty clothes lay in heaps, scattered on the floor. Photos of naked girls flashed on his computer screen saver.

He chuckled. "Too drunk to get it up now."

The room spun as he sat on the edge of the bed and bent to pull off his jeans. His foot caught in the pant leg. He kicked it and fell backward onto the pillow, laughing. Trying to focus, he pulled the other leg out and threw his jeans onto the floor. He closed his eyes, welcoming sleep's abandon. It didn't take long.

Sometime later, he stirred at a sound in the room, but his eyes, too heavy to open, remained shut. He didn't care about the sound. It was probably his imagination. He allowed himself to drift again until something soft and damp fell onto his face, covering his eyes, nose, and mouth.

His eyes flew open. Who was there? But he couldn't see the intruder. Gasping, he tried to sit, clawing at the hands of the attacker, struggling to rip the fabric from his face. But hands stronger than his held it in place. Sucking air, he breathed in the only thing he could— the cloth's sweet sickly scent. Desperate for fresh air but finding none, he succumbed to unconsciousness.

When Jake finally woke, the light of a new day had trickled into his room, spilling its brightness across his face. But he didn't notice. The searing, burning pain in his groin demanded all his attention. His hands groped between his legs. What the hell? Sticky blood covered his fingertips. Moaning, he turned his head and vomited on the pillow.

He tried to sit, blinking the blurriness out of his eyes. The room spun. He looked down.

His pecker was gone.

In its place was a short fleshy stub, the end clamped shut with knotted rubber strip. Blood had pooled around him, soaking the bedspread.

The walls of the room echoed with his screams before he passed out.

Chapter Two

No morning felt the same without Quinn tickling his ear, the breath of her tiny voice saying, "Wake up, Daddy."

Brett stared at the ceiling. A leaky faucet dripped, gnawing at his nerves. He needed to get up and get going, but without his daughter, he dawdled. It was like the air didn't move. The empty apartment reminded him of how alone he was and how unfair the courts had been.

What kind of screwed-up justice system did he work for anyway? He knew the answer: a system that sided with mothers—even addict mothers.

He needed to let it go, but worry had a mind of its own. His fists clenched. Quinn wasn't safe with Ali, but the judge only saw a hot-tempered man, not a drug-addicted mother. Of course he was ticked—what father wouldn't be at a mother who neglected her child?

He dragged his body out of bed and into the shower, trying to scrub his negative thoughts away and wash them down the drain. After he towel-dried, he dressed in his uniform, stepped into his navy-colored pants, and tightened the belt around his waist to the next notch. Anxiety as a diet had a way of loosening a man's pants. *Guess I should have eaten the last piece of pizza last night.* He buttoned his shirt, strapped on his belt holster, removed the gun from the locked drawer, and slid the firearm in place.

His phone rang, playing "Twinkle, Twinkle, Little Star." Quinn's ring, the one he'd programmed to play whenever she called because she was his twinkling star.

He lunged for his cell on his bed and held it to his ear. "Quinn?"

"Daddy?" Her voice quivered. "I'm scared. Mommy won't wake up."

His heart raced as he willed his voice to stay calm. "Are you home?"

"Yes."

"Go lock the front door." He slid into his socks, crossing the room in one sweep, fear squeezing his heart. At the closet, he slipped into his shoes, fumbling with the phone as he bent to tie the laces. Could he get to her in time or should he call 911?

"Okay."

He could hear her breathing like she was moving to the door. In three steps, he dashed across the room to the kitchen and clutched his jacket hanging over the chair. He juggled the phone again as he shoved his arms into the sleeves, first one, then the other. "Sit next to Mommy, and I'll be there soon. I'm going to my car now. I'm coming. Everything is going to be okay."

But it wouldn't. This had happened before, and it would happen again.

Once upon a time he would have called Child Protective Services, but not now. He couldn't wait. They were overworked. It could take them up to seventy-two hours to investigate, and he didn't trust anyone but himself. No one cared about Quinn the way he did.

He grabbed his keys off the counter and headed out his front door, still holding the phone to his ear. "Is Max with you?"

"He's sniffing the garbage. I think he's hungry."

Blast it, Ali. She'd probably forgotten to feed him.

Brett climbed in his cruiser and reached for his sunglasses tucked in the visor. He talked to Quinn as he started the car. "You did good, calling me. I'm sure Mommy will get up soon, but I'll come and fix you breakfast. Do you have eggs and milk in the fridge?"

He envisioned her feet pattering on the tile and thought he

heard the refrigerator squeaking open. "Uh-huh."

That's a shock. But that was Ali—seemingly together in one way, but not in another.

Brett clicked on his flashers, ignoring the speed limit signs as he sped down Wooster Road. Ali's house was on the other side of the highway, but close. Moments like that made him thankful Hursey Lake was a small town.

"I'll be there soon. Don't open the door for anyone except me, okay?" He turned the steering wheel with one hand and held the phone to his ear with the other.

"Okay, Daddy."

Drivers pulled into the right lane and slowed when they saw him coming. After a few turns and red lights, he shut off his flashers and swung the car into the driveway next to Ali's red beater and slammed the car into Park.

On his way to the front door, he scowled as he stomped over cigarette butts littering the concrete, the filters crunching beneath his feet. The lawn needed mowing, and the shrubs had grown spindly and wild. When he'd lived there he'd never let the house get that run-down. The screen door stood ajar, the bottom bent at an angle, not allowing it to close properly. It squeaked in a faint breeze. The landlord had never been good about fixing things.

As he fumbled for the right key, he sucked in a deep breath. *Keep your temper.* He wasn't supposed to be here, but keeping Quinn safe was worth violating the protective order. Besides, Ali had lied. He'd never hit her. Her brother was the one who'd pushed her to lie. And the judge had believed her—not Brett.

Max barked on the other side of the door. "Quinn, it's Daddy." He turned the key and pushed open the door. At least Ali hadn't changed the locks.

Quinn stood before him in bare feet, wearing a pink T-shirt and purple shorts, holding her stuffed lamb she called Lambie under her arm. Her dark curls hung over her dirty face, tear streaks leaving a line of clean skin. Snot dripped from her nose.

He knelt in front of her, scooped her into his arms, and held her to his chest, breathing in her sweet smell, not wanting to let her go. He kissed her cheeks. "Shhh, I'm here now."

Quinn hiccupped like she'd been crying hard. Her arms closed around his neck, almost choking him.

Brett's throat grew tight, and he squeezed his eyes shut, fighting the rage bubbling inside him. How could Ali ignore her child?

Max's tail thumped against the wall. Brett rested Quinn on one leg and nestled the dog's face in his arms, rubbing his ears. Max whined in rhythm to his wagging tail.

"Where's Mommy?"

"She's on the couch." Quinn pointed to their right. Garbage-filled bags sat on the floor along the wall outside the kitchen, smelling like Max had crapped nearby.

Brett dodged the trash and stomped into the living room. Ali lay on the sofa on top of a pile of clothes, her dyed blond hair covering her face. He crossed the room to her, gritting his teeth. "Ali, wake up."

She didn't flinch. His heartbeat raced, suddenly panicked. Was she unconscious? No, this had happened before. But still, was this the one time she wouldn't wake?

Her chest rose and fell. He exhaled, relieved. At least she was breathing. He shook her shoulders and spoke louder. "Ali, wake up."

Her eyes fluttered open and she stared at him, seeming unable to focus. "What are you doing here?" she slurred.

The smell of liquor oozed from her pores. *This was an apt mother?* He wanted to punch the wall at the injustice of the court system. *Easy.* "Quinn called and said she couldn't wake you."

Ali pushed herself to a sitting position, her head bobbing. "I'm awake." But her eyes closed again.

"Maybe I should take Quinn to day care on my way to work."

Ali snorted. "Oh, now you're trying to do me favors?"

No, I'm trying to keep Quinn safe.

Ali folded her arms across her chest, but a few seconds later they fell limp to her sides, her eyes still closed. "She can't go there anymore."

Brett's heart sank. "Why not?"

She waved her hand. "Some stupid rule about being late to pick her up."

Ali loved to blame others. Nothing was ever her fault. But he didn't say that now, not in front of Quinn. He turned to his daughter. "Go wash your hands and face before I make you breakfast."

Quinn nodded, turning toward the bathroom.

Brett lowered his voice and spoke to Ali. "What are you going to do with Quinn when you go to work?"

She shrugged.

"You lost your job again, didn't you?" His fury spiked.

He waited for her to answer, hoping he could stay calm. When she leaned her head against the sofa, he knew. She wasn't going to answer him. She'd lost her job.

He used to pity her, but not anymore. Now, all he wanted was to get custody of Quinn. Maybe now the courts would rule in his favor, and he could prove Ali inept. She had no job and was under the influence of who knew what.

Quinn moved to his side, smelling like mint from the toothpaste. "Daddy, can I go with you today?" She placed her hand on his arm.

"I have to go to work, sweetie." He reached for a tissue on the end table, wiped her nose and her bottom lip where she'd missed a dab of toothpaste. Then he lifted her in his arms, spun her around, and sat in the recliner across from the sofa. She giggled as she tumbled into his lap.

"I have to get the bad guys, remember? But I'll come back for lunch." He wrapped his arms around her. "You hungry?"

She nodded.

"I'll make you breakfast." He lifted her, then placed her on the floor in front of the TV and turned the channel to *iCarly*. "I'll be right back." Before he left the room, she hugged Lambie and watched TV, seeming consoled.

He glanced over his shoulder at Ali on the sofa. She wasn't moving. Of course. She'd slid down, flat on her back, her mouth gaping open, snoring. How was he going to sober her up?

Entering the kitchen, he stared at the dirty dishes, cigarette butts, and beer cans covering the counter and the sink top. *What a mess!* The only time the kitchen had been clean when they'd been together was when he'd cleaned it. Dirt was invisible to Ali.

He clenched his jaw, took a few eggs out of the fridge, and whisked them, beating them until they frothed over the sides of the bowl like the blood foaming in his veins. Oh, how he hated leaving Quinn in Ali's care.

He checked his watch as he added the pancake batter. Fifteen minutes—that's all he had.

He made one large pancake and two smaller ones. Opening

cupboards, he searched for condiments and found a bag of mini chocolate chips balled in a corner. After pulling a few morsels out of the bag, he arranged them as eyes, a nose, and a mouth on the cakes.

The only cup he could find was a dirty one in the sink. He rinsed it, poured Quinn's juice into it, and carried her breakfast into the living room. "Here you go, baby."

"I'm not a baby."

"You're right. I forgot you're five now, so grown-up." He kissed her cheek.

She glanced at the plate of pancakes and threw her arms around his neck, practically knocking over her juice. "You made Mickey." She smiled, plucked the mouse's chocolate eyes off the cake, and dropped them in her mouth.

Her brow furrowed and she pouted. "Don't go, Daddy." She clutched his hand.

"I have to. I wish I didn't." Guilt slammed him in the gut, but what could he do? He'd told the judge about Ali's behavior. It hadn't mattered. She'd passed the drug tests.

Quinn glanced at Ali. "I'm scared."

"Max is here, and Mommy is staying home with you today. I'm going to make her coffee so she wakes up."

When the golden retriever heard his name, his ears perked and his head cocked to one side. The dog ambled over to Quinn and shoved his nose into her hand.

Thank goodness Quinn had Max. It wasn't enough, but for now it would have to do. It was going to take time, but Brett was confident Ali would mess up and give him the evidence he needed to win custody.

Quinn giggled at Max and petted his ear. The dog licked her face and sniffed her pancakes.

She moved her plate away from him. "Okay, I'll give you some, but you have to wait a minute."

Brett stood, sweeping the dog hair off his pants. "Come on, Max. I'll feed you, boy."

Max padded after Brett into the kitchen. Brett found the bag of dog food, nearly gone, stashed on the floor of the pantry. He fed Max, filled his water bowl, and made a pot of coffee. When he returned to Ali, she was still sleeping. He clapped his hands together and the sound jolted Ali's eyes open. "Wake up. I have to go to work. You've gotta get yourself together."

She stared at him and took a deep breath. "Just go."

"I'm coming back for lunch. I made a pot of coffee. Drink it."

Her eyes crossed and she nodded.

Quinn rushed to his side, holding a pancake. "How many minutes will it take before you come back?" She broke off a piece of the cake and handed it to Max, who chomped the morsel in one bite.

"Lots of minutes, but only four hours. You can watch your shows, and before you know it I'll be back."

Should he ask Mr. Ray, the next-door neighbor, to check on her? No, that could backfire, especially if Mr. Ray reported Brett had been there, violating the protective order. It would be better to call every hour and come back for lunch.

Quinn pouted, and tears welled in her eyes. Her lower lip trembled. "Will you check under my bed first?" She put her thumb in her mouth.

"Let's go. I'll scare the monsters away." He growled like a bear, remembering when his father had done the same thing for him. Except, instead of chasing monsters, his dad had chased away dinosaurs.

Quinn giggled and put her sticky fingers in his hand, leading him to her bedroom.

When he saw how she'd made her bed—something he'd taught her to do—a lump formed in his throat. "Nice job." A part of her comforter draped onto the floor, but he pretended not to notice.

He fell to his knees and said, "Hop on."

Quinn giggled and climbed on his back.

"Hold tight. Here we go." He galloped toward the bed, pretending he was a horse, and peered beneath the comforter. "Nothing there." He moved to the closet on the other side of the room, neighing and bucking. Quinn giggled louder. He stopped in front of the closet and deepened his voice. "All monsters, begone!"

Quinn slid off Brett's back and pushed the clothes to one side, tipping her head left and right. "They're all gone. You did it." She hopped on his back, and he galloped out to the living room.

Ali had opened her eyes.

Brett trotted next to her. "You up for the day?" If he didn't go now he'd be docked pay, and he couldn't lose his job if he had any hope of getting custody. He'd already missed more than he should have during the divorce.

Ali nodded. "I'm good. Go."

Brett lingered. "You're not going to start drinking again, are you?"

"Don't worry about what I do or don't do."

"I have to worry. Quinn's here. Don't fall back to sleep." He stood.

Ali reached for a cigarette and lit it.

He wanted to squash the package in his fist. How many times had he asked her not to smoke in front of Quinn?

Quinn latched onto Brett's leg as he walked stiff-legged toward the door. He peeled her off and lifted her into his arms. Smoothing back her mop of curls that had fallen on her face, and staring into her deep blue eyes, he smiled. "I'll be back. You be a good girl for Mommy, okay?"

She nodded, pouting. "I love you, Daddy."

He took a deep breath. "I love you more."

Swallowing the guilt, he told himself he'd done everything he could. Quinn was safe. For now.

After he shut the door and heard Quinn turn the dead bolt, he headed to his cruiser and felt his cell phone vibrate. He unclipped it from its buckle. The screen displayed his parents' number. "Hi, Mom." He opened the car door.

Silence.

Brett paused, then spoke again. "Mom?" He scooted into his car.

"Son?" It was his father.

Brett froze. His fingers trembled at his mixture of emotions. His blood pressure rose, but so did his hopes. "Yeah?" He shut the door.

"How are you?"

"You don't call me for six years and then ask me how I'm doing? What do you really want, Dad?" He shouldn't sound so harsh, but he didn't trust his father's intentions.

The old man didn't answer right away. "I was wondering, uh, since your divorce is final now, uh, if you'd given any thought to going back, of going back . . . to school."

"You don't quit, do you? The real reason you're calling is to rub my divorce in my face, isn't it? You win—you were right. I was wrong. I never should have married Ali. Is that what you want me to say?"

"No, that's—"

"No, I don't want to go back to school, and I don't want to talk to you." He hit the End key on his phone and flung it onto the passenger seat, instantly regretting his words. Tears threatened to sting his eyes. He shouldn't have dissed his old man. *Damn!* But he didn't trust his heart. His father had loved him unconditionally once, a long time ago. If he let him back in his life now, would his father abandon him again?

Where were you four months ago when I needed you, when the judge gave my child to her druggy mother?

Brett cranked the ignition key, threw the car into Reverse, and backed out of the driveway, his tires squealing. Getting to work on time was more important than his father's *conditional* love.

He tried not to care, but he did. Rivulets of perspiration dripped down his back. He pounded his fist on the dashboard, ashamed of his outburst.

Chapter Three

Grady climbed the steep trail that bisected the woods of Hursey Lake, holding his iPhone and occasionally glancing at the GPS coordinates outlining their path. Luke, another boy scout from his troop, lagged behind, panting from the exertion. The early summer air was filled with sounds of birds chirping, bees buzzing, and squirrels chattering. A nearby stream gurgled, the short waves splashing over little rocks. Low tree branches brushed against Grady, scraping his legs.

This was Grady's seventy-sixth geocaching hunt, but Luke's first.

Luke said, "What are we looking for?"

"A container of some sort. A box, or a tin—something the size of a gallon or two, big enough to hold stuff."

"Like what?"

"Random junk, like a whistle." Grady led the way, glancing again at the iPhone, a little perturbed that he'd agreed to let Luke tag along. Grady had felt sorry for the guy. The kid was large and clumsy, and none of the other scouts had wanted to show him the ins and outs of geocaching so he could earn his medal. Being a sucker for the underdog, Grady told Luke he could go with him.

"What's the big freakin' deal about a whistle?"

"It's not about what's inside the box. It's about finding it." Some geocachers collected what they found and replaced items with others, but not Grady. He was only about the thrill of the find.

"If you say so."

Grady glanced at the navigation map on the phone again. "It says we've arrived at our destination." His heart pounded a little faster. They were close. He could feel it.

Luke's eyes darted around. "I don't see nothing."

"It ain't gonna jump out and bite 'cha. We have to look for it—like under a bush or a rock. It'll be hidden." He pointed to the left. "How 'bout if I go this way, and you go that way?" He pointed in the other direction.

Luke shrugged and went to his right, practically tripping over a tree stump. A line of ants marched around a tree.

Grady shook his head and started in the other direction. "Look up in the trees too. The clues said something about Jack and the Beanstalk." Grady veered left and glanced up a large pine tree. He breathed in its deep musky scent. Nothing there. After turning in the other direction, he pushed up his glasses, which had slid down the bridge of his nose, and walked a few feet to the right.

Sunlight peeked through the branches of a large maple tree. Sweat dripped down Grady's neck. He shaded his eyes with his hand and squinted, noticing something about eight feet up. Was there a log lodged between two branches?

He examined the tree bark at eye level, noticing scraped pieces—like someone had recently climbed the tree. The lowest branch was reachable if he jumped and swung himself around. He dropped one shoulder out of his backpack, then the other, then set it on the ground. "Luke, I think I see something."

Tree and bush branches rustled as Luke approached. "Where?"

Grady gripped the lowest branch of the maple tree and swung his legs up. He hung upside down for a few seconds, huffing, before he righted himself and his glasses, straddling the tree branch. He nodded up the tree. "See it between the second and third branch?"

Luke shaded his eyes with his hands and looked. "Yeah. It looks like a log."

"It might be a plastic one." Grady scrambled up the next branch. Flies buzzed, swarming around his head.

Luke waited at the base of the tree. "Throw it down here. I'll check it out."

Grady huffed breathlessly, standing on the second branch on his tiptoes, hugging the tree. He reached for the next branch and missed. Too short. A fly landed on his bottom lip. He spit at it.

"Let me get up there. I'm taller," Luke hollered.

"No way. I can get it." Grady wrapped his legs and arms around the tree and shinnied up like a bear after honey. Dang, he was sweaty! And what was that smell? Phew. He scaled his way up until his fingertips touched the log. He let go of one hand and clutched the log with his other, grasping it in the palm of his hand. Yes! "It's definitely plastic."

Grady's heart raced and he smiled. "Here, catch." He pitched the object down to Luke. "There're too many freakin' flies up here!" He scooted down one branch. His feet dangled until they found the next one.

Luke fumbled the catch below, dropping the cache in the dirt. He bent over it, pinching his nose. "It smells like a dead fish."

Grady scrambled down the tree and jumped with a thud from the last branch. "I know. I hope this ain't no prank." He wiped his sticky sap-coated hands on his shorts and examined the log.

Luke knelt on the ground. "What'cha think?"

"It'll open. See the seams here?" Grady knelt next to Luke and pointed to the hinges on the side.

Luke covered his nose in the crook of his elbow. "I'm not opening it—especially if it's for a stupid whistle. There's something creepy in there."

A buzzard squawked above them, swooped down, then landed in the maple tree close to where the log had been.

Grady stared up at the bird's beady eyes and then down at the log, pinching his nose. "You wuss. It smells rotten, that's all. I'll open it." He took the log, twisting it one way, then another, before it finally split apart, the contents spilling onto the ground. A red yo-yo, a ruler, a comic book, a logbook with a pen, and something in a semi-opened Ziplock bag tumbled out.

Luke said, "Cool!"

Grady lifted a thin stick off the ground. "Yeah, but what's in this bag?" He unzipped the rest of the plastic bag, and an odor wafted from the inside. "Gross. It smells like something died." He turned his head away, burying his nose in the crook of his arm, the stench burning his nostrils.

Luke pinched his nose and took the stick from Grady, poking the contents. "It looks like some fleshy thing." He moved the thing back and forth with the stick, examining it from all angles.

"What the hell is it?"

"I think it's a . . . a body part of some sort." Luke stabbed at the object.

The hair on Grady's arms stood straight up. "Why ain't it bloody then?"

"Hell if I know. Maybe it's from an animal."

"Animals bleed and have fur. This has neither." Grady's brow creased. He turned and looked over his shoulder. Were they being watched?

Luke stood and backed away, his eyes widening. "Crap, I think it looks like the end of some guy's pecker."

Grady looked again and gasped. Damn, Luke was right.

Chapter Four

Brett drove to work, dodging red lights, weaving in and out of traffic like the thoughts snaking back and forth in his mind. Should he call Child Protective Services? He dialed their number, then pressed the Disconnect button, doubt paralyzing him. What if they placed Quinn in a foster home and it took forever to get her back, to prove that he was a fit parent? He'd seen it happen before.

Two blocks from the precinct he thought he'd timed it perfectly, that he'd arrive on time, but a car pulled over to the curb in front of him, blocking his way. What was the guy doing? Didn't he realize he was stopping traffic? He banged his fist against the steering wheel.

A woman opened the passenger door, leaned in, and kissed the driver. Her husband? She got out, closed her door, and opened the back door. She resembled a model from a Victoria's Secret catalog—high-fashion power suit, long flowing hair, lean legs, and high heels—so put together, her teeth so white they seemed to glow. Maybe she used whitening strips. Was she reaching in the back for a briefcase? No, she bent like maybe she was kissing a small child in a booster seat.

Why couldn't Ali be put together like that?

The woman shut the door and blew her family a final kiss. Brett sighed. Ali would never be that poised or confident. He couldn't change her, and nothing he could do would help her gain confidence. He'd tried. For years he'd tried. But he never managed to say the right thing.

The car finally pulled away from the curb, and five minutes later Brett entered the police precinct. He hurried to his cubicle. Chief Dunson shouted from down the hall. "What time is it, Reed?"

Busted.

Brett headed down the hall, ducking his head into the chief's office. "Sorry I'm late, sir."

An unlit cigar dangled from the chief's mouth. "Looks like you're making a habit of it."

"No, sir. It won't happen again." Brett nodded and headed back to his desk.

"That's what you said the last time." Chief's voice trailed Brett down the hall.

A few minutes later, Brett sipped coffee at his desk with Clay, his partner. Clay, at six foot five, filled the room. Some of his body hung over the sides of his chair. He'd played football for U of M while in college, but after ten years of being off the playing field, he'd gotten a little soft around the middle and around his heart. He had a soft heart for underdogs, always rooting for the losing team. His laugh was as snarky as Eddie Murphy's, kind of like a snorting sound, making other people snicker.

But Brett wasn't laughing now. "When Quinn called this morning, I had to go check it out. There've been times when shaking Ali didn't wake her. I had to make sure Quinn was okay."

"Was she?"

Brett nodded. "Quinn was scared, but Ali sat up and spoke to me. She might go back to sleep, but I can't control that." He clenched his fists and lowered his voice. "I think Ali lost her job too. Which totally sucks because Quinn won't be going to day care. As long as she's in the house with Ali, I can't think straight."

"Why don't you call CPS?" Clay nodded toward the phone, then opened his desk drawer and slid a file into place.

"They'll find out I went over there."

"So what? They'll find her messed up too."

"Yeah, but it might take them till tomorrow to check her out, and by that time she could be sober."

"I'll call then." Clay reached for the phone.

Brett placed his hand on Clay's arm. "Don't do it, man."

Clay said, "Why not? You need to nail her."

"I know, but my ass will be on the line for violating the protective order. And there have been cases where the child was taken away for up to a year before the courts resolved the case. You know how messed up and overworked CPS is."

"Maybe you should suck it up and call your old man, dude."

Brett shook his head. His father was a local attorney, known and respected, but he couldn't call him now, and he couldn't tell Clay his old man had called. "He doesn't want anything to do with me. He's made that clear." *And I hung up on him today.*

When Ali had gotten pregnant six years ago, Brett had decided to do the right thing and marry her. He hadn't known her for long—only long enough to be attracted to her. Looking back, maybe a part of him wanted to rescue her. She'd seemed so vulnerable.

Brett reached for the phone on his desk—the one with the blocked number so Ali wouldn't know it was him calling—and dialed her number. No answer. Either she had fallen back to sleep or she didn't want to talk to anyone. Probably both.

Clay arched his eyebrows. "Have you looked in the mirror lately? You have these bulging black bags under your eyes, and your pants are about to fall off. It's not healthy living like you do—this ain't right, man."

Brett's radio cracked with static before he heard the dispatcher. "Base to twenty-five, base to twenty-four. Possible assault and battery at 1246 Ditch Rd. EMS is on the way."

Brett set his coffee down and hurried to the front door.

Clay followed and paused. "My wheels are in the shop. Can I hitch a ride with you?"

Brett nodded and pushed out the door, summer's heavy humidity enveloping him in a sauna. He unlocked the car door. "Hop in." They climbed in and Brett cranked up the air. The clock in the sedan showed 9:10. Maybe he'd get the chance to stop at home after this call. Ditch Road wasn't far from Ali's.

When Brett pulled in front of the house on Ditch Road, the ambulance had just arrived, its lights flashing in the driveway. The front door of the house stood open. Neighbors gawked from their porches and in the street. Brett and Clay hurried to assist.

Three feet inside the door, the victim lay on his back, naked from the waist down in a heap, writhing and screaming. As the EMTs wheeled their gurney into the house, they fired questions at the man. "What happened?"

"Are you blind? My dick is missing. Someone whacked it off." He flapped his arms above his groin.

Clay knelt at the victim's side. "What's your name?"

"Jake"—he paused to catch his breath—"Hunter."

Brett had seen a lot as a cop, but nothing like this. Hunter's pecker was gone, and in its place was a short stub covered in blood with a thin strip of rubber knotted and dangling from the end. Brett's stomach lurched. "Do you know who did this?"

"How the hell would I know? It's not like I gave them permission." Spittle flew from Jake's mouth as he spoke, the alcohol on his breath filling the room. "I wasn't awake when it happened. Someone drugged me and then sliced it off." He winced and groaned as the techs lifted him onto the gurney and inserted an IV needle into his arm.

Brett said, "What do you remember?"

Jake took a deep breath. "Nothing. I was lying on my bed last night"—he pointed to the bedroom—"and woke up this morning . . . dickless." He sucked in another deep breath, clenching his teeth. "It was probably my ex-wife. I'll kill her."

Brett quizzed him about his ex-wife, jotting down her name, phone number, and where she worked. "What time did you get home?"

"I closed Louie's bar." He squeezed his eyes shut. "Maybe 2:20. I don't know." His face gathered in tight wrinkles as if he was forcing the words to come.

Brett made a mental note of the guy's tattoos, his greasy hair and dirty fingernails, and the dried blood on his thighs. "Did you hear, feel, or see anything after you fell asleep?"

Jake stared at the ceiling as if trying to remember. "He put something like a rag over my face . . . smelled like some kind of gas."

Clay glanced around the room. "Have you seen the rag?"

Jake, still lying on the gurney, sat up and lunged for Clay, grabbing his shirt in his fist, sticking his face close to Clay's. "I ain't had time to look for no rag. I've been too busy looking for my dick!

You need to find it, you asshole!"

Clay's large hands shot out and pushed Jake down on the gurney, restraining him. "Keep your hands off me. We'll do what we can."

"Easy for you to say." Hunter nodded toward Clay's crotch. "Yours is intact." He fell limp onto the bed as the EMTs covered his body and rolled him out the front door and into the ambulance.

Brett radioed in the report, telling the dispatcher the victim's name and requesting the crime scene crew. After, he dug out the supply kit from the trunk of the cruiser, and he and Clay each donned a pair of plastic gloves, then unrolled yellow tape around the front door.

By the time they made it back to the bedroom, Clay couldn't hold back any longer. His laugh rolled from deep inside and grew so loud it echoed off the walls. He grabbed his crotch and shivered. "Did you see that stub? This is some scary shit!"

Brett laughed with him. "Makes me want to wear iron briefs under lock and key."

When they heard the crime crew entering the house, they sobered up. Clay spoke first. "Search for the missing part. He'll never piss right again if we don't find it soon. I think it has to be sewn back on within twenty-four hours."

"How do you know that?" Brett said.

"I cut off the tip of my finger when I was a kid, and they had to sew it back right away." He showed Brett the tip of his pointer finger. "I'm assuming it's the same for any body part."

The forensics teams scattered, each going to work in separate rooms, dusting for prints. Clay and Brett combed the bedroom first, finding nothing. "Looks like our guy was thorough."

They searched the rest of the house but only found hidden porn magazines and rolled joints wrapped in aluminum foil in the freezer. There was no weapon or evidence of a forced entry. They collected the bedsheets and clothing and placed them in a bag. Clay pulled the cord on the computer out of the wall socket and placed it in a box with the other evidence.

On the way back to the precinct, Clay snorted, laughed, and squirmed. "It's kinda funny, but it's not. Once this gets out, every guy will be sleeping with one eye open."

Brett dialed Ali again. Still no answer. His clock read 11:34

a.m. "Do you mind if we stop off at my house first? I need to check on Quinn. I told her I'd be home for lunch."

"Sure."

Brett turned down the side street and waved at the neighbor walking her dog. His fingers trembled as he pulled into his driveway.

"Everything looks cool from here," Clay said.

"Give me a few minutes." Brett ran up to the house and turned the knob. This time it opened. Why had Quinn unbolted the door after he left? A panic bell rang. As he entered, he smelled stale cigarette smoke and a hint of the pancakes he'd made earlier. "Quinn? Ali?"

No answer. Where was Max? He always greeted him.

Brett went into the living room. Ali lay under a blanket on the couch—as if she hadn't moved since he left. "Allison!"

No answer. She didn't budge.

He nudged her shoulder. "Ali, where's Quinn? Where's Max?"

Her eyes fluttered. "Hmm?"

Brett gripped her shoulders and shook her. "Where's Quinn?"

"Let me go." She sat, waved her hand, and pushed him away. "I don't know. She was here a minute ago."

"You haven't moved since I left four hours ago."

Brett dashed through the house to the kitchen. "Quinn?" The same mess still cluttered the table and the sink.

He hurried to Quinn's room. The door was shut. He turned the handle, but it was locked. Their rented home had been built more than twenty years ago. The landlord had told them Quinn's room had been an office, which was why it had a keyed lock on the outside. Brett had never removed the lock because they'd never used it— except once. Quinn had been two and hadn't wanted to stay in her room at night. She kept sneaking out, and Ali said she worried Quinn would roam out into the street, so she'd locked her in. When Brett discovered the locked room, he'd been livid with Ali.

Now, he shouted across the house. "Did you lock Quinn in her bedroom? What's going on?" He pounded on Quinn's wooden door.

No answer.

Brett stormed back into the living room. Ali sat hunched over with her head in her hands.

Brett snaked his fingers through his hair. "Did you lock Quinn in her room? Where's the key?"

Ali shook her head, shrugged, and stuttered. "I can't . . . remember . . . where I put the key."

Brett's chest tightened. He ran to the coat closet and fumbled with a hanger, bending it and straightening it as he ran back to Quinn's room. "Quinn, it's Daddy. I'll get you out in two seconds."

There was no sound.

He jammed the long metal side into the lock. "Quinn, talk to me."

Nothing.

His fingers trembled. The hanger was too fat to fit the keyhole.

A strong hand clamped down on his shoulder. He spun around.

Clay stood before him, his eyebrows furrowed in a worried way.

Dread filled Brett's gut. "What? What's wrong?"

"Her window is open on the east side of the house."

"What?" His stomach cartwheeled to his feet. "No!"

Clay took out his key chain and opened a device that contained a thin metal picklock. He gently brushed Brett aside, and speaking in his usual calm, deep voice said, "Here, let me do that. But I don't think you're going to find her in there."

Chapter Five

Static from Brett's radio echoed off the walls of Quinn's empty bedroom. Empty in that she wasn't there. But everything else was—the clothes in her closet, toys in the corner, her lime-green piggy bank on the dresser.

The dispatcher's voice sounded, breaking the silence. "Unit twenty-four, unit twenty-five. There's someone here at the office I need you to see. 10-4." The static clicked off.

Clay finished putting his pick away before he unclipped his radio and spoke into it. "We'll be there in a few. We're about fifteen minutes away."

Brett stood in the center of the room, numb, panic filling every nerve fiber. A low humming throbbed in his ears. Oblivious to the radio, he searched for clues and licked his lips. "Where is she?" He moved to the window. The curtains billowed out and flapped in the wind. "Do you think she left through here?" Brett glanced out the opening and below at the humming air conditioning unit.

"It's possible. All she had to do was step out onto the unit, and away she'd go."

"But what about Max? If someone took her he'd still be here. Unless she took him with her?"

Static from the radio came again. The dispatcher said, "Reed, this is about your daughter."

Brett unclipped his radio, frantic. His heartbeat soared. "Is she there?"

"No, but we know where she is. Chief says to get over here."

"Where is she? Is she safe? What happened?" Brett's voice raised two notches as he fired the questions.

When the dispatcher didn't respond, his eyes darted from the open window to Clay. His heart drummed in his ears. Why wasn't she answering his questions?

Ali stumbled into the room, her eyes squinting and puffy. She leaned against the doorjamb. "Where is she? What happened?"

Brett turned to her, his fists clenched at his sides. "You tell me. You were supposed to be watching her! What kind of mother are you, anyway?" He stormed out of the house, leaving Ali crying in a heap on the floor at the door, still wearing her nightgown and smelling like booze. His heart raced as he wondered where Quinn could be and why the chief wanted him to come to the station.

#

When Brett entered the Hursey Park Police Precinct, the staff turned mute. Officers stared. Was it his imagination or had something terrible happened to Quinn? His heart thundered in his chest.

The receptionist pointed to the chief's office. Brett ran down the hallway. Clay followed.

Mrs. Finkle, an elderly neighbor who lived down the street from Ali, sat in a chair across from the chief. She wore her usual flowered dress—the kind Brett's grandmother used to wear ten years ago. Chief Dunson motioned for Brett and Clay to come in and close the door.

Brett turned to Mrs. Finkle. "What are you doing here? Where's Quinn?"

Chief motioned for Brett to sit.

Brett couldn't. "Is she hurt? What happened?"

He glanced at the chief and then to Mrs. Finkle. "Do you have her?"

Mrs. Finkle wrung her hands and turned to the chief as if waiting for him to answer. Chief Dunson motioned for Brett to sit down again. Brett ran his fingers through his hair.

Clay, who'd taken a seat, reached and took Brett's arm, guiding him into the chair. Finally, Brett slumped into the seat.

Chief spoke first. "It seems your neighbor"—he motioned toward Mrs. Finkle—"found Quinn in the middle of the street a block away from your home early this morning."

Brett scooted to the edge of his chair and leaned toward the chief. "What? Why? Is she okay?" He turned to Mrs. Finkle. "Why didn't you call me?"

Chief added, "Yes, she's okay. Mrs. Finkle said Quinn told her Ali was asleep on the sofa, but she had to find Max because he ran away."

Brett fell back in his seat and exhaled. "Oh, thank God she's okay." He turned to the chief and back to Mrs. Finkle. "Where's she now?"

Chief waved his hand. "She's safe."

Mrs. Finkle's voice trembled, and she moved her thumb over her fingers repeatedly. "She was so upset. Poor thing." She glanced at the chief and then to Brett. "I didn't want to go into your home, so . . . so . . . I brought her here." She looked at the chief as if wanting affirmation for doing the right thing. Her stuttering voice sounded shaky, and the loose flesh on her jowls jiggled as she spoke. "The child was distraught." She paused like she was vamping up courage. "A young child shouldn't be left to fend for herself like that. I've seen her playing outside before, too, unsupervised—in her pajamas, no shoes on. It happens all the time, and it's just not right."

Brett hated knowing Quinn had needed him and he hadn't been there. "I need to see her, let her know everything is okay. Did you see Max?"

Mrs. Finkle narrowed her eyes at Brett. "No, but I saw your car at the house this morning. I figured you knew your wife's, uh, condition." She turned to the chief. "That woman isn't right." She glared at Brett. "And what kind of father would leave a child in her care?"

Acid churned in Brett's stomach. He gripped the arms of the chair before he turned toward her again. "Ali is my ex-wife, and, unfortunately, the courts decided to place Quinn with her. I didn't get to decide."

Mrs. Finkle looked away.

Brett sighed. It wouldn't do any good for him to make an enemy of her. Maybe she could be a witness for his defense. He tried to mellow his attitude toward her. "Thanks for bringing her here, Mrs. Finkle. You're right—the way Ali neglects Quinn is wrong. Would you be willing to tell the courts what you've seen?"

Mrs. Finkle's eyes widened and she nodded, seemingly surprised at Brett's reaction.

Chief motioned toward Clay. "Mrs. Finkle, Officer Rizzo will take you home now."

The old lady reached for the desk, gripping it with both hands, seeming to steady herself as she stood. Her face puffed and turned red as she lifted her large, sagging body. "I don't need anyone to take me home. I drove here, and I can drive myself home." She clutched her purse to her bosom.

Clay moved to her side. "Then allow me to escort you to your car, ma'am."

"Thank you for helping Quinn, Mrs. Finkle." Brett stared at the chief. Where was Quinn? "Clay, can you check at the pound to see if they found Max?"

"Sure."

The lady shuffled out the door with Clay at her side.

Brett turned to the chief, who had come around his desk to close the door.

The chief carried his stout, muscle-tight frame back to his seat, plucked his unlit cigar from the ashtray, and met Brett's eyes. "Obviously, something is amiss with Ali, but Quinn is safe right now. She's with Peggy Turnball from CPS. She took her to a counselor for an assessment."

"Aw, come on. Why did you have to call them?"

"I'm sorry, Reed, but according to state laws we have to investigate this. We have to make sure there hasn't been any neglect . . ." He hesitated. "Or abuse."

Brett jumped out of his chair. "Abuse? Is she hurt? Did she say someone hurt her?"

The chief motioned for Brett to pipe down. He spoke in his usual low, monotone voice, the cigar dangling from his mouth. "I don't know if she's been physically harmed, so let's not get carried away. But an investigation needs to be done. The child said she was locked in her bedroom. The fact that her mother put her there, and then couldn't answer the door, is disturbing." He paused. "I sent Officer Hudson to the house too. She rang the bell, but couldn't get a response either."

Brett stared at the floor and exhaled. "I agree it looks bad. I don't know why Ali locked Quinn in her room. It makes me sick right here." He slammed his fist into his stomach. "But this is what I've been battling for six years. The woman has problems. I'm hoping now the courts will decide that she's an unfit mother." He exhaled loudly. "I want custody. It's the only chance Quinn has." His voice trailed as he rose from his chair and went to the window, where he stared out at the street.

The chief said, "I understand and agree, but you're going to have to play this out. You aren't supposed to be going near her. Don't screw up your chances. Let's take this one step at a time."

"I had to go. Quinn called. I couldn't ignore her."

Chief shook his head. "I'm sure this is difficult. I figured Ali had started using again. Your tardiness, black circles under your eyes—it's putting a toll on you. Most of us here have had domestic problems, but putting a kid at risk is different. Hopefully this will settle soon, and you'll get Quinn. Why don't you stay home for a few days . . . just until this gets worked out?" He stood and crossed the room. Just before he opened his door, he squeezed Brett's shoulder.

"Thanks." Brett met the chief's eyes. "I appreciate that, but I need this job. I have bills to pay."

"I understand." He paused. "But this is your kid we're talking about. For what it's worth, I believe you're a good father. I hope the courts see that soon."

A lump lodged in Brett's throat. Great! He hadn't cried since he was a teenager. He swallowed but didn't trust himself to speak. Thankfully, the department secretary buzzed the chief's office intercom.

"Excuse me, sir, but there are a couple of boy scouts here with something to show you." She lowered her voice to just about a whisper. "I think it might be that guy's, uh, chicken."

"What are you talking about?" the chief bellowed.

"You know"—she cleared her throat—"that guy who had his ding-a-ling whacked off . . . well that *thing* is here. These boys found it."

#

I reached into the backseat for my computer and opened it. Slowly, the machine came to life, whirring and dinging. Courthouse Coffee had great coffee and free wireless. It was one of my favorite spots to do research. Today, like several days a week, I parked in their parking lot facing the lake while Google-searching and eating lunch. The cloudless sky reflected off the water, making the waves look navy blue. I slipped on my sunglasses, and in between bites of my ham sandwich, I researched sex offenders.

To find them, I typed "sex offenders in Stark County" in the search box. Up popped a map and a list with their names, age, eye color, weight, and what they were charged with. There were 108 in our county. They had to register their addresses. It was the law.

I scanned the map, looking for new offenders. There hadn't been any new ones added. I'd already memorized the location of the six on my target list. They were the ones who hurt children. And they lived closest to me. I didn't want to go too far from home.

Next, I typed in the address geocache.com to check for new cache listings. There weren't any. I'd memorized the location of those sites I planned to use several days ago. There were ten within four miles of where I lived. It was fun to find them. I went late at night when people were sleeping. I wore night goggles.

Chapter Six

Dr. Sarah Grinwald, a psychologist and a part-time caseworker for Child Protective Services, waited in her new office overlooking Hursey Lake Beach for her next patient. She sat on the sofa looking out the large triple window watching the lake's waves as they reflected off the afternoon summer sun. She sighed. What a view.

Her old office working for CPS had been downtown, below her apartment, but when she inherited her mother's family estate and no longer needed to pay rent, she decided to splurge on this peaceful lake location and go into practice for herself, taking only occasional CPS cases. When the lake office became available, she'd snatched it in a hurry, knowing her patients would find solace there—as she did. The few who'd been there already had commented on how they wished their lives were as calm as the setting.

Sarah figured if her patients had a view of the lake during their session, they'd be more relaxed, which meant they'd open up more.

To the right of the large picture window was another smaller window that faced a cluster of pine trees, opening up to a hiking trail—something Sarah enjoyed. She kept her hiking boots at the office in case she had a spare hour to hike or geocache—one of her favorite hobbies. She loved the outdoors and the thrill of a grown-up treasure hunt.

With as much snow as they typically got in the winter, Sarah envisioned that sitting in her office would be like living in the middle of a snow globe.

Today, she watched the hummingbirds fly to the nectar she'd left for them outside the window. The birds' colors brought a rainbow splash to the green-treed backdrop behind it.

As she sat there, a robin flew into the window, startling her. She flinched as the bird flapped its wings and hit the glass again. And again. Poor thing. He was going to die if he kept it up. She made a mental note to hang something to deter it from happening again. Hadn't she read somewhere that a fake snake would work? Maybe she could get her brother to help her the next time he stopped by.

She tried to focus on charting her last patient's history. She'd met Eva at the homeless shelter while volunteering. The troubled woman had looked scared, glancing over her shoulder as if someone might pounce on her from the shadows. Sarah hadn't seen fear like that in a woman in a long time, but she recognized it.

Why did some men think it was necessary to harass, intimidate, and belittle women? There could only be one reason—to make the man feel more powerful. Which made Sarah sick. Eva told her she couldn't afford a counselor, but Sarah offered to help her pro bono. Sometimes helping someone who couldn't pay gave her more gratification than a paying client. They were more receptive to change and getting the help they needed.

A knock came from the door. Sarah rose to open it, assuming it would be Peggy Turnball, a fellow caseworker from Child Protective Services. She'd called fifteen minutes ago and asked if Sarah had time to assess a patient.

Peggy stood holding a little girl's hand. The girl wore purple pajamas, and her dark curls hung down past her shoulders. Eyes, translucent like the surface of a swimming pool under a blue sky, stared back at her. The child looked pale and frightened. She bent her head and stuck her thumb in her mouth while twisting her pajama top in her fist.

Peggy said, "Hi, Dr. Sarah, this is Quinn."

Sarah recognized the exhaustion in Peggy's eyes. They'd been caseworkers for CPS for several years at the downtown office. The wrinkled lines of worry in Peggy's brow told how overworked she was, which was why Sarah had decided to go out on her own. She continued to work for CPS on an as-needed basis, especially when there was a child custody case involving a government employee.

Sarah embraced Peggy, then knelt in front of Quinn. "How old are you?"

Quinn looked the other way, avoiding Sarah's eyes.

"I bet you're six, right?"

Quinn shook her head. "Five."

"You're tall for your age. Come on in."

Peggy stepped into the room and shut the door. "I told Quinn you're one of the best listeners around and that you have a horse." Peggy winked at Sarah. "Quinn said she wants to have her own farm someday so she can have lots of animals."

Sarah chuckled. "Oh, I love animals too. Would you like to play with the toys while I talk to her?" She pointed to Peggy.

Quinn nodded. Sarah led her to the corner of the room, showing her the boxes of puzzles and books. She pulled out a little chair for the child to sit on. "Would you like to play with a toy horse?"

Quinn nodded.

Sarah stooped to lift the toy box lid in the corner and handed her a small plastic thoroughbred. "I'll be right back. I'm going to walk Mrs. Turnball to the door, okay? Then we can talk horses for a while."

Quinn smiled.

Sarah sighed as she walked Peggy to the door. "What happened?"

Peggy lowered her voice. "Seems the neighbor found her in the street abandoned and crying. Possible neglect. She was supposed to be under the mother's care, but no one answered her door. Her father's a cop. Divorce situation. He's been ordered to take anger management classes. His wife filed a protective order against him."

Sarah's heart ached for the little girl. Even though she'd seen abuse and neglect before, it still affected her the same way. It was wrong on every level, which was exactly why she had become a counselor.

She'd studied the cop type before too—the power-hungry, macho types—and counseled their battered wives. She scolded herself for judging. As a counselor she was supposed to remain neutral, but it was difficult. "Do they know where the mother is?"

Peggy shrugged. "Not yet. The neighbor thought she might

have addiction problems." Peggy opened the door. "I'll be back at four. I hope to have a family member or a foster family for her by then. I've got to make a few calls. Call me."

"Does she have other family?"

"Not sure if there's anyone else yet."

After Peggy left, Sarah joined Quinn at the children's table. Quinn had taken another toy horse out of the bin and set it on the table in front of her with the other one. Quinn's feet dangled over the edge of her seat, her legs not long enough to reach the floor. She took her thumb out of her mouth and made the horses gallop across the table.

Sarah sat in a chair and pulled it closer to Quinn's. "What kind of animals would you have on your farm?"

Quinn stared out the window, swinging her legs and licking her bottom lip.

Sarah used her soft voice. "I have an Arabian horse named Beauty. She's black like Black Beauty. Have you heard that story?"

Quinn finally turned to Sarah and shook her head.

"I'd love to read it to you, if you'd like. I have the book over there on my shelf." Sarah nodded toward the bookshelf against the wall. "Would you like to go look for it?"

Quinn nodded.

"Go ahead. There are lots of horse books there. You pick one you like. Black Beauty has a picture of a black horse on the front cover."

Quinn sauntered over to the bookshelf seemingly engrossed in finding a book. She thumbed through several until she stopped and pulled one off the shelf.

Sarah stood and bent over Quinn. "Did you find one?"

"I think so." Quinn held up a book. "Is this it?"

"Yep, that's *Black Beauty*." Sarah smiled. "Is it okay if we sit on the sofa while I read it to you?"

Quinn nodded.

Together they sat, side by side, as Sarah read the story and pointed to the pictures. Quinn seemed immersed in the photos and the story, her facial expression showing concern at Beauty's plight.

When Sarah got to the part where the wicked man whipped Beauty, Quinn stopped her. "Why did that man have to be so mean to Beauty? Why didn't he feed him?"

"I don't know. Sometimes people are cruel. It's wrong, isn't it?"

Quinn nodded.

"Has anyone ever been mean to you?"

Quinn shook her head and stared out the window at the lake.

"I'm sorry this part of the story is sad. Beauty didn't deserve to be treated like that, did he?"

Tears filled Quinn's eyes.

"You don't deserve to be treated with cruelty either."

Quinn shook her head, closed her eyes, and put her thumb in her mouth, while rubbing her fingers along her shirt.

"Let me finish the story. It gets better."

Quinn listened and followed along with the pictures. Her thumb fell out of her mouth, and she leaned in closer to Sarah, seemingly more relaxed.

When Sarah read the part where Don came back into Beauty's life, Quinn sighed. "Daddy says sometime we'll all be together in heaven—even if he dies first, or Mommy does."

"What else does your daddy say?"

"That he loves me more."

"Has he ever made you feel uncomfortable?"

Quinn looked at the ceiling, putting her index finger on her temple, a grown-up thinking pose. "No, he always makes me more comfortable . . . like he covers me with a blanket when I'm cold, and he makes chocolate chip cookies on Fridays."

"Has he ever gotten angry at you?"

"Not at me. Just Mom." Quinn rolled her eyes.

"What does he do when he's angry?"

Quinn giggled. "Sometimes he throws things. Like one time he threw a coffee cup, and it broke into pieces all over the floor."

"Has he ever touched you in a place you didn't want him to touch you?"

"Sometimes when my pee-pee . . ." She stopped and whispered, pointing to her bottom. ". . . gets sore, he puts Vaseline on it and it tickles. But he doesn't laugh. He says"—she changed her voice to a low, deep one—"'keep your underwear off so your bottom can breathe tonight.' He doesn't know that bottoms don't breathe, do they?"

Sarah laughed. "I think all skin needs air, but it doesn't breathe

the way you're thinking." Sarah cleared her throat and reached into a basket. She pulled out two cloth dolls. A girl and a boy. She handed them to Quinn. "Go ahead. You can play with them."

Quinn took them and danced them in her lap. "Is he the daddy and she the little girl?"

"They can be anyone you want them to be."

"Then I'll make the girl my mommy and this man, uh, my dad." She danced the puppets in front of her, resting them on her legs. She laid the girl down on her back and snorted. "She's snoring."

"Do you think you can show me what happened today using the dolls?"

Quinn moved the boy doll over to the girl, and changed her voice to reflect a man's. "It's time to get up for work. You can't be late again." She rolled the girl onto her stomach, grunting as she turned her. She danced the boy along her other side and became so absorbed in her playing, she seemed to forget Sarah. The boy doll paced back and forth, put his hand on his head, went back to talk to the girl, but the girl never moved.

When it looked like Quinn was finished playing, Sarah spoke. "It looked like you were having fun. Can you tell me the story?"

Quinn explained how the mom wanted to sleep and the dad wanted her to wake up, but she couldn't.

Sarah said, "Has that ever happened to your mom?"

Quinn nodded.

"How did that make you feel?"

Quinn shrugged and looked out at the lake.

Sarah changed tactics. "Let's play a game. Do you like games?"

Quinn smiled and nodded.

"Tell me something that makes you laugh."

Quinn placed a finger on her chin and looked up at the ceiling. "Max, my dog, when he chases his tail. He looks goofy."

Sarah laughed but stopped when she noticed Quinn's frown. "What's wrong?"

"Max is gone."

"Where did he go?"

"He followed Uncle Mark out of the house and down the street. I watched him from my window until he disappeared."

"Who's Uncle Mark?"

Quinn shrugged. "I think he's Mommy's brother."

"I'm sorry. You love Max a lot, don't you?"

Quinn nodded.

"What about your uncle? Is he nice to you?"

Quinn's lower lip quivered, and she crossed her arms over her chest. "He makes Mommy angry."

"How?"

"He makes Mommy yell."

"Did he make her yell today?"

Quinn nodded again, tears filling her eyes. She brushed them with the backs of her hands. "That's when she locked me in my room."

"I'm sorry." Sarah reached for her hand. "Were you scared?"

Quinn's shoulders shook. "I peeked under the door, and Max was there, scratching. I heard him breathe like this: *hmph*. And I cried, 'Mommy, Mommy, let me out.' But Max barked and Uncle Mark left. I said, 'Max, come here.' But he didn't sniff under the door anymore. That's when I went to my window."

"What did you do then?"

"I opened it like Daddy showed me. Like when we practice fire drills." Tears trickled down her face.

Sarah handed Quinn a tissue and patted her hand. "I'm sorry. I would cry, too, if someone locked me in a room."

Quinn wiped her eyes.

Sarah danced the girl doll on the sofa next to Quinn. "Do you want to pretend this doll is you?"

She nodded.

"Show me what happened next." Sarah gave her the other girl doll.

Quinn took the momma doll. "You have to go to your room. You're making too much noise." Then she changed her voice. "No, Mommy. I'll be quiet. I promise." She moved the doll and disguised her voice again but made the words slow and slurred, acting sleepy. "Go now. Just for a little while. Play in your room."

Quinn looked up at Sarah and said, "I didn't want to go. I didn't do anything wrong. Why did she make me go to my room when Uncle Mark came over? I heard them talking, and I banged on the door, but Mommy wouldn't open it. I cried really, really hard. But no one came. That's when I opened my window."

"Then what happened?"

"I saw Uncle Mark's car driving away and Max chasing it down the street. I jumped out my window and chased after him, calling his name, but I couldn't catch him." She cuddled up next to Sarah, clasping Sarah's sleeve tightly in her fist. Then she put her thumb in her mouth.

"I'm sorry you felt sad and you miss Max. I bet he'll find his way home soon, because dogs don't forget where they live, and he loves you. I can tell."

Quinn smiled so big her thumb fell out of her mouth.

Sarah said, "What's your favorite thing you like to do?"

Quinn shrugged.

"Do you like ice cream?"

Quinn nodded.

Sarah put her hand out to high-five Quinn. "I happen to have some in my freezer—Chocolate Chip Cookie Dough. Want some?"

Quinn high-fived Sarah and scrambled off the sofa. "Yes!"

#

When Peggy arrived to take Quinn to the sheriff's office, Quinn climbed into Sarah's lap, knocking her ice cream bowl to the floor. Sarah felt Quinn's legs tremble against hers.

She held her and explained, "Peggy's going to take you to the sheriff's office. There's a room there where you can wait until they find a safe place for you to go to—just for a while. The room has a TV and tables and chairs. There's a DVD player there too, so you'll get to watch a movie. You'll only be there a few hours."

"Will Daddy be there?"

Sarah turned to Peggy. "Probably not today, but maybe you could see him tomorrow."

Peggy nodded. "We might be able to arrange that. I know he wants to see you too."

With tears in her eyes, Quinn said, "Can't I stay here with you?" She slid her hand into Sarah's and held it tight.

Sarah looked at Peggy, overcome with emotion. She couldn't let the child stay, but Quinn had moved her in a way she'd never been moved before. Why did parents neglect their children? Sarah fumbled for words and stroked Quinn's arm. "Not today, but I'll see you again soon." She was supposed to stay unbiased, but she hoped

Quinn's mother's rights would be terminated until she could start acting like a mother.

"What if I let you take the *Beauty and the Beast* book with you until the next time I see you?"

Quinn nodded.

Sarah reached for a tissue and blotted the tears on Quinn's face. As they stood, Sarah reached for the book and followed Peggy to the door.

Peggy turned to Sarah, glanced at her watch, and took a paper out of her briefcase. "Would you be able to meet me at this address to do an assessment in an hour?" She handed the paper to Sarah.

Ali Reed's address was at the top of the form. "Sure. I can be there."

#

Reading *Beauty* had reminded Sarah of when her mother had read the same book to her: the way her slender, graceful hands had held the book; the way she smelled of lilac bath oil; her soft, soothing voice; and the way she'd sung the words. Usually when Sarah thought of her mother, memories of her father followed—ruining everything good. His anger spilled over and shadowed each poignant thought.

Except today. For a brief moment, while she read to Quinn, memories of her mother weren't interrupted with visions of him. She smiled. For the first time, having children didn't seem so bad. Was it true that some women had mommy genes and some didn't? Did she?

What did it matter? Men screwed up marriages and lives—both in her practice and her life. She didn't want to be a part of that. The perfect man didn't exist. She wanted something simpler, uncomplicated. But with that came loneliness. Was that what she felt when she'd read to Quinn? She wasn't sure.

Now that Quinn had gone, dark memories of her own father flooded back. She tried to repress them and think of Quinn instead, but the room's lonely eyes stared back at her. It was as if an invisible cloud hung over it, making it heavy and dark. Even though the sun reflected off the lake and threw light into the room, Sarah's mood had changed. Emptiness filled her chest. She couldn't stop thinking about Quinn, especially after she'd clung to her when Peggy had arrived.

Chapter Seven

Before Brett left the precinct he approached Officer Katie Williams and asked her to send a patrol out to search for Max. Then he punched the number for the animal shelter and gave them his phone number and Max's description. Clay had already called them, but Brett felt better doing it himself. The shelter said they'd call if someone brought a golden in that matched Max's description, but no one had yet.

He drove to the Child Protective Services office located downtown, a few streets away in the business district of Hursey Lake, next to the Historical Society building.

He parallel-parked in the front at the curb and entered the old building. It smelled like an antique store filled with old furniture that people had left behind in dank, moldy houses. The air felt cold and damp—as if the air conditioner couldn't keep up with the humidity. A receptionist sat at a wooden desk in the lobby.

"Can I help you?"

Brett said, "I hope so. I'm Officer Brett Reed." He reached across her desk and shook her hand. "CPS took custody of my daughter, Quinn Reed, this morning, and I'd like to talk to someone about getting her back. Who would that be?"

"You need to talk to Mrs. Turnball. She's handling your

daughter's case, but she's not here right now." She reached into a dish on her desk and pulled out a business card. "You can reach her at this number. I'm sure she'll want to talk to you."

"There's been a mix-up. I'm perfectly capable of caring—"

She held up her hand. "I'm sorry, but there's nothing I can do. You'll have to talk to Mrs. Turnball."

Brett nodded and took the card from her as she answered a phone call. He moved to a wooden chair across from the girl and sat near the window, then took out his cell phone and punched in the numbers. He recognized Mrs. Turnball's name because of other child protective cases he'd handled, but he couldn't picture her. She answered on the second ring.

"Mrs. Turnball, this is Officer Reed, Quinn's father."

"Yes, I haven't had a chance to call you, but we're in the process of investigating your case right now."

"Look, I'm perfectly capable of caring for Quinn. Where can I meet you to discuss this?"

"We need to talk to her mother too. Can we meet at her house in a half hour?"

Brett nodded. If he told her about the protective order it might delay things further. Besides, with Quinn gone now he didn't care. It changed everything. "Hopefully she'll still be there, but I don't know what condition she'll be in."

"We like to keep the child in her home environment as much as possible. We'd need the judge's permission for her to be placed with you, and that could take time. Quinn is being evaluated right now by one of our counselors. If everything checks out, we'll have to assess your living arrangements too, and then make a decision."

"How long is all that going to take?"

"Realistically, it could take a few days. Is there a family member you'd like Quinn to stay with in the meantime?"

He thought of Ali's psycho mother, who was married to an alcoholic. No way did he want her going there. He couldn't ask his parents either. His mother would love it, but his father would object. No way. "No, there's no one. I'm perfectly capable. Why is it going to take so long?"

"It's paperwork. Things have to be recorded. An investigation takes time, Mr. Reed."

He turned and pounded his fist against the wall. The

receptionist glanced his way. Shoot. He lifted his hand to her and mouthed, "Sorry."

Mrs. Turnball added, "Isn't your father an attorney in town? We could arrange for her to stay with him."

Great. She already knew more about him than he wanted. "No, that's not going to work."

Brett's call-waiting beeped. He glanced at the number. His mother. Should he answer it and ask her to take Quinn? No, he couldn't. That would mean he'd have to talk to his father, and he couldn't bear hearing him say he didn't want to take care of Ali's brat.

#

A hot breeze blew through Brett's hair on the way to his car. The summer heat reflected off his windshield, blinding him. He climbed in his car and threw on his sunglasses, catching a glimpse of himself in the rearview mirror and noticing the wrinkled worry lines creasing his brows. His heart lurched at the thought of not being able to comfort Quinn. He hated thinking about how frightened she must feel.

He drove to Ali's house, his jaw clenched, holding in the anger that wanted to boil over. He stormed up the porch steps with his computer under his arm and pounded on the front door. When she didn't answer, he turned the knob and found it unlocked. He let himself in. "Ali?"

The smell of the garbage still cluttered in the hallway made him gag. What a pigsty. Should he throw the bags in the garage? No, it was better if CPS saw the way Ali lived.

He took three long strides into the kitchen. Ali was sitting at the table still surrounded by dirty dishes. Nothing had moved since he was there last. She gave him her back and moved to the sink.

He went to the table, pushed dishes out of his way, and put his computer down, firing questions at her. "Did you let someone in here?"

She wouldn't look at him. "You aren't supposed to be here."

"Are you into drugs? Owe someone money?"

She turned around and wiped the tears off her swollen red face. "No."

"They're going to put Quinn in a foster home. This is your fault. We're going to go through hell to get her back. And if I have my way, you won't *ever* get her back."

She crossed her arms and set her jaw, looking past him.

Brett banged his fist on the table. Dishes fell, clattering to the floor, and one shattered into pieces.

Ali flinched and shrieked.

"You're not going to tell me what happened, are you? You're just going to stand there and cry?"

Ali crumpled to the floor like a deflated balloon.

"Damn." Brett went to her, plopped down on the floor beside her, and gathered her in his arms, holding her and rocking her as she sobbed into his chest.

He kept his voice low. "I'm sorry. I know you're upset, but please, tell me why you locked her in her room and who was here. I want to understand. All that matters is getting Quinn back. Doesn't that matter to you?"

She beat his chest. "Of course it matters to me. She's my flesh and blood. She's a part of me. I'll never forgive myself if something happens to her."

"What's going to happen to her? What do you know? Tell me. Tell someone." He took her wrists and tried to force her to meet his eyes, but she balled her hands into fists, shutting her eyes and turning her head from his gaze.

He let go of her arms and broke away from their embrace, leaving her alone in a heap on the floor.

The gates to his composure opened, and pent-up rage marched out. "I think the reason you want her back is she's the only one who can make you feel good about yourself. How pathetic. *She's* the parent half the time—always making *you* feel good, telling you how pretty you are. She tells you what you want to hear because she knows if she does, she'll get your attention. You need *her*. Don't you see how wrong that is? You're supposed to be the parent. You were supposed to be watching her!"

Ali buried her face in the crook of her arm, stood, and stomped out of the kitchen toward the living room.

Brett followed, his voice rising. "She has to remind you of everything—which groceries to buy, to turn the stove off, to set your alarm. What happened to you? What robbed you of all your self-esteem?"

She turned on her heels to face him. "Maybe it was you! Did you ever think of that?" She barreled past him and into the bedroom, slamming the door.

He threw his arms up in the air. What had *he* done?

He hadn't bothered telling her the social worker was on her way. He didn't want to give her time to get it together. It was better if they saw her the way he did—surrounded by her true colors. And smells.

His cell phone vibrated. Clay. Brett answered and returned to the kitchen, settling in a chair at the table. The room spun as he forced himself to keep calm. He took two deep breaths. "Tell me something good."

Clay sighed. "I wish I could. I tried. I checked with the CPS director, but because you're a cop they have certain protocols they have to abide by."

Brett clenched his jaw. "So it's worse because I'm a cop? That makes all the sense in the world." He shook his head sarcastically and with disgust.

"Wait it out. Play their game fair, and you'll get Quinn. It's probably going to have to go to the judge first."

Brett's heart sank. He figured this could take longer than one day, especially since it was getting late, but hearing his partner confirm it made it worse. He wiped his clammy hands on his pant legs. "The judge will never let me take her home. She's the one who smacked me with the protective order and sentenced me to the anger management course."

"Yeah, but this is different, dude. Quinn's a child. She can't stay with Ali. Just stay positive. Your girl will be with you soon."

Brett sighed. "Wish I had your confidence."

"Want an update on what the scouts found?"

"Sure. It'll give me a diversion."

"A dick, but it didn't belong to this morning's victim."

Brett stood and paused. "There's another?" He grabbed the broom out of the pantry and swept the floor with one hand, holding onto his cell with the other.

"Looks like it. But we haven't found him yet." Clay snorted. "The coroner said it'd been cut off a few days ago—sliced off a dead man. There was embalming fluid in it."

"Seriously? That's crazy."

Clay said, "We're looking into the obits—men who died in the last few weeks. Medical examiner said that's how long it'd been decaying."

"How many can that be?"

"Exactly? Seventeen local deceased. Twelve of them were men. But we don't know if this guy was local. He could have been from anywhere."

"What's the rap on the guy this morning?" Brett tried to focus on their conversation, knowing the distraction would help, but he couldn't block out Ali's soft crying in the next room. He had no interest in going to her, but the sound grated on his nerves.

"Jake Hunter, previously arrested for domestic abuse, and he's a registered sex offender. He did a kid, served time. Works at the Dayle Foundry uptown. His ex has a confirmed alibi—claims she worked all night—she's a waitress at Stephen's Bar. She said she wished she would have maimed him herself though, said he raped her repeatedly during their marriage."

"What a dirtbag. Any clues on who our perp is?" Brett continued to sweep.

"None at this point, but I'm looking into the victim's family. The dick the scouts found this morning was in a geocaching site."

Brett stopped sweeping. "A what?"

"Geocaching—it's a game hikers play. Someone registers the location of the box at an online site, indicates if it's an easy or difficult find, and lists GPS coordinates on where to find it. The hikers look for the cache using a GPS device. They load the coordinates and off they go. Sometimes the cache is buried. Sometimes it's camouflaged in something other than a box."

"Do they put money in it?" Brett dumped the broken dish into the already-full garbage can.

"No money." Clay explained. "It's usually filled with random stuff—never human body parts."

While Clay explained the game, Brett heard phones ringing in the background and figured Clay was at the office.

"How many of these sites do we have in our county?"

"I haven't researched that yet. When you have time, Google it." Clay paused. "The chief said he sent you home for a few days, but I thought you might wanna stay in the loop." He paused again. "I'm gonna have to take another call here."

"Yeah, keep me updated, but for now all I can think about is getting Quinn back."

"I understand. Don't worry. Quinn will be with you soon."

Brett clipped his phone back on his belt loop and sat at the kitchen table amid the clutter. He strummed his fingers waiting for Peggy Turnball to arrive. Every minute felt like an hour. *Come on, already!*

He opened his computer sitting on the table and waited for the screen to light. He Google-searched "geocaching." When a list of sites appeared, he clicked on the official site and then typed in Hursey Lake's zip code, pressed Enter, and a list appeared. *Four hundred and fifty-nine sites? That's insane!*

The doorbell rang. He shot out of his chair, running in circles, hating the mess surrounding him but reminding himself CPS needed to see the way Ali kept house. He raced to the front door and opened it, but it wasn't Mrs. Turnball.

It was his neighbor, Ray, standing on the porch with his little beagle, Bella. "Hey . . . I-I-I noticed your car here, and . . . and . . ." He stuttered like he always had, but for some reason he couldn't look Brett in the eye. "Is everything okay . . . okay with Quinn?"

"Why? Did you see someone here this morning?" Mr. Ray was a retired widower who often brought Quinn cookies and something special on Halloween and Christmas.

Mr. Ray bent down to pet Bella. "Well, no, I had to take Bella to the . . . to the vet, but . . . but . . . there are rumors."

"About what?"

"You."

"What about me?"

Mr. Ray cleared his throat. "Uh, that you"—he coughed—"hurt Quinn."

"I hurt her? How?" Couldn't people mind their own business?

Mr. Ray shrugged. "They said you"—he cleared his throat—"molested her."

"What?" Brett shot out the door, his voice ringing down the street. "Who's spreading that filth?"

Mr. Ray backed away, lifting Bella tight to his chest, staring at the ground. "I didn't know the person. I heard it at the grocery store. Of course I didn't believe it, but I thought you should know what they're saying. I figured they was lies, Mr. Reed. It didn't make sense. I know you l-l-love Quinn. I-I-I told them that."

Brett lowered his voice. "Thanks for telling me." He squeezed Mr. Ray's shoulder. "I appreciate that you stood up for me too." *Blast Ali for spreading lies about me.*

"I'm sorry to b-b-bother you, Mr. Reed. Tell Quinn I said hello." He nodded and scurried away like the bucked-toothed squirrel he looked like.

Brett took a deep breath and walked back into the house, then slammed the door. He hurried into the living room to open the drapes, but stopped short. Ali was sitting on the sofa—her hair brushed, with makeup and clothes on. "You telling lies about me now too?"

"I don't know what you're talking about." She reached into her purse for a medicine bottle, opened the lid, and took out a pill. She then threw it in her mouth and chased it with a swig of bottled water.

"What did you just take?" He yanked the drapes open.

She ignored him and reached into her purse for her car keys.

"Where are you going?"

"I don't have to tell you." She stood to go.

He lunged for the keys, struggling to take them, but she closed her fist and scratched his arm with her other hand, drawing blood. Then she darted across the room, toward the kitchen.

He chased her, took hold of her arm, and spun her around. "You can't leave."

She jerked her arm out of his clasp. "Watch me."

"Don't you want to get Quinn back? A caseworker from CPS is on her way. She needs to meet you."

Ali paused and her eyes widened, seemingly panicked. Tears spilled down her cheeks again. "Look, I don't remember anything, okay?"

"How can you not remember? Were you that messed up?" He shook his head. "You're disgusting, and you still reek like booze. You aren't in any condition to go anywhere."

Her cell phone vibrated on the coffee table. Brett took a few steps back toward the sofa and looked at the screen. "Your boss is calling."

She paused, crossed in front of him, and snatched her phone. Then she turned, shoving the phone in her purse.

He heard a car in front of the house and glanced out front to see if Peggy had arrived yet. Ali ran toward the back door through the kitchen, her heels clicking on the tile. The door slammed before he could stop her. What kind of mother wouldn't stay to fight to get her daughter back? He knew the answer: a mother who didn't want CPS to see her in the condition she was in.

The fact that she left wouldn't help CPS assess her, but it might help his case. He let her go. It's not like he could stop her.

Her little red Focus, with its dings and large dents—evidence of a reckless woman—squealed out into the street the way a criminal would flee the scene of a crime.

Why wouldn't she talk to him? What was she hiding?

He sauntered across the room toward the front door and stopped when he saw the blanket on the floor—the one he'd wrapped around Quinn. Had it been just this morning that she had told him she loved him? How could anyone believe he'd ever hurt her? He reached for the blanket and found Lambie, the stuffed animal Quinn always carried with her so she could rub its ear while she sucked her thumb. He pressed it into his face, smelling Quinn's sweet smell.

Tears threatened to spill. He swallowed the lump in his throat, folded the blanket, and set it on the sofa, tucking the lamb under his arm. The doorbell rang.

He crossed to the door and opened it. Two women stood in front of him. One was probably in her mid-forties. She had dark hair pulled back and peered over the top of black-rimmed glasses.

The other lady reminded him of Carrie Underwood, his favorite female vocalist, garbed in stylish western wear—boots, jeans, and a ruffled blouse with a country-looking vest. Her large leather briefcase resembled a horse's saddle. The lady's blond hair tumbled past her shoulders, and she stood at least five inches taller than the vocalist, just a few inches shorter than Brett. Something about the way she stared at him with her large deep-set brown eyes made him feel like an insect under a microscope.

The dark-haired woman in the glasses stepped toward him with her hand out. "Mr. Reed? I'm Peggy Turnball."

He shook her hand. "Yes, come in. Call me Brett." Lambie fell out from under his arm. He bent to retrieve it, his face feeling hot.

Mrs. Turnball didn't smile, but she didn't seem cold either, just preoccupied. "You can call me Peggy." She nodded toward the other lady. "This is Dr. Sarah Grinwald, Quinn's assessment counselor."

The doctor reached for Brett's hand, locking her eyes on him and seeming to smirk at the lamb under his arm. "Call me Sarah." Her voice sounded smooth and soothing, the kind of voice a therapist might use to get someone to say how they felt.

He took her hand in his, noticing her firm, confident grip. "Call me Brett." He held the lamb out. "Quinn's lamb. She takes it everywhere." A knot formed in his throat. He coughed, trying not to look as nervous as he felt.

Sarah nodded as if she understood. She didn't look like any doctor he'd ever met. She continued to eye him, as if she could see into his soul and knew his intimate thoughts. It made his mouth dry. What had Quinn told her?

Peggy said, "Was that Quinn's mom leaving?" She pointed in the direction Ali had fled.

Brett nodded. "Yep, I couldn't get her to stay." He motioned for them to enter. "Come in."

Peggy paused in the doorway, cocking her head to the side. "This is her house, but you're here alone?"

"You asked me to meet you here."

"Yes, but I hadn't realized until I read your file that there was a protective order against you."

"Let me ask you something—if your child called you crying, asking for help, would you let a protective order stand in your way?" He paused. "Look, all I want is to do whatever is necessary to get custody of Quinn."

"Do you have your own key to enter any time you want?"

"Yes, but I only come when I think Quinn's in danger."

Peggy glanced at Sarah and back at Brett and then at his arm, nodding. "Did you fight with her?"

Brett followed her line of vision to the scratch on his arm. Great! "It's not what it seems. I tried to take her keys away."

Peggy paused.

He motioned for them to enter. "I didn't hurt her. Come in and we can talk about it."

Peggy exchanged looks with Sarah. "These are exigent circumstances, so we'll come in to assess, but it would have been advantageous for us to talk to her."

"I told her that, but she took off anyway. She probably didn't want you to smell the booze on her breath." He jostled around them to close the door. "I can't make her do anything she doesn't want to do." He motioned for them to head to the living room. "Excuse the mess and the stench. I didn't clean up because I wanted you to see the way Ali lives."

Both women entered hesitantly.

"Look," he said, "I'm a good guy, a cop. My job is to help people in this community, not harm them."

Chapter Eight

Sarah couldn't take her eyes off of Quinn's dad when he answered the door. His appearance startled her. It wasn't because he was in a cop's uniform, because men in uniforms never tripped her trigger. She typically liked the rugged outdoorsy-looking guys. When she'd heard he was a cop, she figured he'd be the typical bad-ass type, but he looked more like a schoolteacher, especially carrying the stuffed lamb under his arm. His curly dark hair hung just a tad over his ears, and his pale blue eyes reminded her of an adult male version of Quinn.

His innocent but desperate look really knocked her off balance too. It was the same look Quinn had displayed before she left Sarah's office. The one that tugged at her heartstrings. He didn't look the type to have anger issues either.

Typically, Sarah was good at staying neutral, but this was difficult. She wanted to believe that Brett was a monster, especially after reviewing his case and learning of the protective order. Her first impression was not what she expected. She almost felt sorry for him, especially when she saw the garbage lined along the wall and smelled the filth. She couldn't imagine raising a child in that environment. What kind of mother was Ali that she would flee even though she knew they were coming? Probably a mother who had something to hide.

When Sarah had seen the deep scratches on Brett's arm she'd almost gasped, remembering another time when she'd been the one who had inflicted similar scratches on someone in her life. When tears had welled in Brett's eyes, she believed his story was different from hers, but how well did she really know him?

As they stood in the entryway, Brett said, "So, you've seen Quinn? How is she?"

Sarah exchanged a glance with Peggy. "She's doing well considering the circumstances. I'm sure you'll get to see her after we finish the assessment."

"Really?" He sighed like he was genuinely relieved. "Thank you. Where is she now?"

Peggy took a few steps into the living room, surveying the home, then moved on to the kitchen.

Sarah stayed in the entryway, facing Brett. "She's in a room at the sheriff's office. It's where we hold children until we assess their situation. The room is equipped with a TV, a DVD player, and a staff that will spoil her." She smiled, trying to help him relax.

"I'm familiar with that room. Has she asked for this?" He held up the lamb. "She never goes anywhere without it."

Sarah shook her head. "She's mostly concerned about her dog."

"I've got a unit out looking for him." He paused and nodded toward the other room. "Can I get you something to drink? Make a pot of coffee?"

Peggy, who had returned to them, said, "No, we don't have time. For now, we need to ask a few questions, search the home, and present you with a few documents."

Brett rubbed his eyes. "Of course, sure." He led them into the kitchen and pulled out two chairs, brushing the crumbs off the seats. "I'm sorry for the mess. Clutter is invisible to Ali." He closed his computer and moved it out of the way before he sat across from the women.

Peggy set her briefcase on the floor, opened it, then brought out a file. "Where do you live?"

"In a one-room apartment across town." He gave her the address. "After I divorced Ali and lost the custody battle, I wanted to keep Quinn in familiar surroundings, so as not to upset her world too much. So I moved out and let Ali keep this place. All I could afford was a one-room apartment."

Peggy scribbled notes on her clipboard.

He said, "Look, this has all been a terrible misunderstanding. Quinn can live with me. She doesn't need to go anywhere else." He exhaled loudly. "Ali hasn't been well for a while, but the courts decided to grant her custody because mothers always get the children. I tried to fight them, to explain her emotional issues, but she lies well. They believed her. And she stayed sober long enough to pass a drug test."

Peggy said, "We've talked to Mrs. Finkle, the neighbor who brought her in, and have Quinn's file here." She motioned toward her briefcase. "According to the divorce transcripts, her doctor said she was taking her meds for depression, holding a job, functioning well. Has that changed?"

"Yes, I think she lost her job, and this morning she had booze on her breath."

Sarah interrupted. "If you were here this morning and saw the shape she was in, why did you leave Quinn in her care?"

Brett's face turned red. He cleared his throat. "What was I supposed to do?" His eyes pierced through her. "I'm not allowed to take her. Ali told me she was okay, that she was getting up."

Sarah didn't say anything.

He continued. "I asked if I could take Quinn to day care, but Ali said the day care center wouldn't take Quinn because Ali was behind in her payments."

Sarah pressed him. "Why didn't you pay for child care?"

"I had. I'd given Ali the money in the monthly child support check. She was supposed to pay them." He rubbed his eyes. "In hindsight I probably should have paid them directly."

He turned to Peggy who jotted notes on her clipboard. "And, for the record, I never laid a hand on Ali. Like I said, she's a good liar." Brett rubbed his hands on his slacks as if they were sweating.

Sarah believed him and was shocked she did. What made him different from the other men she'd met? What made him so believable? Was it because he was the first one who seemed to genuinely care for his child? Maybe it was because he was the type of man she'd always wished her father could have been. Maybe she was seeing him through a child's eyes.

Brett said, "If I had called CPS to report what happened this morning, how quickly would you have been able to respond?"

Peggy's face lit up. "What are you implying?"

"You can't deny that you're overworked." Brett squirmed in his seat.

Peggy exchanged a glance with Sarah. "Let's continue."

Brett hugged himself. "I'm sorry. I didn't mean to offend anyone. It's just that I've spent the last six months trying to work with a system that betrayed me." He cleared his throat and locked his eyes on Sarah, wearing the most sincere expression, as if pleading for her to believe him. "The last thing I wanted was for Quinn's safety to be in jeopardy, but it's been marginal for a long time, and no one would listen to me."

Sarah could tell he was frustrated. In her years of practice, she'd seen it in women. Rarely had she seen it in a man.

Peggy set her papers on a clipboard, clicked her pen, and stood, exchanging a quick glance with Sarah. "Well, maybe we can get to the bottom of all this, but as professionals we need to stay neutral and let the judge decide what's best. Part of my job is to assess the home for safety." She walked to the refrigerator and opened it, then pulled out corked wine bottles, seeming to count beer cans, and made notes. "I'll need to do the same at your home if we're to consider placing Quinn there."

"By all means. We can go there from here. I'll take you right over." Brett stood and followed Peggy.

Sarah reached into her briefcase for her clipboard and followed them.

Peggy opened cupboards, finding one with a bottle of vodka, then scribbled a note. Next, she went into the living room, Quinn's bedroom, and Ali's room. She opened the medicine chest in her bathroom, observing dozens of pill bottles and taking more notes.

While Peggy documented findings, Brett turned to Sarah. "Can you tell me anything about what Quinn told you? I have no clue what happened here this morning."

Sarah bit her lip and answered, again feeling sorry for him. "I read her a story, and she played with dolls. We got acquainted." She smiled. "She said only good things about you."

Brett's eyes watered, and he took a deep breath, looking like he'd waited all day to hear those words. "Thank you." He plopped down into a chair and exhaled again. He looked away, but Sarah noticed how the corners of his mouth turned down like he was fighting tears. He pressed his fingertips into his eyes. She sat in the chair across from him.

Peggy, who approached them from Ali's bedroom, said, "When do you think Ali will return?"

He looked up at her. "I have no idea. She wouldn't tell me where she was going, and she popped a pill before she left."

Sarah placed a strand of hair behind her ear. "You said Ali hasn't been well. Is she struggling with anything else right now? Any other medical concerns that you know about?"

Brett held his head in his hands. "It's not like she has cancer or high blood pressure. But she's been *sick* for a long time. She's depressed, but she won't do anything about it. She denies it, tries to hide it, and won't take her meds. Some days when we were married she'd stay up all night and sleep during the day." He told them about Ali's lack of self-esteem, how sometimes he couldn't wake her. "Some people have a lower tolerance for stress—that's Ali."

Peggy pushed her glasses up on her nose. "Quinn's kindergarten records from this past school year were faxed over. They indicate she was tardy eighty percent of the time. Why's that?"

Brett shifted in his seat. "That was Ali's job. Before the summer break, she took Quinn to school on her way to work. My shift started earlier than hers. But she was always late. She couldn't wake up, so she was late getting Quinn to school. I didn't know she'd been late until I got a call from the principal a few weeks before school let out for the summer." Brett met Sarah's eyes. "Ali can't keep a schedule. If I pushed her about it, she would tell me I was a control freak. I couldn't win."

Sarah set her clipboard on her lap. "Are you controlling?"

Brett's face turned red again, and he squirmed in his seat. He looked out the window as if trying to compose himself. "No. Look, Ali didn't have the best upbringing."

Sarah crossed her arms. "What do you mean?"

Brett sighed and stared at Sarah with such intensity it made her look away. Her face flushed. "Her mother wasn't home very often, but when she was, men would come and go. Ali was sexually abused for more than five years before anyone believed her."

Peggy's brows creased. "I'm so sorry." She scribbled something on her chart.

Brett continued. "Yeah, but her mother made it worse. She wouldn't acknowledge it. She said it was nothing, just Ali's imagination."

Sarah tightened her arms around her chest, working at keeping her emotion in check. "Does she have any siblings?"

"Yes, a brother, Mark."

Sarah straightened her spine and jutted her jaw forward, trying to keep a blank face and her posture composed.

"Why?" Brett leaned forward in his chair toward Sarah. "Did Quinn mention him? Was he here this morning?"

Brett watched her, as if waiting for a clue. Was he holding his breath? She couldn't think of a reason not to tell him, so finally she met his eyes. "Yes, Quinn mentioned he had been here. Does he live nearby?"

"He lives a few miles from here, works at the bank. Did Mark hurt her?"

"Not that I know of. Why do you ask?"

He shrugged. "I don't trust the guy. Never have. There's something about the way he looks at Quinn that makes my skin crawl. What was he doing here?"

Sarah shook her head. "I don't know. Quinn wasn't able to tell me much about him."

He sighed. "He's very protective of Ali and says he feels responsible for not helping her during the abuse. He's four years older than her. When their mother was carousing, he had a job and was rarely home. But there's something shady about him. He better not have harmed Quinn! Do you think he knows something?"

"I don't know," Sarah said.

Peggy sat on the sofa, her head bent toward the clipboard. She looked at Brett. "What did Ali do for a living?"

"She was a cashier at Gale's Mini Mart."

Peggy scribbled on her clipboard again. "I think I have everything I need from here. Like I said, the state's job is to keep your child safe. My responsibility is to assess whether or not she is. At first glance it looks as though she's at risk here." She waved her hand around the room. "If what you're saying is true, your wife is unable to care for her, but we have to assess your background and your residence for the courts to consider changing her custody, even if it's temporary. Five-year-olds don't roam the streets looking for their dogs." She paused to get something from her briefcase. "But we haven't interviewed Ali. We'd like to talk to her once she returns. Do you think you could get her to come to Sarah's office tomorrow?"

Brett nodded. "I'll try, but I can't make promises. What time?"

Sarah took out an iPad to check her schedule. "How's ten?"

Brett said, "I'm not working until this is resolved, so my schedule is open. But Ali might not want me to come." He turned to Peggy. "By the way, talk to Chief Dunson when you check my assessment. He'll vouch that I'm a stand-up guy."

Sarah thought he was going to smile, but he didn't.

But Peggy smiled. "We will."

He turned to Sarah. "Do you think it's possible I'll be able to bring Quinn home today?"

Sarah glanced at her watch. She hated Brett's pleading eyes.

Peggy said, "Don't count on it. Unfortunately, when these things happen, investigations can take at least three to four days, but I'm sure you understand."

He guffawed and clenched his hands into fists. "No, unfortunately I don't understand any of this. All I want is for my daughter to live with me. The *system* is what worries me."

Sarah saw Brett's jaw twitch. Was he ready to show his temper's ugly face?

Peggy put her clipboard in her briefcase and stood. "I'm sorry. We're doing the best we can. I have a half hour to inspect your place. If you're ready, we can follow you there, and then Sarah can perform the psych assessment tomorrow."

Brett's eyebrows creased as he turned to Sarah. "So, if you assess that I'm a good parent, is it likely I could get custody of Quinn?"

Sarah nodded to Peggy, who answered, "It's possible you could get temporary custody, but it won't happen today. I've already asked my office assistant, Robin, to see if your parents can take Quinn. If not, Robin will find her a temporary foster home."

"What?" Brett leaned forward in his chair. "My father has never even met Quinn."

Peggy held up her hand. "We try to find a family member to take the child first. Your father is a reputable man. It'll only be for less than a week—until we can get this report to the judge."

"How long will that take?"

Peggy glanced at the ceiling. "Maybe by Tuesday?"

"Five days?"

"The judge only schedules these hearings twice a week. Tuesdays and Thursdays. We missed today's, so we'll have to wait until Tuesday. I'm sorry."

Sarah watched Brett's ears turn red. He had to be totally frustrated with Peggy, but unfortunately there wasn't anything either Peggy or she could do.

Peggy said, "We need the judge to decide permanency, and that takes time. We just submit the facts. The fact that the judge limited you to only visitation rights until you complete the anger management classes says we need to ask permission for a change. We'll ask and recommend you, but we still need to talk to your ex-wife too."

"For crying out loud, isn't being a cop good for something?"

Peggy didn't crack a smile. "In the court's eyes, child neglect doesn't discriminate. It can be found among the most esteemed professional families."

"But I haven't neglected my child!" Brett ran his fingers through his hair.

"I understand." Peggy turned to go.

Brett shook his head. "No, I don't think you do."

Sarah followed Peggy out the door, once again feeling sorry for Brett, knowing sometimes the system didn't make sense and definitely took longer than expected. She hoped Brett's hearing with the judge would go quicker than the last case she'd handled.

Chapter Nine

The cloud-filled night obscured the moon's light, making the night as dark as Terry Bull's mood. He sat in his living room watching television. He'd grown up with the nickname Terrible and had lived up to the name. His quick temper had often gotten him into trouble as a child, and by the time he reached high school many teachers feared him. He hadn't cared. He still didn't. His mother was the only one who could tolerate him, but she was the one he hated the most—because she'd given him his name.

His mother interrupted his television show. "You need to get off your fat ass and fix the front door you busted. And when you're done, leave it unlocked so I can get in after work."

"What time you working till?" Terry ran his fingers along the nubs of his coarse dark beard.

She stopped to primp in the mirror. "What does it matter? You'll be drunk on the couch anyway."

"Shut up, woman."

She slammed the door, leaving a trail of cheap perfume.

After her car lights faded down the street, Terry scoured the kitchen cupboards for the whiskey. "Where the hell did she put it?" He opened the pantry, the dishwasher, and the microwave, and still didn't find it. He glanced out the front window one last time before he went into her bedroom, where he opened her drawers and the boxes in her closet.

He found the bottle of Johnnie Walker hidden in a boot box on the floor in the corner. The old lady had won it in a poker game from a bartender. "Woo-hoot."

He smacked his lips and smiled, salivating and anticipating the buzz. He unscrewed the top, then threw back a swig. Might as well get started. He needed to finish it all and pitch the bottle so the old lady might forget she ever had it.

No reason to get a glass dirty. He carried the bottle and swaggered back to the living room to watch TV, slipping in his favorite porn DVD. He sat on the sofa, using pillows to support his head. He downed a shot of the scotch whiskey and licked his lips. It tasted better than the cheap stuff he was used to drinking. Johnnie Walker sure made some fine shit. It was sweeter. Better. Smoother.

He turned to the TV, his eyes devouring the flesh on the screen. Man, them women were hot! He took his pants off and held himself.

#

I recognized the sounds of a snoring drunk and David Letterman's voice on the television when I cracked open the unlocked door, doubtful my next victim would hear me. He was in the other room, and his TV was too loud.

I set the backpack on the floor just inside, before clearing the kitchen table. What a mess. Filthy mess. After lining the dirty dishes, forks, glasses, and bowls next to the sink, I grabbed the backpack, unzipped the large compartment, and took out the towel, unrolling it to expose my supplies—the rag, the bottle of chloroform, the ketamine, syringes, and the needles.

Next, I opened the side pocket, took out the retractable scalpel, and set it next to the needles. I opened the bottle of chloroform and sprinkled enough of the solvent on the rag for the job, reached for the syringe, and moved to the living room.

Terry Bull sat on the sofa, his head tilted back, his mouth wide open. Good. He'd made it easy for me. There was no hurry either. His mother would be gone until morning as she worked the late shift. I'd watched them long enough to know their patterns.

And his pants were already off too.

I attacked from behind, wrapping my left arm under his neck and using my right hand to cover his mouth with the rag. He only jerked a little before he succumbed to the chloroform. Afterward, he never flinched. I injected his arm with the anesthetic and retrieved both the towel and the backpack from the kitchen and set them on the floor in front of me. I opened the towel, displaying my tools and wrapped the rubber strip around the end of his penis. In one fluid motion I severed the end that had gone limp in his hand. Wet blood dribbled out, staining his groin and thigh, but not too much. The tourniquet took care of that. He wouldn't feel the mutilation, smell his blood, or feel the way it grew sticky around the rubber band.

Yet.

But he would. I smiled. *You'll never lay another hand on anyone.*

I wiped the scalpel on my towel, retracted the blade, placed all the tools in the middle of the towel, and rolled it into a tight ball. After I squeezed it into the backpack, I zipped the pocket shut.

It was time to go. Now was the fun part. The hide-and-seek part. We'd see how long it took for someone to find the treasure this time. Too bad I couldn't see their faces when they found it. This one will be in the perfect place. I saw it posted on the computer today. I know how to get there—even in the dark.

Humming, I hurried off to the cache site. Tomorrow I had someone else to observe. Someone who'd come to the place I worked, but who hadn't registered himself yet. Shame on him.

Chapter Ten

After Sarah and Peggy left Brett's flat, their assessment complete, he opened the refrigerator. He needed to eat dinner, but his stomach churned with acid. He forced himself to make a sandwich, telling himself it would help him maintain his energy. As he finished his last bite, his cell phone buzzed. Was it Ali? He glanced at the screen, seeing his mother's name appear. Shoot, he'd forgotten to call her back.

"Hi, Mom."

"I'm so glad you answered."

She sounded breathless and like she'd been crying.

"I've been worried about you."

"No need to worry." He spread peanut butter on a slice of bread.

"Child Protective Services called and asked if we could take Quinn for a few days."

Brett sighed. "Yeah, I know. I'm sorry about that. I tried to tell them not to bother you."

"It's not what you think. We want to take Quinn, it's just—"

"You don't need to explain, Mom. I'm sure the last thing Dad wants is to take care of Ali's brat."

The pitch in her voice went up a few notches. "No, no, you're wrong. It's just that—"

"What?"

She lowered her voice. "Dad's sick."

Brett's heart skipped a beat. "He's sick? With what?"

"He didn't want me to tell you, but I have to now. You need to know. Dad has pancreatic cancer." Her voice trembled. Mom had never been real strong or independent. She leaned on Dad for almost everything. "We have to spend the next few days at the hospital for his treatments. He wanted to skip them to take Quinn, but I told him no."

Suddenly, the only sound in the room was the clock ticking. Everything stood still. His father was older, but old enough to die? And had he heard her right? He wanted to take Quinn? That was crazy. "When was he diagnosed?"

"A few weeks ago. He made me promise not to tell you."

No wonder she'd seemed a little on edge the last time he spoke with her.

Had his father really wanted to take Quinn? Or had he said that only because he knew he couldn't? Was it possible he'd changed? "You're right, Mom. He needs his treatments, and if you're going to be at the hospital, it's not a convenient time to take Quinn. She'll be okay for a few days. I should be able to get her next week, once they petition the judge."

"Why won't they give her to you now?"

Brett gave her a condensed version of the protective order, what had happened with Ali, and how it was going to take a few days for the report to be presented to the judge. He didn't tell his mom what CPS had said when they came to assess his flat, that it had been too small and not enough privacy for a man with a daughter. She didn't need anything else to worry about. He broke out in a sweat thinking about where he was going to move, how he was going to afford it, and about Quinn living in a stranger's home, but what else could he do? And there wasn't anything his mother could do either.

#

The next morning, before five, Brett made his bed, tucking the corners in and obsessively smoothing out the pillows, thinking of Quinn. Had she slept okay last night? Was she scared? Was she being well taken care of?

After checking his cell phone for calls and finding none, he took a shower, hoping the water would revive him, give him the energy he needed after tossing and turning all night. He dressed in plain clothes instead of his uniform. Afterward, he busied himself in the kitchen, washing dishes, but stopped and paced. He couldn't focus. He found himself washing the same dish for so long his fingertips were beginning to shrivel. On the counter was the Notice of Temporary Removal of Child and Right to Hearing form. It was the same one Peggy had left at Ali's. He still couldn't believe this was happening.

Peggy and Sarah had only stayed a half hour—long enough to assess whether Brett's place was a safe environment for Quinn. Of course, he didn't have anything to hide. It was neat and clean and void of any liquor. Heck, he couldn't even go out for a beer with the guys anymore without feeling repulsed. The smell of alcohol reminded him of Ali and made his temper flare.

Overall, there were no safety issues, but they said he'd have to get a bigger place to be granted custody. Since Quinn was a girl, she needed her own room, and since his entire apartment was only one room, it wouldn't work. There was no privacy.

Where was he supposed to get the money for a bigger place? He clenched his jaw, picked up the dish in the sink, and was about to throw it across the room, but stopped. He sighed heavily, put his head in his hands, and rubbed his temples. Getting angry wouldn't help. He'd only have another mess to clean up.

As he continued with the dishes, visions of Sarah seeped into the corners of his mind. It had been difficult to read her. Had she known something more about Ali's brother? Should he go to Mark's house and have a chat with him, find out what really happened yesterday? If he was with Ali when Quinn was locked in her room, he might know something. Could Brett trust himself not to lose his temper? He and Mark had gotten into it before. The guy thought his sister was perfect. What if Brett wasn't prepared for what Mark had to say and rage got the better of him? He'd totally screw up his chances of getting Quinn. But still, he had to know.

He dried his hands on a towel and glanced at his watch: 6:50. Just as he reached for his phone to call Clay, Clay's number appeared on the screen. Brett answered. "Hey."

"What's happening?"

"Washing dishes. Waiting for my appointment to see Quinn's counselor at ten. Any word on Max?"

"Nothing yet. Sorry, man. I wanted to check in on you—see how you're doing, give you an update on the whacker."

"The who?" Brett set the towel on the rack to dry. "Oh yeah, never mind. My head's mush."

"I'm in your driveway. I'll be right in."

Brett met him at the front door.

Clay stood on the porch in full uniform, his squad car parked out front. He carried a few manila folders under his arms and two coffees in his hands. He plowed through the door with the posture of a rhino, his large dark frame filling the entryway. Clay set the coffee and folders on the kitchen table and gave Brett his usual animal-type hug. "I'm praying for you, man."

Brett wished he had Clay's strength—physically, emotionally, and spiritually. He'd been a rock, always reminding Brett of his own lack of faith. Brett wished he could be as calm and sure of God as Clay always seemed to be.

Brett fell into a chair, shook his head, and pressed his fingers into his eyes. "I think Mark was at the house yesterday."

"Ali's bro?" Clay scooted a chair out and sat down in front of the folders.

Brett nodded. "I want to pay him a visit, but if I find out he's hiding something, I'm afraid I'll kick his ass and blow my shot at custody. Do you think you could go see him at the bank, rattle him a little?"

Clay nodded. "Sure. He works at First National, right?"

Brett filled him in on the details. "Find out why he was at Ali's and if he has the dog."

Clay said, "I'll go after I leave here and get back to you." He slid one of the folders across the table. "How you holding up?"

"I'm hanging in there. All I can do is wait." Brett told him about Peggy's visit and how he had to move to a larger place.

"What are you going to do?"

Brett frowned. "I'm not sure I can do anything. I'll need a security deposit, and I don't have the cash."

"Why don't you check out Tudor Apartments? They've had enough crime over there, they'd probably pay *you* to stay there."

Clay chuckled. "Having your cop car out front might cut down on incidents, and maybe they'd waive your deposit."

"Thanks. That's a great idea."

"Have you talked to Ali?"

Brett shook his head. "She disappeared, won't even answer her phone, and she needs to be at this appointment with me at ten, but shoot, if she doesn't show, it might help my situation."

Clay patted Brett's back. "I agree. Let's hope she doesn't show."

Brett opened the folder. "What's this?"

"It's the dirt on our sex offender, Jake Hunter." He took a sip of his coffee. "Seems he has quite a reputation. Hangs out at the local bar. He served four years at Clarion County Jail for doing that kid."

"Pedophile?" Brett studied the photo of the man.

"Yep."

Brett whistled. He stared at the photo—troubled eyes, mustache. But if he'd seen this guy on the street he would never have known he was a convicted sex offender. Too bad offenders couldn't be forced to wear a tattoo across their forehead labeling them a perv. "What about the kid he did? Anyone from the family hate him enough to do this?"

"Not that I could find. The kid he was convicted of molesting would only be twelve right now, and he's moved to Ohio with his family. I've got Officer Holmes on that—trying to locate them."

Brett studied the profile sheet, pretending to care because he still had a job to do, and the diversion was healthy, but trying to focus on what Clay was saying was difficult, at best. "So our pecker-whacker has a thing against pervs. That's not a bad thing. I kinda like this guy." Brett grinned.

Clay's radio squawked, and he turned the volume down. "There was another victim last night."

"Who?"

"His name was Terry Bull. A low-life registered sex offender living with his mother." Clay handed Brett the other file.

Brett opened it to find a profile sheet very similar to the first one.

"What happened?"

"Same thing. Best we can tell is that the whacker went to great lengths to stop the bleeding with his little tourniquet. I think he wants his victims to live without their rods for a while." Clay snorted a couple of times.

"Has anyone found it?"

"Not yet, but we're searching cache sites."

"I saw that there are close to five hundred in our county!"

"Yeah, I saw that too. Let's hope he's not going to hide the next one in one of those places. We'll have to recruit every officer within a hundred-mile radius to help cover them. Chief put me in charge of organizing a team that will rotate some of the larger sites. Some of them are micro sites, not big enough to hold the loot." Clay blotted his forehead with a napkin, absorbing the perspiration lining his brow. "The blood work on Jake Hunter came back. Seems he had high levels of ketamine in his body. It's a drug used to put patients under before surgery. We only found a few fibers at the site. Not sure they'll amount to much. This person seems meticulous. Hasn't left any real clues yet."

Brett nodded.

"We suspect he knocks the victims out with a chloroform rag and then injects them with this drug. They don't feel a thing until the drugs wear off. Then, wowsa!" He sipped his coffee. "No prints found. The neighbors didn't see anything either. But two days ago they saw a man in a truck parked across the street, watching the house."

"What'd that guy look like?"

"Thirty-something, balding, wore sunglasses, drove a light-blue truck—older model, lots of dings and dents."

"What can I do to help?" Brett needed to stay in the game, keep his mind occupied because eventually he needed to get back to work. Idle time only gave him opportunity to worry about Quinn.

"Thought you'd never ask. Feel like hiking?" Clay smiled.

"Where?"

"There're a few sites near here. I could use another man on the hunt team. You can use your iPhone to find the coordinates for the cache box. Hand me your phone." Clay held out his hand and waited.

Brett took his phone out of the clipped case and handed it to Clay.

"It's not every day you can hunt for dicks-in-a-box." Clay snorted.

Brett chuckled.

Clay added. "The media has leaked this, so there's a good chance there'll be more geo-hunters looking for caches than ever before. We can't keep the press out of it. We can't block off every site, and game players are adding new sites every day."

Brett couldn't believe there were so many geo-hunters in the county when he'd never heard of the sport until yesterday. He moved his chair next to Clay, looking over his shoulder at his iPhone. "Show me what I need to know."

#

After Clay left, Brett searched in the little shed outside his flat for his old hiking boots. He hadn't worn them in years. He used to hike trails but hadn't for a long time. He glanced at his watch: 8:05. Maybe he had time to pay Mark a visit first.

When he saw Max's spare leash hanging on the wall, an emptiness filled him. Too bad the dog wasn't here; Brett could use his expert sense of direction. Brett could get lost even if he had a compass.

Where are you, guy? We miss you.

The side door into his shed creaked open. "Brett?"

Brett jumped. Ali stood in front of him. Her short blond hair stood flat on one side and straight up on the other. It looked like she'd just rolled out of bed. Her blue eyes looked almost purple from being bloodshot red. She leaned against the doorjamb as if she might fall over.

"What are you doing here?"

"We need to talk." Tears fell down her face. She wiped them with the back of her trembling hand.

He should have felt sympathy, but her tears didn't matter anymore. "Okay. Come into the apartment. Give me a minute to shake the dirt off these boots."

"Where are you going?"

"For a walk, but not till later, that's all. Nowhere right now. We have an appointment with the counselor at ten. I've been trying to reach you, but you probably know that. You're ignoring me, aren't you?"

She avoided his eyes.

"That's typical." He turned his back to her, walked outside the shed, and hit the boots together, knocking off clumps of dried mud. He hit them with a little more force than necessary, dreading talking to her, knowing she'd probably lie again.

He left the dirty boots outside his door and invited her in.

She sat on a kitchen chair, reaching into a pocket for a tissue, while her eyes seemed to roam across the room. "Your place is really tidy." She balled the hanky in her hand and pressed it against her temple. "I have such a headache."

Brett nodded. "Of course you do. You have a hangover." As soon as he said it, he regretted it.

She shed more tears and spoke in a whiny voice. "I want to go see the counselor today. What was her name?"

"Dr. Sarah Grinwald." He sat across from her. "Tell me who was at the house yesterday."

She looked away, swallowed, and met his gaze. "Mark."

"Why? What did he want?"

"I don't remember. That's the bad part. I couldn't wake from my fog." She hesitated. "But I didn't want Quinn to see him. I'm not sure if I was dreaming, but I locked Quinn in her room to keep her safe."

"Safe from your brother? Why? What did he try to do to her?"

Ali shook her head and stood, then moved toward the kitchen sink. "Nothing. I don't remember. Can I have a glass of water?"

Brett nodded and held his temper in check. She knew. She just didn't want to tell him. "Help yourself."

She opened a cupboard and took out a glass, then poured herself water from the spigot. After that she opened her purse and fumbled through its contents. She finally took out a medicine vial, then threw a pill in her mouth and chased it with a swig of water.

"What are you taking?"

"The muscle relaxer for my neck." She massaged her neck and closed her eyes.

"Ali, you don't need those. You need to quit popping pills and drinking. Sleep at night instead of during the day. See a counselor. See someone who can help you." He tried to say it as gently as he could, but he wanted to shout it at her. He'd said it over and over again for the last year. "How many different drugs are you taking?"

Her eyes darted out the window and then back to him again—

the telltale sign that she was going to lie. "Just this one. I can't help it. My neck hurts all the time."

"Sure it does. You rear-ended someone six months ago. Remember?" He wouldn't forget. Her insurance had skyrocketed. He sighed. "You need help, and I can't do it anymore. I'm going to fight for Quinn. It's not going to be pretty this time. I want you out of her life. For good."

Her cries grew louder. "I'm sorry. I'm trying to do the best I can. I hate being alone to take care of her and have to work too. I'm in constant pain. All you have to think about is yourself. You never talk to me; you never look at me."

"Ali, we're divorced. I tried for six years to make it work. It's not my job to make you happy. You are not my responsibility anymore."

She reached for his arm. "I need you. I'm sorry. I don't want to be like"—she hesitated and waved her hands at herself—"this. I hate who I've become, but it's like I don't know how to stop. I'm in pain all the time. It won't go away. I want to be a good mother." She stopped and hiccupped a deep sob.

He shoved his hands in his pocket. All she did was whine. "Yeah, yeah, I know, I've heard it before. And I'm sorry for you, but your problems aren't my problem anymore. I don't understand them, and I don't have time for them." Her blubbering tears had worked once. He'd succumbed to her needs and empathized with her pain. He still did, but after being separated from her for months, it was easier to walk away from the guilt.

He had to force himself to stay calm, refrain from taking her by the shoulders and shaking her. He raised his voice a notch. "Quinn is living with another family—because *you* neglected her. Do you understand? I can't accept that—nor should the courts."

She reached for his arm and squeezed it. "Please! I promise I'll quit drinking. I'll go to AA. I want Quinn back too. She's everything to me. Please, don't take her away. I have nowhere to go. My mother won't let me live with her. Please."

Brett unhooked her hand from his arm and lowered his voice. "I can't talk about this anymore. It's nonproductive. I'm sorry for you, but I can't help you. I have to let the natural consequences happen. Go home and get ready, and I'll pick you up at 9:45. But after that, I'm done!" He turned and stormed out the door.

Chapter Eleven

Dawn showed its pink-clouded face as twenty-two-year-old Nikki pleaded with Justin, her boyfriend, who sat eating his breakfast. "Come on. I watched two hours of football reruns with you on Saturday. You said you'd do this with me."

Justin sighed and took his last bite of an egg. "You don't waste time, do you?"

Nikki sat next to him on the sofa tickling his ear with her fingertip. "It'll be cooler if we go now. Tory said she's found a hundred and two caches. And hiking is great exercise."

Justin smiled at Nikki. "You don't quit."

She bounced toward him like she was cheering for the winning team. "Yay, you'll do it?"

Justin stood. "I promised, didn't I?"

She clapped and moved across the room to her desk. "I already have an account all set up. I want to find the one I showed you yesterday titled 'Under the Bridge.'" She opened her laptop and waited for it to boot up. "Bring your iPhone over here so we can program the coordinates."

Justin placed his iPhone on the desk, slipped on his tennis shoes that were sitting next to the sofa, and grabbed his sunglasses. "Do I need one of those safari hats too?"

"Nope, none necessary." Nikki copied the GPS coordinates of the cache into the iPhone from the geocaching site. The site was west of Hursey Park. "I think this one is along the trails behind the doctors' offices. Listen to what it says about the site:

"'In 1924 developers of the west side of Hursey Lake considered using this site as the location of the new sugar mill. The nearby creek and abundant trees made the area very inviting. Unfortunately, construction crews began to complain about the terrible smell and eerie noises coming from the wooded area adjacent to the bridge. Several residents reported seeing a large apelike creature moving through the woods in the early morning hours. Construction crews aborted the project in 1926 when one worker—Richard Tracker—had a face-to-face encounter with something he described as a large manlike ape that had stepped out from under the bridge. It howled and made a sound Tracker said he didn't want to hear twice in his lifetime.

"'The cache is hidden near a tree alongside the bridge. A longtime resident of the area claimed the tree was sacred to Indians that lived there in the nineteenth century. The tree was called "Walking Bearman." The area has never been developed due to the persistent sightings of this apelike creature stalking the bridge until the late 1970s.

"'Move fast and don't linger too long. Hikers have reported mysterious shadows moving in the woods in the late-night hours, and unusual noises on moonlight nights. Dogs may be spooked in the area too.'"

Nikki said, "Ooohhh, doesn't that sound mysterious?" She didn't wait for Justin to answer as she reached for her sunglasses and the hiking backpack and threw it over her shoulder.

"Very cool, yes."

Minutes later, Justin drove to a community parking lot closest to the trails and parked.

Nikki couldn't believe she'd finally convinced him to go. He was always surprising her. She thought he'd try to find a way out of it, but not this time. She hoped once she got him outside and he felt the excitement of the hunt, he'd love it, and they could geocache more often.

He held her hand as they walked along the roadside of the industrial park medical district, his dark coarse hair hanging over his ears.

People drove by on their way to the hospital, a doctor's office, or a pharmacy. None would suspect where Nikki and Justin were going or what they were after. Nikki felt a little like a private detective. What a thrill.

She glanced at the navigation system, but the sun's bright rays made it almost impossible to read. She put her back to the sun, making a shadow on the screen to determine where they were going. "It says we're seven-tenths of a mile away. How far is that?"

"Oh, from about here to there." Justin pointed across the street.

"Where over there?" Nikki squinted to see.

Justin laughed and pointed again. "Somewhere over there."

Nikki slugged his arm. "Quit teasing me. You know I have no sense of direction."

Justin smirked. "I think we're supposed to go west now through this parking lot since the bridge is over that way. Right?" He pointed to a little sidewalk between two doctors' offices.

They headed toward the office door, but instead of going into the building, they continued their trek behind it, toward a field that led into the woods.

When they got to the trail entrance, Justin motioned for Nikki to go first.

She led them along the worn trail. "I read somewhere that it's important to act like we have a purpose—not to look like we're hunting for the prize. There could be other hikers searching for the same cache, and you don't want to spoil their fun or give away that we're searching."

Thick weeds scraped at Nikki's legs and arms. The sounds of automobiles driving by and horns honking faded as the trees and the brush absorbed the sound. Soon, all that was left were the sounds of bees humming, frogs from the nearby creek croaking, and the rustling of the bushes they walked through. Nature followed them to the bridge. Little bitty eyes lay hidden in the trees, watching them.

A fly flew into Nikki's ear, and she let out a little scream. "That little insect just smashed itself onto my face." She wiped the wet spot with the bottom of her shirt.

Justin took her hand and drew her closer to him. "Come here."

She hopped over a large prickly weed.

He pulled her into his arms. "I was hoping we'd have a moment like this." His lips pressed into hers. He reached down to her buttocks and brought her even closer. Then his fingers walked up her back to the long tendrils of red hair that fell loosely on her back.

She shivered and felt the hardness of his body against hers and the way his fingers pressed possessively around her waist. A sliver of sunlight peeked in between the shade of the tree branches shining a light on Justin's brow. Oh, she could stand here a very long time. But she pulled away. "Hey, stop that." She giggled. "We came here to find the cache." She took his hand and led him further along the path.

Justin laughed and slapped her bottom. "You can't blame a guy for trying."

She flinched and giggled. A squirrel's paws crunched on dead leaves on his way up a nearby tree. Nikki looked ahead. "There's the bridge up that hill. See it?" With her hand over her brow, she said, "Check out that humungous tree!" A large tree hovered over the bridge at the far end.

"I bet that's the one called Bearman. Look out. He's probably lurking nearby." Justin laughed.

"Stop!" Nikki turned to give him the evil eye. But then she broke out in laughter.

Justin checked the GPS. "I think we need to get to a clearing. I don't have a good signal here."

They hurried about ten feet to where a bike path opened into a less dense area. Justin stopped to study the reading.

Nikki gazed at the bridge. "Do you remember reading the book *The Three Billy Goats Gruff* when you were a kid?"

"Uh, no."

"This reminds me of the story. The Billy goat tries to cross the bridge, and the troll, who's lurking under the bridge, says, 'Who's that tramping over my bridge?' But in the end, the Billy goat wins. He pokes the troll's eyeballs out and crushes him to bits, body, and bones."

"Except today, instead of the Billy goat, it'll be Bearman, right?"

"It does feel kinda creepy here. Can't you just picture the troll waiting under the bridge and hear the clippity-clop noise of the goat on the top? Shhh, listen to how quiet it is." They froze and listened. The only sounds were the chirping of birds and the gurgling water under the bridge.

Justin abruptly placed his hands on Nikki's shoulders and shouted, "Boo!"

Nikki screamed and jumped, slugging Justin on the arm. "Don't do that!"

Justin held out his hand. "Wait." He inhaled. "Do you smell that smell?"

She sniffed and wrinkled her nose. "Yuk, what is that?"

"It's the Bearman! *Rooaarrr!*" He laughed.

She swatted his arm again, giggling.

"I couldn't resist." He glanced at the GPS. "It looks like it must be under the bridge here somewhere." He pointed to where a stream ran perpendicular to the bridge, where the water gurgled only a few inches deep. Rocks jutted out along the way.

Nikki ducked under the bridge along the side of the water, trying to balance on the rocks, holding onto the metal support beams on the side. Her eyes followed the beams above. "I bet it's in one of these steel pieces on the side. You look down at that end, and I'll look down at this end."

"If you find it first, don't open it. Wait for me," Justin said as he headed in the other direction.

They searched all around and underneath until they heard someone riding a bicycle, its spokes clicking along the top of the wooden bridge, and then past them deeper into the woods.

"Let's check out the top side." Justin waved Nikki over.

Together they walked with their heads bent, looking down in between the wooden boards. They started at one end of the bridge, walking to the other side. When they got to the end, Justin noticed a loose board. When he stepped on one side of the board, the other side rose.

Nikki knelt next to the raised board and peered underneath. "Cool. We found it!" Lying in the dirt was a dark-green metal box. The words *Geocache Box* were written on the outside in red nail polish. Flies buzzed all around it. Nikki waved them away and handed the box to Justin, jumping like a cheerleader on the balls of her feet and squealing. "I can't believe we found it!" She hopped in a circle. "I know it's silly, but it's the thrill of it."

While Nikki jumped, Justin knelt in front of the box. "Hey, what's this? Look what I found."

Nikki knelt next to him. Justin met her eyes. He held a tiny square box. Slowly, he flipped it open. Inside sparkled a princess-cut diamond ring—her favorite kind. She gasped.

Justin, still on his knees, said, "Nikki, will you marry me?"

"What?" Her hand covered her mouth. "Was that in the cache box?"

He chuckled. "No, I haven't opened the cache box yet. This is the box I brought. Do you really think someone would put something this valuable in a metal box for anyone to find?"

Nikki's heart felt like it would hop out of her chest. "Then this is for real? You're really, really asking me?" Her voice grew higher with each word.

"I'm really, really asking."

Nikki took the ring with trembling fingers. Justin slid it on her finger. Tears streamed down her face.

"Well?"

"Well what?"

"Do I have to ask twice? Will you marry me?"

"Yes! Yes!" Nikki stood and stared at the ring in the sunlight, twirling and admiring how it sparkled and lit up her hand. "I can't believe this. You had it planned all along, didn't you?"

"I wanted it to be a surprise."

She threw her arms around him, and they tumbled onto the ground, laughing, with Nikki still squealing. "I love you, you tricky guy, you!"

Justin held her and kissed her tenderly. He wiped her tears with the bottom of his shirt and gave her a totally serious look. "I'm really looking forward to spending the rest of my life with you."

"Me too, me too." She smiled.

They stayed that way for a few minutes, wrapped in each other's arms and looking into each other's eyes. Nikki didn't want the moment to end.

Justin said, "Let's open the cache box and sign in as the future Mr. and Mrs. Justin Prescott. This is history. We're now an engaged couple!" He pulled Nikki to a sitting position, reached for the box, and then opened it. Inside was a logbook, a plastic bag, a Spiderman sticker, an old six-inch wooden ruler, and a bottle of nail polish that jiggled on the bottom.

"What's in the Ziploc bag?"

Justin picked it up by the corner, holding it up to examine it. "Ew, I don't know." He moved the contents around inside the bag.

"It looks bloody and squishy." Nikki reached over and pressed her fingers to it. She peeled apart the Ziploc seal and opened the bag. A stench as bad as a spraying skunk filled the air, making them both gag. Nikki screamed and threw the bag down.

Justin pulled his phone from his pocket. He put his nose in the crook of his arm and resealed the bag using just the tips of his fingers. "I think I know what it is. I'm calling the police."

Nikki pinched her nostrils shut. "Why? What is it?"

"You don't want to know."

Chapter Twelve

At 8:50 a.m. Brett drove his cruiser downtown toward the corner of Main and Third—a block from Mark's house—and pulled into the Kroger parking lot. Mark was supposed to be at work, so Brett thought it might be a good time to check his house for Max. Things didn't add up, and Brett didn't want to wait for Clay to talk to Mark.

Brett still trembled, visibly rattled from his discussion with Ali, and called the animal shelter again.

When the girl answered, it sounded like there was a pack of barking dogs in the room.

"This is Officer Reed, just checking back to see if anyone turned in a golden retriever? I called yesterday."

The girl paused. "Max?"

Brett's heart raced, hopeful. "Yes."

"I see the note here, but no goldens have been turned in. I'm sorry." She promised to call if they found him.

Brett exhaled, feeling hope fade. It wasn't rational to think that if they found Max Brett would be closer to gaining custody of Quinn, because one had nothing to do with the other, but finding Max would give him hope.

Maybe the dog had followed Mark home. There was one way to

find out. He had forty-five minutes before he had to pick up Ali for their appointment. Not much time, but he would get in and get out. It would be worth it if he found Max and could bring him to see Quinn.

Brett could have called Mark and asked him, but ever since the divorce they hadn't been close. Mark had made it clear that he loathed Brett. He'd been the one to push Ali into filing the protective order.

Just as Brett was about to get out of the car, his phone vibrated. Clay.

Brett answered. "Did you see Mark?"

"No, sorry. He was out of the building at a meeting, but I'll try back later."

"Thanks." Brett got out of his car and headed toward Mark's house, taking the alley behind his home. Brett was acting impulsively, but sometimes he couldn't help himself.

"I've got an update on the whacker though—two hikers found another dick in a cache box this morning. We think it's Hunter's, but it's too late to sew it back on. It was sent off for DNA testing."

"Ouch! Where did they find it?" Brett heard paper rustling in the background.

"Under the bridge near the Walking Bearman tree."

"Didn't you say the first was found north?" Brett turned down the alley behind Mark's.

"Yeah. I have a map identifying the site locations. Stop in after you meet with the counselor and pick it up. It looks like we're going to need a lot more support to cover these cache sites."

Brett, with his phone to his ear, listened to Clay as he continued his walk toward Mark's. The summer sun peeked in between the trees and houses along his way. He was glad he'd dressed in his khaki shorts and a short-sleeved shirt instead of his uniform. At least he'd be cooler. "Chief might not want me at the precinct. Maybe you could meet me somewhere. I'll give you a call after my appointment."

"Where are you now?"

Brett approached Mark's backyard from the alley. "Uh . . . you don't want to know. I'll call you later."

After Brett clipped his phone back onto his belt, he climbed the steps and knocked at the back door. No answer. A row of hedges bordering the property hid the neighbor's view of Mark's yard. Perfect. He knocked again, and when no one answered, he turned the knob.

Locked.

He walked down the back porch steps to the side of the house, checking the bathroom window, which was slightly ajar. After taking out his pocket knife, he dug at the corner of the screen and pried it open, then set it next to the house, behind a bush. He pushed the window open and lifted himself into the house headfirst, coming face-to-face with the toilet.

He stood and froze, listening for sounds of life. Nothing.

"Max?"

Nothing.

Tiptoeing, he made his way into the living room, noticing the furniture—not much—a few tables, a futon, and a few tall lamps. It looked the same as the last time he'd been there. No sign of Max or Mark.

He went into the kitchen. A toaster and a coffeepot sat on the counter, dishes lay in the sink. Unopened mail littered the countertop: Netflix, phone bill—nothing out of the ordinary.

Brett hurried into the office and sat down at the desk in front of Mark's computer.

He tapped the space bar, and the machine began to whir. A leopard appeared as the screen saver. Brett clicked on the browser, and Google appeared. No passwords necessary. Sweet. He clicked on the History bar and then Show All History. Everything Mark had recently Googled appeared—mostly Amazon and Facebook pages. He clicked on some of his comments and his friends' Facebook pages. No secrets there.

Brett continued scrolling. He clicked on yesterday's date. Lines of geocaching sites appeared. "Whoa! What the heck?" He leaned forward and hurried to click on the first one. It was a YouTube video of a couple on their first hunt. His heart raced. Why would he be researching geo-sites? Brett was certain Mark had never hiked a day in his life. Another site was a recording of a difficult find. All were in this county—Stark County. Brett scoured the desk for a piece of paper and a pen. He jotted down the specific site locations and stuffed the paper in his shorts pocket. He was about to move the cursor to a Word file, when he heard a car door slam outside. *Crap!*

He hurried toward the window and looked out. Mark's truck had pulled into the driveway. *Damn!* What was he going to do now? This had been a really stupid idea. Nothing he could say could get him out of this one. He scanned the room and looked for a place to hide. The only option was the closet. He slipped into it and left the door ajar, and concentrated on keeping his body still and breathing as quietly as possible. He only had fifteen minutes to get to Ali's. How the hell was he going to get out unseen?

The back door opened, footsteps followed, and then the refrigerator squeaked opened. A minute later, footsteps headed down the hallway.

Peeking through the crack of the closet door, he watched Mark, dressed in a navy suit, pop the top of a Coke, take a swig, and set it on the desk. He plopped into the chair. The back of his balding head stared at Brett. Mark clicked the keys and hesitated. He gulped a few sips of his Coke and paused.

Brett's phone vibrated. *Shit!*

Mark spun around in his chair and faced the closet. "Who's there?"

Brett decided he had two choices: come out now or come out later. What did it matter? He was caught. He stepped out of the closet and into the room so Mark could see him, holding his arms up in the air. "Hey, bro."

Mark jumped out of his chair. "Bro, my ass. What the hell are you doing in my closet, in my house?"

"What are you doing home from work?"

"I don't need to answer that. What's it to you anyway?"

"I'll tell you what I'm doing here if you tell me what you were doing in my house yesterday."

Mark returned to his chair. "You scared the crap out of me."

"Why are you so jumpy?"

"I'm not used to men jumping out of my closet, okay? Where's your car?"

"Never mind. Just answer my question."

Mark looked at Brett and held his gaze. "Ail needed to borrow some money."

Brett's stomach turned. "Did you lock Quinn in her bedroom?"

Mark shook his head. "What are you talking about? I didn't see Quinn when I was there."

"Why don't you start from the beginning and tell me what really happened."

"There's nothing to tell. I stopped by, Ali was sacked out on the couch, and I figured Quinn was in her room sleeping. End of story."

"Did you give Ali money?"

Mark's eyes darted away from Brett's. "Yeah, she woke up long enough to take it."

"Did she say what it was for?"

"Day care."

"How much did you leave her?"

Mark looked away. "About three hundred."

Was Mark hiding something? "What about Max? Did you see him?"

Mark averted his eyes again, for a few seconds, long enough to drum up a lie. Lying seemed to run in the family. He nodded and scratched his nose. "He was at the house, but when I turned to leave he went psycho, barking and growling at me. I ran out the door to get away from him, but he followed me. The SOB bit my ass. I have the bruise to prove it." He reached back and rubbed his behind. "I wasn't about to stick around after that. I don't know where he went."

"You asshole." Brett turned to go, clenching his fists at his side, wanting to beat the truth out of Mark but knowing it was better to keep his temper in check—at least for now. Max never bit anyone. If he'd turned aggressive toward Mark, it was for a reason.

Mark followed him out of the room. "You're the asshole. What gives you the right to break into my house?"

#

Brett hurried into the alley after Mark pushed him out the door and slammed it in his face. Just as well. If Brett had stayed much longer, he might have decked the guy.

He jogged through the alley past garbage cans, barking dogs, and a gold cat, then into the street toward his car at the grocery store. Running helped simmer his boiling blood. He slowed as he approached the parking lot as shoppers were coming and going.

Taking two deep breaths, he wiped his sweaty palms on his shorts and climbed into his car. He drove out of the parking lot tempted to switch on his flashers, but held back. It would be better if he didn't draw attention to his car, but he needed to haul butt if he was going to make it to Sarah's on time. Ali had better be ready. It was 9:40.

It felt like a week since he'd seen Quinn!

He unclipped his phone and dialed Clay's number. Clay answered on the second ring. "What's up?"

"If I give you the URL addresses of two geo-sites can you tell me if either is one of the crime scenes?"

"Maybe. Why?"

Brett dug in his pants pocket and retrieved the addresses from Mark's computer, then read them to Clay. "I found them on Mark's home computer."

"You were there?"

Brett shoved the piece of paper back into his pocket while watching the traffic, and sped to Ali's. "Yes, but you don't know that."

Clay chuckled. "I'm not sure I like the sound of that, but I'll check them out and get back to you."

"Thanks." Brett disconnected his call and dialed Ali's phone. No answer. Of course. She better be ready.

He pulled onto her street and noticed a van marked WMDU, the local television station, parked out front. His stomach tumbled. What were they doing there? Had something happened to Ali? He flew up the driveway and threw the gearshift into Park. As he got out of his car, a thick-bodied news reporter approached him with a microphone. A short guy with a beard followed with a camera resting on his shoulder.

"What's wrong?" Brett said, approaching the men.

The reporter shoved the microphone in Brett's face. "Officer Reed, is it true that CPS took your daughter?"

"Who told you that? What business is it of yours?" His temper rose, furious with the gossip hounds in his neighborhood, especially Mrs. Finkle. Why couldn't they mind their own business?

"Is it true?"

Brett turned away and continued his trek up the driveway. "No comment."

"Are you hopeful that you'll get her back?"

As he walked toward the front door, the reporter followed.

"Your neighbor said your daughter was found wandering the

streets. Is that true?"

"No comment." He reached for the doorknob, but it was locked, so he rang the bell. *Come on, Ali. Where are you? Let's get out of here.* The summer humidity suffocated him as he felt his insides bubble to the top. A rivulet of sweat trickled down the middle of his back.

"Officer Reed, there are rumors that your daughter was sexually abused—is that true?"

"What?" That did it! Brett balled his fist and hauled at the reporter, hitting him square in the jaw, barely making the guy flinch. The reporter staggered, but only a little. His hand went to his jaw and he cussed.

Brett's hand stung like he'd hit a brick wall. He shook the burn away, wincing. He'd never been much of a boxer and weighed probably fifty pounds less than the reporter, so it was no wonder he hadn't made a dent in the guy. "Get the hell out of here. Now! And don't come back." He fumbled for his key, shoved it in the hole, and pushed through the door, shutting it and closing out the reporter.

He scolded himself for losing his temper. He'd be in deep trouble for decking the guy. But how could anyone believe he'd molest his own daughter? The thought of it made him sick.

The walls of the garbage-infested home stared back at him, and a heavy feeling of doom spread through him. The house was too quiet. Something didn't feel right. "Ali?" His stomach somersaulted.

He hurried to her bedroom. Clothes were scattered across the floor and the bed. The dresser drawers had been emptied. Her suitcase, typically in the back of the closet, was gone too. His hand went to his stomach as if someone had sucker-punched him. She left? Where did she go? She'd never left before. Did she go to her mother's? Should he call her mother? No, she was the last person he wanted to talk to.

He took a deep breath. Okay then. This was what he'd wanted, wasn't it? She had made it easy for him. He was okay with her being gone. Right?

Why then was his stomach turning? Why did he feel panic?

He bolted to Quinn's bedroom. Clothes from the closet were thrown all over the room. Drawers were open and emptied onto her bed. Quinn's stuffed animals and her suitcase were gone. What was happening? Had Ali planned to take Quinn somewhere? Was she kidnapping Quinn? How could Ali know where Quinn was?

There was one person who might know—Sarah Grinwald.

He glanced at his watch: 9:56. He was going to be late, but she'd know if Quinn was taken from her foster home. Certainly CPS wouldn't have allowed Ali to take Quinn, would they? No, that would be kidnapping.

He plucked Sarah's business card from his wallet to look up the address and raced out the front door to his car. The news reporter and his crew had left. Brett turned on his sirens and sped down the street, leaving smoke from the burning rubber of his tires.

The entire time he sped down streets to Sarah's, all he could think about was Quinn and how reckless Ali could be. Nightmares of Ali driving drunk with Quinn flooded his mind.

When he pulled into Sarah's office parking lot, there were three other vehicles there—and none were Ali's.

Chapter Thirteen

Earlier that same morning, about eight fifteen, Sarah had pulled into the parking lot of Hursey Community Church a little behind schedule. Her morning hike had lasted longer than she'd anticipated. There had been ten new geo-sites posted, and one was so close to her home she'd ventured out to find the cache, hoping to get to her office by eight thirty for her client. But she never found it. She had the coordinates right and arrived at the destination, but no luck. It was the first time she aborted a hunt before she found the cache.

The summer sun beat down through the sunroof in her Ford F-150, warming the top of her head and shoulders. She parked away from other cars, hoping to avoid door dents, and walked to her office.

Four hours a week she volunteered her services for free at her church for men and women who couldn't afford a counselor. It was her way to give back. There had been times in her life when she'd felt she had no one to turn to. She vowed she'd be there for others someday.

She primarily counseled women because she could relate to them better, but occasionally she accepted a male client. Men scared her. She knew it was irrational—not all men were abusive, but fear was never rational. She'd seen many women who'd suffered at the hands of a man, herself included. She never wanted that to happen again, so she figured if she didn't allow intimacy in her life, she'd be safe.

Today's patient was Mr. Michael Moore. She'd met Mr. Moore once before—and talked to him long enough to know he was harmless. He'd recently lost his job and moved to the area to be closer to his mother. He was seeing a counselor because he needed confidence, someone to help him feel good about himself, so he could interview better.

Soft-spoken Mr. Moore, in his mid-forties, looked like the true stereotype of a nerd. He usually wore black polyester pants and a short-sleeved cotton plaid shirt, tucked in. The top of his pants sat high on his waist, almost to his chest. His belt looked too big, and the excess flapped in the air and hit his arm when he moved. His black-laced shoes clunked, making him lift his legs high as he walked—as if they weighed too much. They looked too big for his feet—kind of like Bozo the Clown's.

Sarah's goal today was to encourage him to go for a makeover. She knew the person to help too. Maybe if he could improve his persona it would boost his self-esteem. In order for him to find a job, he was going to have to improve his self-image first.

Sarah led him into her makeshift office she used at the church. He held the door open for her when they reached her twelve-by-twelve-foot room. Like a gentleman, he waited for her to sit before he did. They made small talk about the weather, and then he asked her a question. "Can you give me some tips on how to meet nice women like you?"

This gave her the perfect opportunity to talk about a makeover.

#

Yesterday, at work, I smelled him right away. The name on his file was Michael Moore, but I doubted it was his real name. It was probably an alias, a cover-up. He wore his pants up to his chest, and his oversized belt flapped against his arm when he walked. He pretended to look like someone he wasn't, but I knew. I didn't have to check the online sex offender list to know, because I could smell him. But I checked the registry anyway. Just to be sure. He was new to our town, moved from Ohio, but I found him on the Ohio sex offender list. His real name was Calvin Moore.

He smelled like all the other slimy pervs. He would be my next victim. It wouldn't be long, and everyone would know his true identity. I could leave his prize in the new cache box near his house. And Moore would never be able to use his pecker again.

The thrill of the game made my heart race.

I followed him out of the office, pretending I was going to run an errand. He pulled into the driveway of a small home in the heart of downtown, across from the Dental Solutions office. I parked in the doctors' lot, facing Moore's home, pretending to look at a map. A car pulled up to the curb in front of his house, and a lady with two little girls—one with blond hair and one with dark curly hair—got out of the car. The lady looked like my seventh-grade music teacher, Melody Stookey. Wasn't she retired now? How did she know this creep? She carried something in a bowl to his door. The girls skipped alongside her. Were they her grandchildren?

Don't go in his house! I broke out in a sweat thinking of Moore being near the girls. He answered the door, took the bowl, and Mrs. Stookey left with the girls. I exhaled. Moore watched as they turned to go.

As I spied from across the street, memories came flooding back, the ones I wanted to go away. They saturated my mind. I squeezed my eyes shut, and put my hands on my head. But the memories came anyway.

The dead don't choose when they die. Because, if they did, Mama would have chosen to die long before she did.

I peeked through her cracked bedroom door listening. Mama was gone, but the bedsheets were the same as the ones she used to sleep on. I remember lying beside her and smelling them and thinking how they smelled of her—like the blooming rose bushes off the front porch. But now they only smelled like him. She'd been gone too long. No matter how hard I tried, I couldn't smell her anymore.

I stared at the rumpled sheets through the crack of the door, wishing she was there, calling my name to come and cuddle with her. But instead, I heard little muffled cries. I couldn't go in. I wouldn't dare. I was too afraid. Besides, it would only make things worse. I listened to his lies through the door. They were the same ones he'd told me, only now he told them in a different way. I shouldn't have believed, but I had, and now I hated him.

"Your mother would want you to be strong. She's looking down from heaven, so make sure she sees you smiling and not frowning. She'd want you to be a good girl, and do what Daddy says."

My eyes jerked open. A door slammed across the street. I wiped perspiration from my brow. Moore was leaving his house. But now he looked different. He'd changed his appearance. This *other* Moore wore fashionable jeans and cowboy boots, and he smoked a cigar. His dark hair was slicked back Elvis-style. Even his walk was different—confident, cocky. I had to look twice to make sure it was him, but it was.

How did Mrs. Stookey know this guy? I turned in my seat, reaching for my computer in the back. I slipped it onto the seat next to me and opened it. Four bars of wireless lit up from the Dental Solutions office. No password necessary. I typed in Melody Stookey, Hursey Lake, IN. Several links appeared with her name and "Foster Care" next to them. Were the girls foster children? Possibly. I clicked on a few more links. Mrs. Stookey's husband, Bruce, died several years ago. She retired from the Hursey Lake School District five years ago. She had one son. Her maiden name was Moore. Was Calvin Moore her son? I doubted the girls were his. They must be foster children.

My stomach knotted and my skin prickled thinking about Moore being anywhere near children.

I hurried back to work.

#

By nine thirty Sarah had returned to her office on the lake. She squinted as the sun reflected off the waves and onto her office windows. Peggy had arrived with Quinn. They were waiting in the office until Brett arrived. Sarah stood outside, lakeside, with her brother, Dean, who had come to help clean her windows and install a snake deterrent to keep the robins from slamming into the glass.

She handed Dean the ammonia cleaner and a stack of newspapers, pointing to the windows that needed washing. She showed him the shed, where he could find the ladder. Dean took the ladder, carried it to the side of the house, and hung the rubber snake with a nail under the gutter.

"Do you think it'll work?" Sarah asked.

Dean nodded as usual, limiting his words. He'd always been more of a silent type.

As Sarah turned to head back into her office, a siren blared down the street. For a second she panicked, thinking someone was hurt, but then remembered Brett was coming. Guess he was using his power to get there.

Sarah waved to Dean. "I've got an appointment, so go ahead and start, and let me know when you're finished. Thanks for doing this."

He waved and smiled.

She entered her office through the lakeside door and returned to where Peggy and Quinn were waiting. They sat at a table in a little room adjacent to Sarah's lounge area, putting together a hundred-piece horse puzzle. Sarah turned to Peggy and gave her the signal that Brett had arrived. "I'll be back in a minute." After closing the door, she moved toward the front door, waiting.

The police siren stopped, and within seconds Sarah heard the rapid knock at her door. She opened it and Brett rushed in, seemingly out of breath, with Quinn's lamb tucked under his arm. He wore hiking boots, shorts, and a short-sleeved shirt. Sarah couldn't believe how different he looked without his uniform on. This Brett looked more like an outdoor enthusiast, natural and carefree, the type she was typically attracted to.

"Ali's gone." He panted as his words tumbled out. "She packed her stuff and Quinn's and took off in her car. Is there any way she found out where Quinn is staying?"

Sarah closed the door behind him. "It's possible, but I wouldn't know how, and she didn't take Quinn. She's here—in the office." Sarah pointed to the adjacent room.

"She's here?"

Sarah nodded.

Brett exhaled loudly and put his hand on his heart. "I thought Ali had found her and taken her. Thank God Quinn's here. I wonder where Ali is. Are you planning on tracking her down?"

"If she doesn't show, we'll do what we can."

Which meant they'd do nothing. Impatient, he shook his head and pointed to the office door. "Is Quinn in there?" He took a step toward the door.

Sarah held up her arm. "Whoa." She motioned for him to stop.

"Before you go in there, we need to go over a few things about visitations. Let's sit over here for a minute." She waved for him to join her at the sofa.

Brett hesitated, glancing at the office door as if he was contemplating whether he wanted to see Quinn now or sit on the couch. He took another deep breath and finally sat, wiping his hands on his shorts. His eyes followed Dean, who stood outside the office on the ladder.

"That's my brother. He helps me out around here. He won't be here for long." She sat in the chair across from Brett. He met her eyes. "You and Ali are the most important people in Quinn's life. Seeing you is one of her basic needs. Stop and think a minute what you're going to say. Don't discuss when she's going to come home—not yet. Because you don't know. You don't want to confuse her or get her hopes up."

"I'm not stupid. I know how to be sensitive to my child's needs."

Sarah's face heated at his rudeness. She wanted to say, do you know how many parents don't know what their children need? She calmed herself. Obviously Brett was anxious to see Quinn. "There are books, games, and puzzles over there that you can take into the room." She pointed to the same alcove in the corner of the room that Quinn had visited for *Black Beauty*. "I'll need to ask you a few questions after you visit with her, for my report." She glanced at her watch. "Maybe Ali will show up."

"Don't count on that happening."

Sarah began to rise.

Brett placed his hand on her arm. "Wait."

Sarah withdrew her arm from his reach, not because it repulsed her but because a strange tingling sensation shot through her.

Brett said, "Oh, I'm sorry, but you don't know Ali. I don't trust her. I think she's going to try to take Quinn. What's the procedure for getting a custody hearing, and what can I do to speed that up?"

Trying to keep her composure, Sarah settled back in her seat. "You have the right to request the immediate return of Quinn to your care. You'll have a hearing in front of the judge within three days of your request. But you might want to consult an attorney first. Sometimes there are reasons to postpone this hearing." She reached across the table to a manila file and took out the form for the request and handed it to him.

"I don't understand. Why would I want to wait?" He studied the form.

"To make sure you render her mother incompetent. It might take a little while for the investigative report to prove that Ali is an unfit parent—if in fact she is. By waiting for the complete report, you could benefit from a more thorough investigation. If you go to the hearing now, you run the risk of Quinn ending up in Ali's care again."

Brett stroked his chin, looking anxious. "I don't have the money for an attorney." He paused. "I want a hearing in three days. I don't want to wait. I'll take my chances."

Sarah nodded.

"Are you certain that Quinn is safe where she is? She's in a good home?"

"Positive. Foster parents have to have completed home studies, and they're monitored. The woman she's staying with is a retired teacher."

Sarah watched as he seemed to relax, sinking into his chair.

He sighed and his shoulders fell, and his bloodshot eyes stared at the door. A long, deep breath escaped his lips. "Can I see her?" His voice dropped two notches, as if all the energy he'd had when he walked in had disappeared.

Sarah hesitated. Was he okay? He seemed emotional, but that was understandable. Maybe he was acting the way most loving fathers would. She felt sorry for him.

She stood and led him to the office. He followed.

Immediately after opening the door, Quinn turned and saw her father. She bounced off the chair and ran into his arms. "Daddy!"

Brett knelt on the floor and held her to his chest, kissing the top of her head, her forehead, and her cheeks. Tears brimmed his red eyes. "Hi, baby."

Sarah tried to look away to keep her own tears from spilling, but she couldn't. She was drawn to the way his hand naturally and tenderly caressed Quinn's cheek and how the child was his only focus. He seemed to examine her from top to bottom as if looking for any sign of neglect. He spun her around and danced the stuffed lamb in front of her.

Disguising his voice, he pretended to speak for the lamb. "I've missed you so much. Where have you been?" He rubbed the lamb into Quinn's neck, tickling her. She giggled and reached possessively for her toy, hugging it to her chest. "You brought Lambie. Thanks, Daddy!"

There was something about the way his dark curls fell onto the top of his ears and his eyes sparkled for his daughter that gave him almost a playful baby-boy look. But his thick muscled legs and broad shoulders seemed steady enough to hold the weight of five children.

"I didn't know when I was going to see you again." She looked around him at the door. "Where's Mommy?"

Brett, who still stooped on the floor with Quinn, looked up at Sarah. She shrugged.

"She's sick, honey. I'm sorry. She wanted to come, but she wasn't feeling well. She loves you."

"What about Max? Did you find him yet?"

"No, but we're looking. We're not giving up." Brett pulled away from the embrace, still eyeing Quinn up and down as if inspecting her for bruises or broken bones.

"Can I come home now?" Quinn pouted, which had probably won many battles before.

"Not yet." He smoothed the hair off her forehead and bent to kiss it again. "Is the family nice to you where you're staying?"

"Yes, Sadie is there too. She's my age and my best friend. We swing together and play hide-and-seek, and they have a kitty, Daddy! A little white kitty, and I get to hold her and sleep with her."

Brett stood and took Quinn's hand. "How exciting. I know how much you've wanted a kitty."

Quinn bounced on her toes. "The lady is a music teacher too. She's going to teach me how to play the piano."

Brett gave her a high five. "Wow, that's awesome! Are you eating well?"

"Yes." She giggled. "She doesn't make my eggs dippy like you do, but I ate them anyway." She whispered, "I did what you told me. I didn't tell her they were yucky." She wrapped her arms around Brett's legs. "I miss you."

As Sarah witnessed the exchange, she found it more and more difficult to swallow the lump of tears in her throat. It was obvious that Brett was a strong part in the child's life, but Sarah knew the courts, and typically the mothers came out way ahead of the fathers. Unless they could prove Ali was unfit, Brett didn't stand much of a chance.

Sarah couldn't believe that, for the first time in a long time, she was attracted to a man. She wanted to do everything she could do to help Brett get custody of Quinn.

Her skin prickled. She'd better keep her guard up.

Chapter Fourteen

Brett played two games of Memory with Quinn and read *Black Beauty* to her. She told him how Sarah had a horse that looked just like Beauty, and how Sarah had said she'd let Quinn ride him someday. When it was time for their visit to end, Brett swallowed the knot in his throat. He coughed and scooted his chair next to Quinn. "You have to go now, but I'll see you again soon. It's going to take a little while to sort this out, but I'm working at making sure you can come home with me forever, okay?"

Quinn looked away and nodded, tears filling her eyes. "You have to find the bad guys, right?"

"Yes." Brett kissed the top of her head. "Pretend you're on a camping trip with your new best friend, Sadie. Have fun, and soon you'll be home."

She nodded again and bit her lower lip as Brett held her hand, ushering her out to the main lounge area, where Sarah waited. Brett approached Sarah, still holding Quinn's hand. Quinn slipped her other hand into Sarah's, like they'd been friends for years. Sarah smiled, seemingly comfortable with how Quinn had warmed up to her, so uninhibited. "When can I meet your horse?"

Sarah glanced at Brett. "Hopefully soon. Maybe your dad could bring you sometime. I know my Beauty would like you."

Quinn swung her arms back and forth, smiling at Sarah and then back to Brett. "Will you, Daddy?"

Brett raised his eyebrows at Sarah, surprised she'd offered. "That would be fun. As soon as we get you back home, we'll go meet Beauty. Meanwhile, you have fun with Sadie, okay?" He squeezed her hand.

Quinn jumped on the balls of her feet. "Okay, I promise."

Peggy, who'd been in the bathroom, approached and reached for Quinn's hand. "All set to go?"

Brett cleared his throat and excused himself to use the bathroom. He needed to regroup and gain control of the emotions that threatened to take over and pull him under. No way could he stand there and watch Quinn walk out the door. He couldn't meet Sarah's eyes either. He had to stay focused for the interview portion of the appointment, and he needed to appear stable—even though the earth had never rattled under him as much as it did right then. He held it together until he shut the bathroom door and turned the lock, then he sat on the edge of the tub and dropped his head into his hands. He swallowed a sob, took a deep breath, and stood. He crossed to the sink, turned the cold water on, and splashed it on his face.

When he returned to Sarah, she was sitting in the chair with a notebook and a pen in her hand. She motioned for him to sit across from her on the sofa. Quinn's absence left the room empty. The fingers of loneliness pressed into his heart. He cleared his throat and took a seat, picking at the sharp, jagged edges of his fingernails where he'd bitten them half off.

There was something he needed to know. Something he hated to ask. "I need to know something."

Sarah nodded. "What's that?"

"Did someone—" Brett hesitated. "Was Quinn okay? I mean, no one tried to . . ." He covered his face with his hands.

"Was she sexually molested?"

Brett met her eyes and nodded.

"No."

Brett collapsed deep in his seat and exhaled loudly. He stared up at the ceiling. "It's just that I don't know what happened. Anything was possible."

"I understand. I'm sure you're relieved." Sarah hesitated before she began her questions. "So, when you left for work yesterday, did you realize Ali had been drinking or using drugs?"

Brett clasped his hands together, feeling the bruise from punching the reporter. He rubbed his hand and stretched it and placed it in his lap, forcing a calm demeanor. "She was sitting up and promised she was okay. But it wasn't the first time she told me she could handle Quinn, but then didn't. I hoped she could, of course. Obviously. She'd had bad cycles before and turned it around, so I hoped she would this time too. But what could I do? I had to go to work. And I wasn't supposed to be near her." He leaned forward in his chair with his elbows on his knees, cradling his head.

"If you were to get custody of Quinn, what would you do for child care?"

Brett shook his head and looked away. He'd filed bankruptcy last year, broke from Ali's ongoing medical expenses. Sarah had probably already done a background check, so she had to know. He could ask his mother for money, but she'd tell his old man. His dad had never wanted him to be a cop; he had wanted him to go to law school and be a part of his father's firm—make it Reed and Reed. When Ali had gotten pregnant, and Brett decided to marry her, his father had gone berserk. But Sarah didn't need to know about all that drama. "I'll find a way to pay for day care."

She paused as if waiting for him to say more, but he didn't. She continued. "Tell me about your childhood. Do you have siblings?"

"Nope, I'm the only child. I know what you're trying to do, and it's not going to work." Brett watched a sailboat glide by the front of the window, struggling to stay afloat in the wind.

"What am I trying to do?"

"You want to see if there's a pattern of abuse or neglect in my family. Well, there isn't. Never was. It's just that my father and I don't speak."

"Do you want to talk about it?"

"Not really. It has nothing to do with getting Quinn back. But Ali's problems do. If she doesn't show up here today, it'll help my case, won't it?"

"That depends."

"On what?" Brett squirmed in his chair.

"On what you tell me, and if you're telling the truth."

Brett exhaled and straightened his legs. "Where do I begin?" He stared out at the sailboat again. "When I first met Ali she seemed calm, reserved, and in control. She was nonconfrontational, simple. I liked that. I liked how agreeable she was too." He paused to make eye contact. "She'd go along with anything I'd say and support my opinion. We were teens. I thought she acted a little shy and that, eventually, once she felt more comfortable around me, she'd loosen up, have her own opinions. But after we were married, I realized she didn't like to make decisions. She couldn't. She was agreeable to whoever was in control at the moment. She wouldn't stand up for herself.

"After she had Quinn, she slept all the time. I'd worry, wondering if she'd wake up after I'd gone to work. Or if Quinn was in her crib crying and waiting to get out. I never knew what Ali was doing—was she drinking or under the influence of some drug? Was it safe for her to drive? And then there were days when she'd go manic. She'd stay awake all through the night." Brett watched a Jet Ski turn circles in the water. "She can do that for days. When I pushed her for answers, or an explanation, she'd curl up in a ball and cry."

He stopped to clear his throat and wiped his hands on his shorts. "The doctors said it was postpartum depression. Then they diagnosed her with bipolar disorder. They put her on so many drugs that some mornings I couldn't wake her. I'd shake her and shake her, and she wouldn't budge." He turned then and met Sarah's eyes, lowering his voice. "She didn't confide in me about the abuse until we'd been married for several years."

"What abuse are you referring to?"

Brett looked away. "Sexual abuse. Her mother's boyfriends. For years. She never really went into great detail."

Brett explained how Ali didn't have many friends, how the only people she confided in were needy people on drugs or people down on their luck. She'd listen to their stories and feel bad for them. He told her how Ali flitted from task to task without ever completing one. How disorganized she was with keeping a schedule—even for sleeping.

Sarah crossed her legs and leaned forward in her chair. "That must have been difficult for you."

He met her eyes. She seemed sincere. Nobody had ever validated his feelings before. Yes, it had been tough, real tough.

Brett exhaled deeply again, and his heart raced as he swallowed a lump in his throat. "I'm sure there are others who are far worse off than me. The only reason I'm sharing this is I want custody of Quinn. I don't like talking about it. What's the point? I left Ali because I couldn't live with the dysfunction anymore. I've moved on, but I never expected to lose custody of Quinn."

"Maybe it would help if I explained abuse in a way that will help you understand Ali better."

"Why? I don't need to understand her. I understand everything there is to know about her. I don't want anything to do with her anymore."

"Unfortunately, she's the mother of your child, and you'll always have that connection, so you can't erase her from your life." She uncrossed and recrossed her legs. "I'm not saying you need to make excuses for her. I only want you to see an illustration." She reached for her water bottle sitting on the coffee table and took a swig.

Brett watched, noticing Sarah's boots, jeans, and her pink top. She was poised in a casual sort of way, nonthreatening yet confident. Something Ali could never pull off.

"Let's say one day, hypothetically speaking, you're not in uniform, but you're at the corner of a crime district. You're distracted—maybe you're texting someone. A guy on the street attacks you, steals your wallet, and beats you over the head. You blame yourself for being distracted, for not paying attention to your surroundings, and for letting the guy get away. You chase him down, but you're injured and you're too far behind. It's not your fault, but you scold yourself for not being more alert. You mull the incident in your head over and over again, wondering where the guy came from, what you could have done differently. And sometime afterward, you decide it'll never happen again because you won't let your guard down."

Brett nodded, thinking, *Does she know me, or is she guessing?*

She brushed a strand of hair out of her face, and crossed and uncrossed her legs again. "Now, imagine if you're a child like Ali with immature thoughts, trying to make sense of when and why abuse is happening—and it's occurring much more frequently than what happened to you with the mugger. One week something happens, and she tells herself it was because she glanced at her mother's friend a certain way, or didn't listen to him. After a while she gives herself bizarre explanations for the abuse, thinking she was responsible. She believes she did something to cause the abuse, and wants to figure out how to get it to stop, to prevent it from happening again.

"In many abusive families the child is taught to hide the family secrets, and so the child never develops normal healthy relationships. Their concept of a healthy relationship is distorted. And in Ali's case, maybe it was the only way she felt loved. So, she learned to be ashamed to love."

Sarah shifted in her seat, but kept her honey-brown eyes on Brett, suddenly making him feel warm all over. She spoke with passion. Was she speaking from her own experience?

She continued. "Ali's problems are complicated. It's going to take a long time and a lot of counseling to break through the barriers of her abuse. I can understand why you wanted to divorce yourself from her. It must have been difficult living with a person who couldn't show love, who possibly struggled with why she did, and still does, certain things."

Sarah seemed so connected, understanding, and nonjudgmental. Brett didn't know if it was the setting or just being in her presence that made him more than comfortable. He'd never shared this much information with anyone—not even Clay—and it felt liberating. Was Sarah just good at her job? Or was he attracted to her? He better get that thought out of his mind right away. He didn't trust his judgment where women were concerned. He sighed and leaned back in his seat, crossing his leg over his knee. "You sound comfortable talking about this, like you speak from experience."

She avoided his eyes before she responded. "This is my job. I hear abuse stories all day long. It happens far more than you think." She continued looking out the window at the lake.

He figured she had patients with problems, but he suspected again that she had personal experience with abuse. "I can sympathize with Ali's predicament and her family abuse, but I can't fix her. I'm not responsible for her actions. I learned that a long time ago."

She shifted her eyes back to him and smiled. "Bravo. You're farther ahead than most people."

"Ali denies she has problems. She insists she forgave her mother years ago."

"Which makes it even more difficult for you, because until she realizes she needs help, she won't seek help or get better."

"Don't I know it. But if you're telling me I can't have custody of Quinn because I left her yesterday when her safety was compromised, then I can't win. You're telling me that it was my responsibility to make sure Quinn was safe, but I'm not responsible for Ali's behavior. Do you see my point?"

"Totally." She nodded.

Her eyes finally locked onto his, and something made him believe that she understood better than anyone. A spark flickered inside him. Shoot, he was attracted to her. Was he crazy? This wasn't the time to think about having a relationship with someone, especially someone who was his ticket to getting Quinn.

He rubbed his palms on his shorts, not realizing how sweaty they had become. Leaning toward her, he smiled and said, "So, after hearing about my predicament, does it help my case? Do you think I'll get sole custody?"

"I can't answer that."

He sighed. "Divorcing her was the selfish thing to do. It made my life easier because I didn't have to live with her dysfunction." He threw his hands up in the air. "But in the end, it didn't change anything. She's still dysfunctional, and I'm not around to ensure Quinn's safety. I only worry more because I ended up with less control."

"I'm sorry. I'm sure it's frustrating." Sarah turned the clock on the table toward her. "Ali probably didn't show up because people like me scare her. She's not ready to spill her guts."

Brett leaned back in his seat. "Well, I hope she keeps screwing up, so she doesn't have a chance in hell to get our daughter back."

#

I sat in my truck across from a counseling office, eating my lunch, when I saw the same dark-curly-haired girl that was with Mrs. Stookey yesterday. The girl wasn't with Mrs. Stookey today. She was with another woman. They were coming out of the doctor's office building and getting into a car together. Where was the lady taking the girl?

I wonder if she's that little girl I heard about at work—the daughter of a cop? The pervert cop. Mrs. Bailey, a customer at work, said they took the girl away from both parents. Was this the girl?

I turned the ignition key. The truck rumbled, and I followed them. The lady drove across town to the same street where Moore lived, but one block farther. The lady parked in the driveway. I parked one house away and watched.

The little girl climbed out of the car and skipped to the front door. Mrs. Stookey and the other little girl answered. They opened the door for the dark-haired girl and let her in. Shortly after, the lady drove off alone.

I sighed. Didn't they know Mrs. Stookey's son was a pervert? Probably not, since he hadn't registered yet. I'd better get to him tonight then, before something happens to those girls.

Chapter Fifteen

Shortly after noon, Brett called Clay on his way home from Sarah's office. Clay agreed to meet him at Chloe's Sports Grill off Center Street for lunch. The restaurant had a wireless Internet connection, and Clay wanted to bring his laptop.

Brett pulled into the parking lot, entered the restaurant, and waited for Clay in a booth. An older couple, probably in their seventies, sat in an adjacent booth side by side—just the two of them. They smiled and waved at Brett. He didn't know them. They just seemed like a friendly couple. He tried not to stare, but couldn't help watching how they rubbed arms and laughed together like they were telling each other jokes, like they were new lovers. Would he ever find that? He thought of Sarah. What was her story? Why was he attracted to her?

Clay interrupted Brett's thoughts as he entered the restaurant, his long stride bringing him across the room in five steps. He took a seat across from Brett and set his laptop in the middle of the table. "You doing okay, man?"

Brett nodded. "For now. I filled out some form asking the courts for a hearing in three days to grant me custody. Say some prayers that the judge approves."

"Still don't want to call your old man?"

Brett shook his head and stared at his hands. Clay didn't know about his father's cancer, but Brett couldn't talk about it. Not yet.

The waitress brought them water and took their orders.

Clay placed a county map on the table, pointing out the geocache sites he'd marked. "Here's where Jake Hunter lives." He pointed to the spot on the map marked with a red circle and the number 2, then pointed to another red circle with the number 1. "This is where our dead guy's piece was found. There's a YouTube video online of this location. It's one of the URL addresses you gave me from Mark's computer history."

"Really?" Brett studied the map. "What about the other URL?"

Clay pointed to Terry Bull's house, indicated with a yellow X, and the other cache site where Hunter's penis was found at the other red circle and the number 3. "The other URL address from Mark was not this site. It was from another local geo-site."

Next, he showed Brett where the county sex offenders lived in that general vicinity. They'd been circled with black X's. There were fifteen.

Brett saw a pattern and possible correlation between where the items were found and where the offender lived. Jake's penis was found near his house.

Clay drew a circle around the geocache site near Terry Bull's house. "This is where I think you should look for his dick. It's the closest site to Bull's house. I had several guys looking for it with no luck." He smiled and looked up at Brett. "You sure you're ready to hunt for a dick-in-a-box?"

Brett chuckled. "I can spot them a mile away. Besides, I'm not doing anything else, and I need to stay busy. This will be a challenge." In more ways than one. He'd never geocached before, and he didn't have a keen sense of direction. "What about Mark? Have you talked to him?"

Clay nodded. "Yeah, I did a background check on him. He owes a lot of cash to investors after soliciting funds for a start-up that tanked. He's had a few speeding tickets, but other than that, he's clean. I met him at his office, and we chatted about Ali. He claims he didn't have anything to hide, that he told you everything he knows."

"Did you believe him?"

"No. He seemed too nervous."

"Do you think he's the whacker?"

"I doubt it. He had an alibi. A woman friend, but not sure if she was covering for him or telling the truth. He said he'd heard about the geocaching thing from TV and Googled it out of curiosity." Clay chuckled. "He was pissed that you broke into his house though. Are you crazy?"

"When it comes to my daughter, yes."

Clay reached for his PC. "I put a tail out on him, so he'll be watched." He turned the PC around so he could see it. He typed, clicked, and turned the machine back around for Brett to see.

Clay pointed to a spot on the screen. "Every geocache site listed at geocaching.com is a waypoint. The website generates a unique GC code associated with every geocache listing. Once the reviewer finds the cache, they sign a logbook that's usually found in the box. We're interviewing those who have registered and signed the logbook, asking questions about other caches they found along their way, who they saw, that type of thing. So far it's a bust. We've archived these two sites here where we found the prizes." He pointed to the screen. "By archiving them, it removes the listing from public view." He clicked on another screen. "We temporarily closed down the site for our county an hour ago. Cache hikers are out hunting in herds. They think it's funny. I've got Officer Greer monitoring the site for any newly posted sites."

Brett read the screen. There were 587 sites in the county. "Do you have a team inspecting every one of these sites and taping them off?"

"We don't have the manpower to cover them all, and some of these boxes are tough to find." He chuckled. "Plus, we don't want people to panic. Chief says we'll block off as many sites as we can near here. He's planning on making an announcement this afternoon for the public to avoid geocaching in our county because they could be potential crime scenes, but that might just stir more trouble. People will blatantly ignore that request." He rolled his eyes.

Brett studied the site. When he looked up, Clay was watching the TV that hung in the corner of the bar, behind Brett.

Clay gasped. "Check it out, Reed."

Brett turned and followed Clay's eyes and watched what Clay was viewing on the TV screen. It was Brett with the mic in his face at Ali's house. The reporter asked his questions, the last one being about sexual abuse, and then the clip ran of Brett pummeling the guy's jaw. Brett shook his head and rubbed his hand. Dread filled his gut. "I'm hosed. That was really stupid."

"It was. If you're going to hurt the guy, you gotta do better than that." Clay snickered.

Brett didn't. He covered his face. "Let's hope the judge doesn't see that. This could totally ruin any chance I have at getting Quinn."

Clay's forehead creased. "You have another problem too. Let's hope the perp doesn't see that and think you did your kid. You'll be hunting down your own dick in a box somewhere."

Brett froze. "You aren't serious!"

Clay laughed. "I don't know, but if I was you, I'd be sleeping with both eyes open."

Brett threw an ice cube at Clay, hitting him in the chest. "He's after *convicted* sex offenders, not the accused ones."

Clay's laugh rang across the room, deep and strong. "You sure? You could be the first accused."

The waitress brought their food and set it in front of them. Brett was no longer hungry.

Clay bowed his head. "Dear God, please guide us to find this guy before he whacks off my partner. Keep Brett strong and able to sleep with his eyes open." Clay chuckled, hesitating. "Seriously though, give Brett the strength to battle against the courts to get his daughter back. Show him your love, and give him the courage to stand alone. Help him to see that he is a good and loving father. Amen."

Brett avoided looking up and into Clay's eyes and stared at his food instead. He didn't trust his composure. "Thanks. No one has prayed for me like that before."

"I think you need to start saying a few of your own." He chuckled again. "Let's eat."

Brett told Clay how Ali had disappeared with her clothes and Quinn's and how he feared she'd track Quinn down and take her.

"I don't think you have to worry about her going anywhere. She's not strong enough to take Quinn, dude. She can't even take care of herself."

Brett nodded. "You've got a point."

Clay wiped his mouth with his napkin and took another bite of his burger. "Listen, you're going through a crisis right now. You can't see it, but you'll come out stronger."

"Will I? Not sure, but you're right about one thing—I can't see it. I don't have the same faith you have."

"You can change that. Just ask God into your life. Develop a friendship with the Guy. You'll see that amazing things happen when you do."

#

Brett parked the cruiser at Hursey Lake Park, the closest parking spot near the trails. He'd have to hike the rest of the way on foot. This cache was buried somewhere off the beaten path. The clue had been "fools look for gold." What was that supposed to mean?

Clay had had to get back to the precinct to organize a team of searchers, so Brett went on his own.

He opened the trunk, took out his backpack, and slung it over his shoulder. He remembered the last time he'd hiked. He'd been eight years old, and the backpack had been too heavy for him to carry.

He'd gone with his father on a two-day trip through the Hoosier National Forest. His father had showed him how to use a compass, and how to identify poison ivy and poison berries, and they'd brought two magnifying glasses to inspect nature's world. They sat on the ground and watched ants dance up a hill, and identified animal tracks. They saw spiders in their webs and a praying mantis up close.

His father had showed him the beauty in nature and how to listen to their sounds. They once sat on a tree stump next to each other and played a game. Dad said, "Close your eyes and listen."

Brett heard a strange sound, a chattering noise. He played the guessing game and said, "Is it a monkey?"

His father laughed. "Nope, just a squirrel."

Brett opened his eyes and looked to where his father pointed. In a tree, out on a limb, a squirrel faced another, sounding like he was shouting at the other, making a noise Brett had never heard before.

They had played the game until Brett recognized all the sounds on the trail—the wings of a bat, a cardinal's call, a crow, the difference in the buzzing sounds of a fly and a wasp, and the creek's water lapping over rocks.

Would he recognize all the same sounds today?

As he trudged toward the trails, he saw people sitting on picnic benches, and children running on the playground, glancing his way. They must have seen him getting out of his car. Cops had a way of drawing attention, even when they weren't dressed in uniform. Concrete trails leading into a greenway bordered the park alongside a large creek that fed into the lake miles away. Cyclists, joggers, and dog-walkers filled up the scenery.

He welcomed the hike, avoiding the time when he'd have to go home to an empty house. He checked his map and his iPhone, studying the coordinates he'd transferred from online—the one closest to Terry Bull's house.

The sun beat down on his back until he reached the trail where he lost the sky in the woods. He welcomed the trees' shade. Flies buzzed, birds called back and forth, and a nearby stream gurgled. Leaves rustled, making him think someone was near, but each time he turned he only saw squirrels skipping over the ground and scurrying into the trees foraging for nuts.

After swatting at a half-dozen mosquitoes, he stopped, opened his bag, and took out a can of insect repellent, then sprayed himself. His cell phone vibrated. He unclipped it from its strap and glanced at the caller ID. His mother. He didn't want to talk to her, but if he didn't take her call now, she'd keep calling.

"Hi, Mom."

"Have you heard how Quinn did last night?"

"Yes, I saw her this morning. She looks great and seems to like her foster home. I'm good."

She sighed. "Thank God."

"How's Dad?"

"He's okay. We're at the hospital waiting to talk to his doctor. I hope you get Quinn soon."

"Me too."

"Dad wants to see you. It's been too long since you two spoke. This is the perfect opportunity to get you two back together."

"I'm not sure of the timing right now."

A young girl, maybe in her twenties, jogged past him. Her long ponytail swished from side to side. Another man walked by with a large white fluffy dog. The dog's tail wagged as he pulled his owner down the path.

"Mom, can I call you back? I'm in the middle of something."

"Are you eating well?"

He rolled his eyes. She always thought about food. "Yes, I had lunch with Clay. Thanks for thinking of me. I'll call you when things are back to normal. I promise."

He disconnected the phone. Would things ever be back to normal? How much time did his father have? Pancreatic cancer was a killer. He worried about his mother. This had to be difficult for her. She and Dad had always been close.

Would he ever have the kind of love his parents had? He checked his cell again. Had he missed a text from Ali? Nope. None. He returned his phone to the clip and put the thoughts of his family on another shelf, continuing down the path.

After another quarter mile the worn path continued one way, but the coordinates of the GPS directed him down an area where there was no path, in another direction. It wound its way around a creek and through dense woods. He avoided tree roots and stumps threatening to trip him. Mosquitoes buzzed in his ear and swarmed around his head. Locusts chirped all around him. He trudged up a steep hill, watching the GPS. He was getting closer. He hoped he'd be able to find his way back. Finding his way with the navigation system was easy, but he'd never asked how to program it for his return. His stomach churned thinking about finding his way out of the middle of the woods.

He panted as he climbed. Man, he was out of shape. He listened to himself puffing like an old man. Pitiful. When had he let himself go?

When he reached the top of the hill, the sun beat down through a clearing, but the trees and bushes rustled as a breeze kicked up, cooling the air for a moment. Brett stopped to sip water from his canteen. The GPS indicated the cache was approximately twenty more feet, but he had to go down a narrow dirt path and over the pebble creek first. His steps were smaller now, not as surefooted. He leapt over larger rocks, slipping often.

A clicking sound whirred toward him. It came out of nowhere and seemed to be getting closer. He turned, looking behind him. A cyclist weaved in and out between the trees. A neon orange flag waved to and fro from the back of the seat. Brett hid off to the side, watching from the shadow of a tree as the cyclist flew down the path next to him and splashed over the shallow creek in the same direction Brett was headed. As quickly as he'd come, the cyclist was gone.

Brett continued in the same direction and stopped when the GPS displayed "you are at ground zero."

Really? He didn't see anything that looked like a cache box. He unzipped his backpack and took out his flashlight. It wasn't dark, but the dense cluster of trees blocked the sun's light. He shone a light under the brush. Nothing. He picked up a stick and searched in the nearby bushes, moving the branches from side to side. Sticks and leaves brushed up against him. Besides mosquito bites, he'd probably end up with poison ivy.

Clay had said the first cache had been found up in a tree. Brett flashed the light up one tree and down another. Nothing. He moved to his right and followed the same procedure, shining his light up, down, and under the brush. Still nothing.

What was the clue? Fools look for gold. Where does a person find gold? In the ground? In rocks? What about fool's gold? Wasn't it near the creek? Was the cache buried near a rock?

On his last circle of the area, his foot struck a large rock. He tripped and paused. He bent down, flashing his light over the ground, and found several larger boulders. He kicked the first one. It wouldn't budge. He kicked several others until he kicked one that tumbled over. It was a hollow piece of plastic, disguised as a rock.

After sitting in the dirt in front of the boulder, he opened his backpack and took out a pair of gloves. He tapped the rock and turned it upside down, looking for a way to open it. Underneath was a six-by-six-inch hinged area. He needed a coin to turn the notch. He stood, reached into his pocket, and pulled out a nickel, then twisted it in the groove until the latch clicked open.

He shook the contents onto the ground. A tiny deck of cards, a small notepad, a pair of red fluffy earmuffs, and a plastic bag fell onto the dirt. Inside the bag was something liquid, red, and squishy. He held the corner of it away from his body and flashed his light on it, examining it closer, shivering at what he saw.

A fly landed on his hand. He shooed it away. Fighting nausea, he threw the bag back into the boulder, lifted the rest of the other contents, and shoved them into a different bag. After placing them all in his backpack, he rolled the gloves off his hands, balled them up into another bag, and zipped his backpack shut. He unclipped his phone to call Clay, but when it lit up, he noticed he only had one bar of service. He'd have to wait to make the call when he got to a clearing.

Just as he stashed his phone in its clip, a voice rang out.

"You can't steal the cache. That's cheating."

Brett swung around, dropping his backpack, and faced the direction of the voice.

Huh? What was she doing here?

Chapter Sixteen

Sarah stood with her arms across her chest, her bike leaning against a tree, waiting for Brett to say something. She almost laughed at how she'd made him jump and how frightened he looked, and at the mosquito bite welts covering his face. Obviously, he wasn't a seasoned hiker.

Still bent over his backpack, Brett said, "Are you trying to scare me to death? What are you doing here?"

"I'm hiking for the same thing you just found. What are *you* doing? Why are you taking the cache?"

"Police evidence."

"What?"

He shuffled through the backpack in front of him. "There's someone whacking—" He took out a roll of wide yellow Caution tape.

Sarah cocked her head to the side. "You're not going to finish your sentence, are you? What was in that rock?"

"Have you seen the news today?"

"No, why?" She left her bike at the tree and moved toward him.

"Let's just say I'm not authorized to talk about it. I've got to close off this area. He stood, throwing the backpack onto his shoulder, and draped the tape around the trees within a ten-foot perimeter, four feet from the ground. "Sorry I can't share it with you. This is one find you'll have to give up." He tore a piece of tape with his teeth.

He scratched at a mosquito bite on his neck. "Do you know your way back to Hursey Park from here? I'm a little turned around."

She chuckled. "A cop without a sense of direction?"

"Yeah, it's embarrassing. Don't let it get out, okay?"

"I'm a professional. I keep lots of secrets." She helped him hold up the tape. "I know these woods like the back of my hand. I grew up around here. My house is just over the creek and up that hill." She pointed to her left.

"Perfect." He tied the last bit of tape in a knot and put the roll in his backpack, then zipped it shut. "I guess you probably think I'm crazy for working while Quinn is gone and Ali's missing."

"I don't judge."

"Don't you?" He stared into her eyes as if looking for something.

She didn't back away. "No, I don't."

He held his gaze. "What am I supposed to do? Go to my apartment and stare at the walls?"

"I'd probably do the same thing." Sarah was queen of the "keep busy" strategy, always looking for ways to keep her mind and body occupied. She averted her eyes and moved toward her bike, taking the handlebars, and turning to go. "I'm sure it's easier to keep busy."

Brett followed. "How many of these cache boxes have you found?"

"Forty-eight." Sarah led him out of the woods and toward the clearing.

Brett whistled. "Not that you're counting, or anything." He grinned. "All in this county?"

"No, I've searched in six other counties, but all in Indiana."

"What's the most bizarre thing you ever found?"

Sarah turned her bike toward the trail, its tires crunching on debris. "Hmm, I'd have to think about that. Probably a toilet seat. Although there have been some crazy things."

"A toilet seat? That must have been one large cache box."

"Yeah, it was in a large trunk, hidden in a cave."

"When was the last cache you found?"

She paused, noticing something different in his tone. "A week ago." Why was he asking her these questions? The trail narrowed. He let her go first.

"Where was it?"

She spoke over her shoulder. "On the other side of town. Why?" He sounded suspicious of her. Why?

"Did you see anyone out of the ordinary on the trails or near the caches?"

She hesitated. "Like?"

"I don't know. Anything or anyone different than you normally do."

She paused. Did he suspect her of something? "Nothing and no one I can remember."

"Why do you do it?"

"I enjoy being outdoors, being one with nature, and as a child I didn't get to play too many games. I guess this is my inner child coming out."

As they approached the clearing, Brett's phone vibrated. He stopped and unclipped it from his belt clip. "I haven't had service since I entered the woods, and now it's catching up to me. I missed five calls. Can you wait while I call my partner? I need to ask you a few more questions."

She glanced at her watch. "I have five minutes."

He pushed a few buttons on his phone and said, "Hey, I found what we were looking for." He paused.

Sarah watched as Brett's expression changed from victory to concern. What had happened?

A frown creased between his brows. "No!" He shook his head. "When? Where is she now?" There was another pause before he disconnected the call and turned to Sarah. "Ali has been in an accident. She's at the hospital."

"I'm sorry." She didn't know what else to say. He surely didn't need one more thing to go bad.

#

Brett's sirens blared, and the colors of his flashing lights pulsed like the throbbing in his head as he headed to the Hursey Lake Hospital's emergency room. He pulled up to the automatic doors, the ones he'd been to before as a cop doing his job, following the victims or perpetrators after a crime had been committed.

Clay had said someone died in the accident. A woman in her twenties. Ali's fault. Brett's stomach lurched, bile rising in his throat. A woman was dead because of Ali.

Maybe he could have prevented it if he'd taken her keys away. Had she been under the influence of drugs or alcohol?

He hurried inside. Nurse Becky greeted him at the receptionist's desk, knowing him well from his frequent cop visits with drunk drivers. But tonight, Nurse Becky looked at him twice before she seemed to recognize him, probably because she'd rarely seen him out of uniform. "Oh, Brett. Come on back."

She led him through double doors and into another area lit with fluorescent lights and enclosed in curtains. He expected the room to smell like a usual sterile hospital room, but instead, he smelled . . . nothing. It was as if there was an air purifier in the room that eliminated all smells. Or was it because there wasn't much life left in Ali?

Beeping sounds echoed off the walls. A swooshing sound like air being pumped in and out of a machine joined in the noise. Men and women in blue scrubs surrounded Ali. One woman wrote something on a chart. At first, all Brett could see was the color of Ali's spiky bleached hair. IV tubes, breathing tubes, and oxygen nasal tubes protruded from her body. Even on her worst drinking days Ali hadn't looked this bad.

The room spun. Nurse Becky, who'd followed him into the room, pulled up a chair next to Ali and motioned for him to sit.

He shook his head, standing to the side. "I'll be okay. Do you know what happened?"

The nurse said, "We were told she ran a stop sign and hit the driver's side of another car."

Brett cringed. "Was anyone else injured besides the lady who died?"

"Not that we know of." She patted his shoulder before she quietly left the room.

Brett stared at Ali's face, trying to find some resemblance. Had there been a mistake? This wasn't Ali. Her face was as round as a blowfish, but as pale as his cotton T-shirt. He took a deep breath and moved closer, recognizing the birthmark on her small hand resting on the bed. Yes, this was Ali.

A man in blue scrubs, with a head of graying hair and a bulbous nose, approached Brett. "I'm Dr. Nesbitt, the neurosurgeon." He extended his hand.

Brett shook it. "Brett Reed. How is she?"

The surgeon, in a somber voice, said, "She's lost a lot of blood from a cut on her neck here." He pointed to a large bandage that ran from just under her left jaw. "She wasn't wearing a seat belt, so there was trauma to her brain from the impact, and she can't breathe on her own."

Brett nodded, noticing the bandages along her neck.

The doctor continued in his medically grave tone. "The tube coming out of here is to drain the fluid." He pointed to a tube running from behind her head. "See this meter here? This checks the pressure. We have to monitor it. If it gets below this mark here— well, let's just say that we don't want that to happen."

Brett whispered, "What are her chances of living through this?"

The doctor looked away and then back to Brett. "The next twenty-four hours will tell."

Brett held the doctor's eyes. "If she lives, what kind of life . . . I mean, will she have brain damage?"

The doctor shrugged. "We never know. Every person is different, and sometimes miracles happen. Hope is your friend. Hope and prayer. But the longer she stays in this coma, the stronger her chances are of being severely disabled, if she lives."

"Was alcohol in her system?"

The doctor hesitated, not meeting Brett's eyes. Was he holding something back? "We haven't gotten the toxicology reports back yet." The doctor took her chart and wrote something on it, and started to walk out of the room but turned to Brett and squeezed his shoulder. "I'm sorry. I'm sure this is difficult. I'll let you know if there are any changes, but for now she's stable. I'll be back after I make my rounds."

The doctor left the room, and one at a time the nurses did too. The machines continued to beep and swish, and occasionally the blood pressure machine would click, pumping air into the cuff.

He reached for her hand, amid tubes protruding and crisscrossing around her. Her hand was warm but limp, and her fingers felt like sticks—thick and lifeless. Red gashes and scrapes covered her arms and face.

The sounds of the machines echoed off the walls, keeping the rhythm of an artificial heartbeat, breathing for her.

Brett released her hand and moved to check the dial on the tube at the back of her head. The long lever seemed to pulse and hover right around the danger zone.

What could he say to her? If he had one wish, would it be for her to return to her life as it had been before the accident? If that miracle happened, she'd have to face prison for killing someone. Would he stand by her side? What kind of life would she have behind bars?

There was no going back for Ali. For any of them. She had had time to change before the accident and chose not to. If she came back to her life now, would she seek help? He doubted it.

Thank God Quinn hadn't been in the car with her or she'd be dead now. Dizziness circled him. He inhaled sharply. What was he going to tell Quinn? Poor Quinn.

Ali's fingers twitched. His heartbeat quickened. He leaned toward her. "Squeeze my hand if you can hear me."

He waited. Nothing. Had it been his imagination? He watched her eyes. Nothing. Not even a flutter.

He squeezed the tears shut in his eyes and lifted Ali's hand, kissed it, and left the room.

On his way to the waiting room, Brett passed a young man sitting in the corner who had bandages on his head and his arm. His elbows rested on his thighs as he sobbed into his hands. Dr. Nesbitt stood over the young man with his hand on the man's shoulder. Between muffled sobs, the young man said, "Why did this have to happen? We were getting married next month. My whole future is gone. Just like that." He snapped his fingers and glared at the doctor as if waiting for answers.

The words cut into Brett, making the hair on his arms stand up. He took a seat across the room, but he was still close enough to hear what was said next.

The man's face reddened. "Was she drunk? If so, I'll sue her. I swear I'll sue her and her entire family." His face wrinkled in a tortured expression.

Brett looked away. He was sure Ali had killed the man's fiancée. Tears filled his eyes, blurring his vision. The room spun. He needed air, fresh air. Air that would give him hope in a life that didn't have meaning. Wandering down the tiled corridor, he saw a sign for a chapel. He went inside and sat in a pew. A wooden cross hung on the wall behind a white altar. One elderly lady, bent over and hunchbacked, exited the room in short, shuffling steps, wiping her eyes with a tissue.

He sat alone in the dark, empty chapel for a long time. It had been a long time since he'd stepped into a church. The evening's darkness engulfed the room and his mood. There was no reason for him to stay at the hospital with Ali. He couldn't do anything to help her. All he could do was pray, and he wasn't very good at that either.

He went to the front of the chapel, closer to the altar and the wooden cross. He sat on the wooden pew, leaned forward, and clasped his hands together. Now what?

Footsteps fell on the tiled floor. Brett turned to see Clay tuck in and kneel beside him. Clay placed his hand on Brett's shoulder and squeezed. "I'm sorry, man. Do you want me to pray with you?"

Brett nodded and watched as Clay's eyes closed and he bowed his head. Brett dropped his head too.

Clay said, "Oh, heavenly Father, bless this man and his family. Help him to see your plans for him. Let him feel your powerful love. Remind him that in times of turmoil he can turn to you for guidance and approval. Protect Ali and Quinn, and keep them safe until they are with you in eternal peace. Amen."

Brett turned to Clay. "Thanks, bro."

Clay leaned into Brett, wrapping his large arms around him for a brief man-hug, patting his back. "No problem. I'm sorry you're going through this."

"Yeah, me too. This sucks." Brett ran his fingers through his hair. "I need to get the evidence to you. It's out in the cruiser."

"No need. I found it."

"You found it?"

"Yeah, you left the car running outside the ER, so I took the backpack and parked the car." He reached into his pocket, pulled out the keys, and handed them to Brett.

Brett hit his forehead with the palm of his hand. "Thanks. I guess I was in a hurry."

Clay stood to go. "Come on, let me buy you dinner. You gotta eat."

\#

I sat in the dark, hiding in the row of pine trees along the side of pervert Moore's house. As soon as his lights went out, I'd proceed. There wasn't much time though. Mrs. Stookey dropped the girls off a half hour ago. She was crazy for leaving them with the creep. I'd watched from across the street.

Pine needles stabbed at my thighs, making me a little more crotchety than usual. It was a good thing I packed a Snickers bar. I opened my backpack and pushed the other stuff aside until I found it, unwrapped it, and took a bite. Maybe now I could stay awake long enough.

A car's lights flashed up the road and headed down the street. The fat lady next door stood on her porch waiting for her poodle to potty. She called to him, "Hurry up, Biscuit. Mommy wants to go to bed."

The car continued past the house, so I scooted a little deeper into the trees. It passed, and the yard returned to darkness. But not before Biscuit saw me. He growled. I froze. He barked louder and louder as he approached. When he was a few feet away, the lady came running over. I held my breath.

"Biscuit. Get over here," she whispered, and grabbed him in her arms and waddled home. She hadn't seen me. She shuffled into her house and turned off her porch light.

Darkness filled the yard again. All I had to do was wait a little longer. I took out my iPad and played a few games of Angry Birds. I wanted to kill the pigs for taking the eggs.

Then, I woke with a jerk, forgetting for a second I was waiting for Moore to go to bed. My iPad was still in my lap. It must have shut off after I'd fallen asleep. Darn! I'd have to wait to see my scores later. I shoved the iPad in my backpack and took out the flesh-colored nylon, pulling it over my face and adjusting it around my nose. After throwing my backpack over my shoulder, I proceeded to the side door of the house.

Quit humming. Deep breath. *Do it, do it, do it. Not scared now. Not scared. I'll show him. I'm brave now.*

I turned the knob of the side door that led into the house. Unlocked. *Score!* I tiptoed into the kitchen. Brownies.

No, I can't eat them now.

Someone snored. I lifted the backpack onto the kitchen table and gathered the rag, the syringe, and the tourniquet. I hummed softly. After pulling on my gloves, I applied the liquid to the cloth and gathered the syringe and the rubber band.

Do the deed, do it. I followed the snoring noise down a hallway and peeked into the room. The pervert's dark hair showed against the white pillow. The bedsheets lay in a crumpled mess around him, reminding me of Mama's bed. And then the lies. I wadded my fists.

I entered the room. Shut the door. Lock it. Go to the pervert. Cover his face with the rag. Hold it down. Wait. A little longer. He's done kicking. Get out the syringe. Poke him. Only a little. Doc Spear uses this all the time. It won't kill. It's okay, it's okay. Get out the rubber band. Wrap it tight, knot it. Pull it tighter. *I know how to make a double knot.* Open the bag. Get the scalpel. Slice, slice. Red blood, go away. Damn blood.

A whimper. From under the bed. Who's there? "Don't cry; don't listen to the lies. Shut your ears. I'll save you this time. Daddy can't hurt you now. I promise." Let me stop the blood first. Wrap the piece in the plastic. Put everything away, wipe it on the towel. Tuck it in the backpack.

"I'm coming. I'm a big boy now. I'll save you. I see you under the bed. Scoot to me. I'll help you." It's the little girl with the dark curly hair. "Come to me, come to me." Aw, she's crying. Poor baby girl. So sorry. "Mommy is looking. Smile. Don't be scared. I'm not scared. I'm a big boy. Come to me. It's all better now. Daddy's gone."

Chapter Seventeen

Brett and Clay turned to leave the chapel but stopped short when a small voice called out from the back of the church. "Are you happy now?" Ali's mother, Mrs. Mable Greer, stood in the doorway, glaring at Brett.

Give me a break, crazy woman. What was she talking about? His temper soared at the sight of her—big dirty T-shirt, polyester pants spread too thin across her dimpled pear-like bottom, and curlers dangling from her thinning hair.

Despite her short frame, Mable's love for control could dominate the largest room. Her presence suffocated him. She loved making him feel inferior, questioning his motives, telling him how worthless he was. But what was she saying now? No, he wasn't happy. Especially seeing her. She was the last person he wanted to talk to.

She shuffled double-time up to the front of the church, tears streaming down her face, her nose bulbous and red. Her voice sounded higher pitched than usual, as if she was on the verge of hysteria. "Ali could die! This is all your fault. She's really out of your life now, isn't she?"

Brett kept his voice low. "What are you talking about? I didn't do this to her. I never wanted her out of my life this way."

She slammed her fist into his chest. "This never would have happened if you hadn't divorced her. She'd still be at home, safe."

Brett crossed his arms over his chest. "Are you insane? Ali's self-destruction started way before I divorced her." Brett started to turn away, but stopped, years of pent-up anger spilling over. "I gave Ali every chance to get it together. Did she tell you that she's the reason Quinn is in foster care right now?"

Mrs. Greer's mouth dropped open.

Brett had turned to go, Clay at his side, but stopped and turned to the lady. "Yeah, that's right. CPS took her away because Quinn was found wandering the streets in her pajamas a block from home. Guess where Ali was? At home hungover, asleep on the sofa."

The old lady put her hand across her heart melodramatically and reached for a pew. She sat down, fanning herself.

"She didn't tell you that, did she?" Brett asked.

Clay touched Brett's arm, but Brett flung it off. He was tired of taking the blame for Ali's behavior, and he didn't care about Mrs. Greer's theatrics. He'd seen her antics before, and tonight he was too tired to care about her loss. His voice boomed off the walls of the small chapel. "Since when do you give a care anyway? If you want to go throwing stones, maybe you should pitch one at yourself. If you hadn't left your boyfriends home alone with Ali to abuse her, maybe she wouldn't have been so messed up!"

Mrs. Greer shriveled against the pew, throwing the back of her hand up to her forehead.

Clay pressed his arm against Brett's chest. "Maybe you two should take a deep breath. Obviously you both care for Ali."

Brett threw his arms up in the air. "I'm done. I'm not sure what I'm doing in here anyway. Prayer has never worked for me." He turned his back on Clay and Mrs. Greer and headed out the chapel door.

Clay's radio chirped. "Unit twenty-five, do you read?"

Clay snapped the radio off his belt and answered. "Ten-four."

"We have a report of another amputation at 621 West Shady Lane. The victim's mother also reported the assailant kidnapped her foster child. Do you know where Agent Reed is? Copy?"

Brett, who had moved to the other end of the chapel, ran back and grabbed Clay's radio. He spoke into the mic. "This is Agent Reed. Does this have anything to do with Quinn?"

"Ten-four."

"Where is she?"

"Appears our mutilator took her with him, sir." She didn't offer any more information.

Radio static filled the church and shook every nerve fiber in Brett's body. His knees buckled. He leaned against a pew. How could this happen? What the hell was Quinn doing in the home of a sex offender? Hadn't Sarah promised she was safe? He swung a fist into the cushioned seat of the pew.

Mrs. Greer cried out. "What did she say? Did someone take Quinn?"

Clay placed his hand on Mrs. Greer's arm. "We need to go. We'll find out what we can and let you know."

Brett's adrenaline raced and fueled him with energy. Quinn had been kidnapped! He ran ahead of Clay. "I'll meet you there."

Clay grabbed a hold of Brett's arm. "Slow down. You're not in uniform, and you're not in any shape to handle this."

Brett chucked Clay's arm off him. "This is my daughter! Who else is better able to handle this? I'm tired of giving everyone else control. No one is doing a good job of keeping my daughter safe. I'm done! I'm taking matters in my own hands."

Clay tightened his grip around Brett's arm. "Don't be stupid, Reed. You're going to get yourself into trouble. You're all Quinn has right now. Leave your cruiser here. Come with me."

Brett turned and charged out of the chapel, leaving Mrs. Greer racked with sobs, sitting alone in a pew. He heard Clay's footsteps following him.

When they stepped outside, Brett followed Clay to his cruiser and slammed his fist into the hood of the car, growling like a mother bear. "Grrrrr, how the hell did CPS place my child in the home of a *sex offender*?"

Clay shrugged. "We don't have all the facts yet. You don't know for sure if he was a sex offender."

"Why else would the perp slice him? My gut is saying this reeks. This reeks bad." Brett flung open the cruiser's door. He tore his cell phone off his belt clip and reached into his pocket for Sarah's card, then punched in her number. He didn't say hello. He didn't care that she answered in a sleepy voice, and he didn't waste time on pleasantries. "Quinn's been kidnapped by some psycho penis mutilator. You said she was in a safe home. If she was in a safe home, how did this happen?"

"What?"

"If I find she's been harmed, I'll have your ass and the county's ass hung in court."

"Slow down."

"Is this what the state calls *a safe environment*? I want answers, and I want them now!"

"What happened?"

Brett explained what he knew and gave her the address of where he was headed.

"I'll be there shortly. I'll call Peggy. Give me a few minutes to throw on some clothes."

Brett put his phone back on his belt clip and stared out at the dark highway, his back rigid and his jaw clenched. Cars and trucks moved to the side of the road, their brake lights flashing red on the highway.

Clay sped between them, weaving in and out of the lanes. The cruiser's siren blared, and its lights flashed.

West Shady Lane was at the other side of town. Brett watched as they zoomed by dark houses and businesses. Few people occupied the streets. Everyone seemed to be sleeping. It didn't seem right that the town could sleep while Quinn was in danger. It was wrong. Like they needed to grieve and search with him until she was found.

When Clay turned down West Shady Lane, Brett stared at the dark homes they passed and the shadows along the road. Was Quinn in one of these homes, or hiding in the trees? Was she crying for him? If she was with a madman, she wouldn't understand. How could she possibly know the mind of a criminal? No five-year-old could. She'd never met anyone mentally unstable, and he was certain, if she really had been kidnapped, that the man was deranged. Only an angry person could do what he was doing. But maybe, just maybe, this was all a sick joke. Maybe Quinn was safe with her new friend Sadie, and the dispatcher had gotten it all wrong. He could only hope. Besides, why would a penis mutilator kidnap a child?

Clay slowed when he saw the ambulance flashers in the driveway. He pulled to the curb.

Brett opened his door and raced to the ambulance, not bothering to close his door. The patient lay on the gurney in the van, moaning like a cow in labor, reaching for his crotch. The techs busied themselves with their patient, taping the IV to his arm and checking his vitals. Brett scooted in between them and took a hold of the patient's shirt, lifting him to within an inch of his face. "Who are you, and where's my daughter?"

The patient looked cross-eyed at Brett.

"Did you touch her, you pervert?"

Each tech grabbed one of Brett's arms and pulled him off the patient. "Easy, easy."

Brett relaxed his grip and looked from one tech to the other. "Who is he? Is he a registered sex offender?"

One tech said, "Name is Calvin Moore but he's been using Michael as his alias. His mother is inside. She said he just moved here from Ohio."

Brett lowered Moore's head to the gurney. But once Moore's head relaxed on the pillow, the jerk smiled. His words came out slurred, but Brett swore he'd said, "You have a real sweet daughter."

Brett thrashed and struggled to break free of the techs' grips, ready to bust Moore to pieces.

Clay took hold of Brett's shoulders and held him back. "Take it easy, Reed."

The techs let go of Brett and lifted Moore into the van. Clay held Brett off until the van doors shut. "Look, Reed, I'll release you if you promise to keep your head on, okay?"

Brett nodded and Clay released him.

"Give me your radio." Brett held out his hand for Clay's device. He radioed the precinct, gave them Moore's address and name, and asked them to check it out.

A middle-aged woman in a white blouse and brown polyester slacks stood on the porch with a little girl dressed in *Dora the Explorer* pajamas. The girl held a yellow square pillow and sucked her pointer finger. She yawned.

Clay approached them, reaching into his pocket for his badge. He showed it to the woman. "I'm Officer Clay Rizzo. This is my partner, Officer Reed. Quinn's father. Obviously he's not in uniform right now, but he's a cop. We need to ask you a few questions and examine the evidence."

The lady twisted a tissue in her hands. "I'm Melanie Stookey, the foster mom." She nodded toward Brett. "I'm sorry. I'm so sorry."

Brett gritted his teeth. "Not as sorry as I am. Where is she?" Brett's eyes darted around the woman to the inside of the home.

Clay looked at the neighbors gathering on their lit porches and nodded to Brett. "Let's go in."

The woman cried, wringing her hands. "She's gone. I'm so sorry."

"You're *sorry*?" Brett shook his head.

Clay motioned for Mrs. Stookey and the girl to go into the house. He took hold of Brett's arm and ushered him in after them.

Brett stepped over the bloodied beige carpet. A brown leather sofa and a black worn recliner stood in the middle of the room. Exotic animal posters hung on the walls—cheetahs, monkeys, snakes. The home smelled like mold growing in a wet crawl space. Brett shivered. Quinn had been staying here in this dump? He shook his head.

Mrs. Stookey said, "I dropped her and Sadie off here around ten this evening. I had to go to the nursing home. My mother is dying." She twisted her hanky.

Clay said, "Is Sadie a foster child too?"

Mrs. Stookey nodded. "When I returned and saw the blood, I knew something was wrong. That's when I found my son and— realized Quinn was gone."

"Exactly what time was that?" Brett said.

"Around midnight. Sadie was sitting there, crying." She pointed to the sofa. Mrs. Stookey put her arm around the girl.

"You left the girls with your son?" Brett's voice boomed off the walls.

She shirked and nodded. "I had to go. There wasn't anyone else."

Brett wanted to scream. "But he's a registered sex offender!"

She whimpered and lowered her voice. "He was, but he just moved back from Ohio. He hadn't registered yet."

Brett noticed Sadie looking down at her bare feet, curling them in as if she was pigeon-toed. Tears ran down her cheeks. She sucked her finger and held her pillow up to her cheek.

Brett knelt in front of her. "What a beautiful name for a pretty girl. Quinn told me about you. She said you're her best friend."

Sadie smiled.

"I'm her daddy. Were you sleeping with her last night when Mrs. Stookey left?"

Sadie nodded.

"Did she snore?" he said, teasing.

Sadie giggled and shook her head.

"Where were you sleeping?"

Sadie nodded at the sofa she was sitting on and swept a strand of her straight blond hair out of her eyes. "But he took her to his room."

"Who's he?" Brett's blood boiled.

"Mr. Moore." Sadie pointed down the hall.

Mrs. Stookey gasped.

Brett ignored her, keeping his eyes on Sadie, ready to lose it but forcing himself to stay calm. "How do you know?"

"I saw him, but I pretended to be asleep."

"Did he ever take you to his room?"

Sadie looked at Mrs. Stookey and then back at Brett. She slowly nodded.

Mrs. Stookey gasped again and twisted the tissue in her hand faster. "It's not what you think. It can't be. He hasn't done anything like that in a long time. He went through counseling."

Brett's stomach lurched. He ignored the woman sniffling beside him and stayed on his knees in front of Sadie. "I'm sorry he took you. I hope he didn't hurt you."

Tears pooled in her eyes.

Brett said, "Where did he hurt you?"

She pointed to her groin.

Mrs. Stookey collapsed onto the sofa, shaking her head. "No!"

Brett held Sadie's hand. "He's a bad man. You were very brave. You're going to be safe now. I promise. No one is going to hurt you anymore."

Her shoulders shook as she hiccuped a sob. Brett put his arms around her and held her to his chest, letting her tears spill, and wishing he was holding Quinn instead. He wiped her face with a tissue until all the anger inside him erupted.

He stormed to where Mrs. Stookey sat and came within inches of her face, shouting, his spittle flying. "What kind of person are you to let your pervert son take care of innocent children? Are you mad? This is all your fault."

The woman sobbed louder.

Clay took Brett's arm. "Easy."

Brett turned to him. "Easy? We should cuff her and make her sit in the slammer."

Sadie let out a cry. Brett turned and saw panic in her wide eyes. The child trembled, making Brett feel guilty for his outburst. As he moved back to the child, he saw Officer Beth Hudson, a rookie cop in her late twenties, enter the house. Brett waved her over and knelt in front of Sadie again.

He lowered his voice. "This is Officer Beth. She's going to take you to a safe place and buy you some ice cream. You like ice cream, don't you?"

Sadie nodded.

Beth, who was short, thick, strong, and loud, took Sadie's hand. If anyone could reassure a child, it was Beth.

He asked one more question. "Did you see the person who took Quinn?"

Sadie nodded and put her finger back in her mouth.

Brett's heart raced. "What did he look like?" Brett held his breath.

Sadie shrugged.

Brett pressed. "Was it a man?"

Sadie shrugged again. "I don't know. There was something over his face."

Clay placed his hand on Brett's shoulder. "Let it go for now, man."

Was he crazy? This child may be the only one who'd seen the perp. "Would you tell Officer Beth if you remember something about him?"

Sadie nodded and took the officer's hand. They headed toward the door.

Brett locked eyes with Officer Hudson, begging her to find out something. He waved good-bye to Sadie, hating how she would be tossed into another foster home like some kind of unwanted animal. He promised her he'd bring Quinn to visit her soon. And he meant it. Sadie smiled.

Why wasn't she with her parents? Why did people have children if they couldn't take care of them? Why had Ali? Why had he ever thought that marrying her was doing the right thing? That all she needed was to be rescued?

Mrs. Stookey, slumped in a worn recliner, whimpered. "I'm so sorry, so, so sorry."

Brett didn't want to listen to her apologies. He wanted answers.

Clay stood in the center of the room, his large dark frame towering over the scene, his voice booming and commanding authority. "Mrs. Stookey, are you ready to tell us the truth now, or should Officer Reed read you your rights?"

Brett moved to the sofa, working to keep his temper in check, clenching his fists and releasing them, clenching and releasing.

"What do you mean?" Mrs. Stookey wiped her face with a tissue.

Clay shifted his weight. "Where did you go tonight? Why weren't you here, and how were you able to get a foster license with a sex offender living in your home?"

She averted her eyes. Tears fell down her face.

Clay said, "It's better if you tell us the truth straightaway."

Brett added, "You could be charged with aiding and abetting a sex offender."

"No, I promise. I had no idea Calvin would harm these girls. He's been without work, so I left the girls here for him to watch until I returned. This isn't my home. It's the one Calvin's renting."

Brett leaned forward in his seat, staring at Mrs. Stookey. "I can't believe you left two young girls with a sex offender!"

His voice shook. He pounded the table with his fist.

Mrs. Stookey squealed. "Calvin's been through counseling. He hasn't, er, done that, uh, in a long time. He's been good." Her voice trembled.

Brett shook his head. Was she so blind and stupid that she hadn't heard what Sadie had said? Between clenched teeth, he stood with his back to her so he wouldn't have to see her, and said, "How often have you left them in his care?" He squeezed his eyes shut and held his breath waiting for her answer.

Mrs. Stookey hesitated before she quietly said, "Just the last two nights."

He exhaled and stormed out the front door, shoving the handle with so much force the door hit the side of the house. *Just long enough for your son to cause permanent damage to my daughter and somebody else's daughter*. He was glad her son lost his dick. Maybe this butcher perp was making the community a better place after all.

He stared into the star-filled sky and let his tears fall. *Where are you, my twinkling star? Daddy is going to find you!* But as far as Brett knew, there were no leads.

Why would this person take Quinn? Wasn't he only intent on maiming sex offenders? Wouldn't he hate anyone who harmed a child? Why then would he have taken Quinn?

Chapter Eighteen

When Sarah arrived at West Shady Lane, Brett and another officer, clad with rubber gloves, were dusting for prints and placing soiled sheets and garments into bags. Sarah stood outside the bedroom door watching the men. She didn't want to interfere, but she needed to know what had happened. She stood on shaky knees waiting to hear.

Brett glared at her with pursed lips. He dusted off his clothes and introduced her to his partner, barely making eye contact. "This is Officer Rizzo." He turned to Rizzo. "This is the counselor who placed Quinn in a *safe* home."

Officer Rizzo nodded at Sarah. "Name is Clay." He continued to the other side of the room, dusting for prints.

Brett's sarcasm pelted Sarah, but she understood. He was pissed. Guilt bled through her. This had been her fault. He was right. She'd promised him that Quinn would be safe and now look. He wore the same clothes he'd worn when she'd seen him at the geo-site, before the hospital had called about Ali. His eyes were bloodshot, and his face was still pocked with mosquito bites. As he approached, she could smell that he hadn't showered either. Obviously he'd never made it home. "I haven't heard back from Peggy yet. I woke her and begged her to look into what happened."

Brett glowered at her. "It kind of doesn't matter now, does it? Quinn's gone."

"I'm really sorry. Tell me what happened." She wished he would meet her eyes.

He looked away.

"How's Ali?"

He shrugged, continuing his work. "Brain-dead, for now. Not sure she's going to live. And now, Quinn . . ." He squeezed his eyes shut, paused, and turned to Sarah, speaking between gritted teeth. "Her friend Sadie, the other *foster* child living here, admitted she was sexually abused by this perv. Did you know that?" Brett had moved to within inches of Sarah, close enough for her to see his red-rimmed eyes. "Which means Quinn may have been abused too!"

She backed up, tears filling her eyes. "No, please no! Don't assume that. Don't let your mind go there. I'm sorry. I don't understand how this happened. Mrs. Stookey had an impeccable reputation. She's been fostering children for five years."

Brett shook his head, his voice booming. "And *now*, Quinn's with . . . some madman, and who knows if she'll . . ."

He didn't finish his sentence, but Sarah knew what he was going to say. *If she'll make it out alive.* Sarah hated how defeated Brett looked and sounded. Seeing his little-boy face in such turmoil caused a surge of protectiveness in her heart. What could she say to give him hope? She leaned against the doorjamb. "Tell me what you know about the guy who took her."

Brett said, "He's a penis mutilator who targets sex offenders." He turned his back to her, continuing his work.

Sarah said, "He's only harming men, right?"

Clay nodded. Brett seemed to ignore her.

"Maybe this guy thinks he's saving Quinn from the sex offender. Obviously, he targeted the guy who lives here. Maybe he hates men who harm children. And quite honestly, I agree. Who doesn't hate pedophiles? But if I had to profile the guy, I'd say he thinks he's doing something good, like he's saving people from these perverts."

Brett strolled to the TV, dusting for prints, his back to Sarah.

Was he thinking about what she'd said?

She continued. "Maybe the guy took her to a safe place."

Clay nodded to Brett, smirking. "Let's hope the guy doesn't

target you."

"Why would he do that?" Sarah turned to Clay.

Clay said, "Rumor on the street is that Quinn was placed in protective custody because Brett was harming her."

"That's crazy. Who said that?"

Brett turned to Sarah. "Does it matter? Once the press gets wind of a rumor, it's truth no matter if it is or not."

"That's wrong, so wrong." She wanted to wrap her arms around him and give him hope, take away his worry. Her heart ached for Quinn. That poor, poor child.

Brett's shoulders sagged. He turned to Sarah. "So if he really hates sex offenders and rumors are spreading about me molesting my daughter, he'll probably show up at my house in the middle of the night and whack off my—"

"That's not true. Think about it. How does he know that Quinn is your daughter? If he saw her in this offender's home, maybe he thought he was rescuing her from *him*, right?"

Clay interrupted and nudged Brett with his elbow. "Check out the floor."

Brett bent down and knelt, scanning under the bed. "Hand me the flashlight."

Clay reached for his pencil light on his belt and handed it to Brett. Brett flashed the light under the bed and gasped.

"What?" Clay fell to his knees beside Brett.

Brett lifted Quinn's lamb and put it up to his face, tears filling his eyes. He sat in the middle of the floor, clutching the lamb, his eyes squeezed shut. He moaned, its sound reverberating across the walls, rocking the silence. "No!"

Clay sat beside him, placing his hand on his back. "We'll find her, man. I promise, we'll find her."

Sarah looked away, overcome with emotion. There was something about seeing a man cry that made her shudder. Seeing Brett cry tore her insides to pieces. She remembered his visit with Quinn and how he'd embraced her. Tears spilled as she remembered Quinn's tight grip on the lamb too. If the child had been under the bed, then she must have been hiding. Sarah understood. She'd hidden under beds before too. And since the stuffed animal had been in this room there was a good chance that Quinn had been molested too. Dread filled Sarah. She hoped her intuition was wrong.

\#

Brett placed Lambie in a crime scene bag, knowing he had to, but wanted to keep it with him. He and Clay finished their work while Sarah watched. They were on their way to load the patrol car with what little evidence they could find, when a lady carrying a small dog came running over to them from the house next door. Sarah, who'd walked out with Brett, stopped to listen too.

The lady wore thick glasses and had red Keds on her feet. "Excuse me, but my little Biscuit was barking last night at something over there." She pointed to a group of pine trees next to the garage. "Biscuit barked and growled, and I thought it was strange because he doesn't usually go over this far to Mr. Moore's house."

Sarah, who held her keys in her hand, paused and stared at the lady. "Mr. Moore?" She turned to Brett. "Is that the name of the guy who lives here?"

Brett nodded.

Sarah turned to the lady. "What was his first name?"

The lady stared into space for a few seconds before she said, "Uh, he told me it was Michael, but I think it was Calvin because shortly after he moved in I got his mail by mistake, and it said Calvin Moore. But I didn't know him personally."

Clay asked the lady to point to where her dog had been barking.

She pointed to the row of cedar trees.

"Did you see anything or anybody?"

"No, I never did. Is Mr. Moore going to be okay? What happened?"

Brett answered. "We're not able to discuss that right now, but if you think of anything else, please call."

Clay handed her his card.

Sarah butted in. "What did this Mr. Moore look like?"

The lady put her hand on her hip. "Let me see. He had dark hair and wore his pants real high—hiked up to his chest. But at night he'd get all dressed up and go out looking like Elvis. The transformation was amazing."

Brett studied Sarah's face. Why did she look shocked?

The neighbor lady started to turn toward her home but stopped. "Am I safe?"

Brett wanted to say, no one is ever safe. Instead, he said, "Just lock your doors." Once the lady was out of earshot, Brett turned to Sarah. "Do you know this guy?"

She nodded. "Yeah, I thought he was a harmless man, a perfect gentleman. He's a patient. Just goes to show I'm not a very good judge of character."

"You're right. You're not." Brett couldn't help lashing out at her. She should have done a more-thorough investigation on Mrs. Stookey's background. He moved toward the row of pine trees, where the neighbor had pointed, his head down, looking for clues. He kicked over dead needles. A Snickers wrapper surfaced. "Hand me a crime kit," he said to Clay.

#

On the way back to the precinct, the dark night surrounded Brett and Clay. Few drivers were on the road.

Brett sat with Lambie enclosed in plastic on his lap and rested his head against the seat, thankful Clay was driving. Thoughts swirled in Brett's head like dead leaves in a tornado, dizzy from the flitting and bogged down from the rain. The lack of sleep didn't help contribute to his emotional state, but how could he sleep now?

Why had the perp taken Quinn? Had she watched him sever Moore? Oh, he hoped not! Had he found her hiding under the bed crying and wanted to rescue her? Brett wanted to believe the latter. Sarah had. She'd looked sincerely upset about Quinn. Her whole demeanor toward Brett seemed to change. There was something in her eyes that made him think she understood. That she wanted to help. That she felt miserable about assuming Quinn had been in a safe home. Or was he a fool?

Was Sarah the vigilante? She was an avid geocacher and he suspected she'd been sexually abused. Her comment about hating pedophiles seemed personal too. On the other hand, she was trying to keep him confident by saying the perp wouldn't harm Quinn. He wanted to believe this, but bad thoughts seeped in his mind, like black tar oozing between cracks. They tortured him. Did Sarah know more than she was saying?

Clay called the chief and put him on speakerphone.

Chief answered. "Dunson here." His voice sounded gruffer than usual, like he'd been woken from sleep.

"Hey, it's Rizzo and Reed."

"Reed, we're working to find your daughter. Officer Hudson has an artist working with the other child who was at the house—what was her name?"

Brett leaned forward in his seat. "Sadie. Did she think it was a man?"

"Not sure. The kid said *he* was dressed in black with clunky shoes, but he had something over his head, maybe a mesh cap. I have units out now searching sites. I've called in all local units and those from Jasper, Livingston, and Pulaski counties. We should have a force of about a hundred officers by seven a.m. We're going to cover all these geo-sites and find your daughter, Reed. Soon." He cleared his throat. "Officers Pierce and Rankin are checking with Moore's neighbors as to whether they saw anything."

"Thanks." He appreciated how much help the officers were giving. They'd find the guy or a clue soon. They had to.

After Clay disconnected the call, Brett phoned the hospital. The operator connected him to a nurse in Ali's ICU room. Ali's condition hadn't changed. At least he wouldn't have to tell her about Quinn. Not yet.

Clay interrupted his thoughts. "You sure you want me to take you to your car?"

Brett nodded. "Yeah. By the way, do you have that list of deceased men from the county?"

Clay pointed toward the floorboard in front of Brett. "Yeah, they're in that folder there."

Brett reached for the thick accordion folder.

"They're filed under 'W' for Whacker."

Brett opened the folder and shuffled through the tabs for the "W" file. He grabbed the papers and pulled them out. Using the light of his phone, he glanced at the names and ages of the deceased. They didn't mean anything to him. No name looked familiar. "The whacker's only victim who doesn't fit in with the others is dead and probably on this list, right?"

"Assuming he lived in this county, yes."

"Finding him would help." Brett tucked the papers under his arm as Clay pulled into the hospital parking lot.

Clay pulled alongside Brett's car. "Officer Hunt is working on that list too. Why don't you try to get some shut-eye—even if it's a few hours?"

"Are you crazy? I can't sleep. Looking over these names will give me something to do. I need to shower and get in my uniform. I'll be at the precinct as soon as I can." He opened his door. "Call me if you hear anything—anything at all."

"Of course. I'll head to the lab first and drop off the piece you found from the geo-site. I'll have them check the bedding from Moore's. They'll know whether Quinn was in that bed. I'm praying her DNA doesn't show up."

Tears filled Brett's stinging eyes. "I am too." As he climbed out of the car, he handed Lambie to Clay.

#

I paced the wooden floors in my living room, twirling the bottom of my shirt, my feet clunking on the planks. Now what? The girl was sad. She didn't like me either. Why didn't she feel safe? Didn't she realize I'd saved her? Why wasn't she happy to be with me?

She sat in a chair near the fireplace and crossed her arms, glaring at me.

"Would you like to play a game?"

"No, I want my daddy." Tears fell down her cheeks. She sniffled.

"No, please don't cry." I'd seen tears so many times before, and there had been nothing I could do. My stomach twisted at the memories. I paced.

Maybe she was cold. "Would you like me to build a fire? Momma always said a fire made everything inside feel better, that it warmed her heart."

She turned her back to me.

I rubbed my fingers across my lips, over and over again. What should I do? "You'll be okay now. I'll take care of you. We could watch TV."

She stood and stormed across the room to the bathroom. "No. I don't want you! I want my daddy. You aren't my daddy." She slammed the door and turned the lock.

I stomped my foot. I didn't know how to get it right. I wanted her to feel safe, to like me. She didn't want to look at me. Pressing my ear up to the bathroom door, I listened. Her whimpering made me cringe. Had I done this to her? No, not me. But someone else. Why then did she want her daddy?

#

Brett pulled up to Ali's home around three a.m. exhausted. He went to Ali's because it was closer to the precinct, and he wanted to feel closer to Quinn, to another time when he'd held her.

He needed to shower and change his clothes. Maybe then he'd get a second wind. Thankfully, he kept a spare uniform in his trunk.

Ali's street was dark and quiet; few homes were illuminated, but he noticed a parked car a few doors down that wasn't ordinarily there. His heart raced. He thought he saw a silhouette of a person in the front seat. He pulled his cruiser into the driveway, climbed out, and popped the trunk. After gathering his clothes, he headed toward the door and placed his clothes on the porch, ducked behind a few bushes, and examined the car from a distance.

It looked like Mark's truck, but he couldn't be sure. What the hell was he doing?

Brett dashed, squatting toward the back of the vehicle. When he was within twenty feet, the engine started and the driver sped away with only his parking lights on.

It sure looked like Mark. Jerk!

Brett reached for his phone and called Clay. "I think Mark was just parked out front. Not sure why he was here. He's heading east toward Main Street in a white truck. I'm afraid if I go after him I'll lose my cool."

"I'm on it."

Clay's sirens blared through the phone.

Brett climbed back into his sedan. "I'm going to chase him from behind."

"I don't think that's a good idea. Let me handle this, Reed. Stay put. I'm not that far away, and if I don't find him we'll park a car at his house and wait for him. I'll let you know when I've got him."

Clay had a point. Brett needed to let him handle this. But what if Mark got away? Ugh! Giving up control was not an easy thing, especially when Quinn was involved. "Okay, but call me."

Brett stepped out of his car and headed back to the porch to gather his uniform, but when he heard a scratching sound coming from the side of the house, he froze. He set his uniform on the front porch again and slowly moved toward the other side of the house—toward the garage in the back. He hid in the shadows with his back up against the house. Where was his weapon when he needed it?

He crept inside the side door to the garage and reached for a shovel that hung on a Peg-Board hook. He held the blade in the air and tiptoed out the garage and along the sidewall toward the noise. He heard another sound and paused, listening, and waited. It sounded like something was dragging toward him. It was moving closer, scraping the ground as it went. What if the guy had a gun? It was better to wait. He forced his breathing to slow, but his heartbeat sounded like drums banging in his ears. He listened. More scraping. Then he heard a whimper.

Max?

Brett turned the corner, the shovel raised above his head, ready to strike. But it was Max. He lay in the grass on his stomach, doing the army crawl. When he saw Brett, his tail thumped slowly against the ground, and he stood.

"What's wrong, boy?" Brett leaned the shovel against the house and bent to examine the dog. Prickly burs were tangled in his hair around his ears, neck, paws, and abdomen. His back leg was caked in dried blood. Brett scooped him into his arms, and Max yipped. "Sorry, boy. Shhh, let's get you inside and take a look at you."

Max relaxed, slapping a wet kiss across Brett's cheek.

Brett went to the back door that led to the kitchen. He jostled Max in his arms and fumbled in his pocket for the keys. After he opened the door, he carried Max into the house and placed him on the kitchen counter. Maybe it was exhaustion or raw emotion, but Brett couldn't hold the tears from flooding his eyes. *Quinn, Max is back! He's back. Now it's time for you to come home too.* He wiped his tears with the back of his arm. "Where have you been, boy? We've been worried."

Max wagged his tail again, but Brett could tell it took great effort.

"I wish you could talk." Brett cut the burs out of Max's fur and washed his leg wound, which didn't look as bad as he'd originally thought, as the dog could stand on it now. When Brett finished, he lifted Max and placed him on his doggie bed on the floor next to the kitchen table.

"I bet you're hungry." As Brett filled Max's bowls with food and water, the dog scrambled to stand, his legs quivering as he moved. He sauntered over to his bowls and ate and drank like he hadn't eaten since before he left. Brett remembered the last time he fed him and how Quinn had stood within arm's reach. Oh, how he wished she was standing there now. Had that only been two days ago?

His phone rang. Clay.

"Yeah?"

Clay said, "We found him at his house, in bed. Said he never left. He said even if he had been parked in front of your house it's a free country. We couldn't book him with anything. Sorry, guy."

Brett swung his fist in the air. "He's lying! I *know* he's up to something!"

"I'm keeping Riggs parked nearby in an unmarked car. If Mark's our guy, we'll get him."

Had Mark known where Max had been? It seemed strange that Max showed up when Mark was parked out front.

Chapter Nineteen

A horn honked in the distance. Brett woke with a start. Darn! He'd fallen asleep at the kitchen table, next to Max, who slept on the floor. The computer and the list of deceased men lay on the table next to Brett. He glanced at the clock on the stove: 6:28. He'd slept for two hours. His hands tingled from sleeping in an awkward position. Guilt punched him in the gut. How could he have possibly fallen asleep when Quinn was out there somewhere, needing him? He stood, rubbing his eyes. It felt like someone had thrown sand in them.

Just before he'd fallen asleep, he looked over the list, reading the names and addresses but not seeing them. He couldn't focus, and he hadn't been able to make calls because it was too late.

He shook the tingle out of his arms.

Max stirred and hobbled to Brett. He knelt in front of the dog, enveloping his head in his lap and rubbing his ears. "We're going to find her, boy. We will."

As if Max knew who Brett was talking about, he limped to Quinn's room. Brett followed and watched Max sniff her bed, the floor, and the toys on her shelf.

The doorbell rang. Max barked. It was probably Clay. He hoped it was him bringing good news.

Brett hurried to the door and opened it. A tall blond woman stood on the porch with a bald man who held a camera on his shoulder. Not another news crew!

The woman spoke first. "Officer Reed?" Her voice squeaked. She cleared her throat. "Could you answer a few questions for us?"

He didn't have time for this. He needed to call the station, talk to Clay, get out of there. He started to close the door.

"Wait! You haven't seen the morning paper, have you?" She handed him a newspaper. "This was in your driveway."

He took the paper and pulled it out of its plastic wrap, then shook it open to read. On the front page was a photo of him with Quinn. Seeing Quinn's face made him gasp. *Officer's Daughter Kidnapped by Sex Offender Mutilator.*

Brett stared at the words, his mouth agape. Seeing the headlines made his nightmare even more of a reality. He glanced over the names of the victims, the crimes, and the profile of the perpetrator. The words blurred. He leaned against the doorjamb, overcome with vertigo.

The woman put the mic in front of him, and the camera's red light flashed. "Why did Child Protective Services take your daughter?"

Brett stared into the camera, his voice barely audible. "Leave me alone."

"The paper said your wife's blood alcohol level was twice over the legal limit. Do you expect your wife will be charged with vehicular homicide?"

"What?" His ears buzzed.

"What's her prognosis?"

"Go away."

"Will you sue the state for putting your daughter in harm's way?"

Brett grabbed hold of the door, using its weight to lean on. "Go, just go! I need to find my daughter." He shut the door, wishing he could shut out the same questions that drilled through his own mind.

The lady spoke through the door. "The community wants to help."

He ignored the reporter and stoically walked to the living room. Ali had been drunk? He sat on the edge of the sofa and read the paper. Next to the article about Quinn's kidnapping was one about

Ali. Her wrecked car and the victim's were also on the front page. It was a miracle Ali had lived. Her driver's side was practically gone.

Ali had run a stop sign going ten over the speed limit. The victim, Holly Daby, was only twenty-five years old and engaged to be married soon. She and her fiancé were studying to be dentists and were finishing their schooling in Indianapolis. She'd come home to Hursey Lake to visit her family. She died at the scene of the accident.

Brett closed his eyes and pictured the young man waiting at the hospital. He dropped his head into his hands.

Tears stung his eyes. He shook his head and pressed his fingers into the sockets. He wasn't going to cry. Not now. There wasn't time. He hurried into the bathroom, but the first things he saw were Quinn's yellow duck towel hanging on the hook and her Barbie toothbrush in the holder. He stopped and rubbed the towel against his face. *Daddy will find you, baby. He'll find you.*

When he opened the drawer to grab his razor, he saw a tube of Ali's lipstick. He remembered a time when she'd put it on her lips and then Quinn's and how they giggled. Memories of Quinn surrounded him. He sat on the stool and wept.

When no more tears would come, he took a shower while listening to his usual AM talk radio station. The announcer discussed how easy it was to get information about sex offenders. A person only needing to do a computer search by state. Indiana was broken down by counties. In one click, search engines brought up the names, addresses, ages, and photos of the offenders.

People were calling in saying how that was a violation of privacy, but other callers disagreed, complaining that all citizens had the right to know who their neighbors were for their safety and the safety of their children. He shouted at the radio and clicked it off, disgusted. "What about those sex offenders who move to a new town without registering?"

After he lathered his body and his hair, his phone vibrated against the countertop. With wet hands, he reached for it. His mother. *Oh, crap!* She'd be frantic. He couldn't answer now. He'd call her later. Right now he needed to get to the precinct.

#

Brett retrieved the uniform he'd left on the front porch last night and shook it, hoping the wrinkles would fall out. There was no time to press them. He dressed quickly, the damp clothing bogging down his mood even further. When he was ready to go, he opened the car door for Max and helped lift him into the backseat. No way was he going to leave him home alone now. He doubted the chief would mind, given the circumstances, but it didn't matter because right now he didn't give a damn. Having Max nearby made him feel closer to Quinn.

After putting on his flashers, he drove to the station. He was about to call Clay, when his phone buzzed. He glanced at the screen. His mother. "Hi, Mom."

"Hi, Son," his father said.

Dad? Brett froze. His father's voice sounded foreign—older and deeper. Why hadn't he noticed how it had changed when he called earlier? "Uh, hi."

"Your mom was worried."

Nothing about him being worried. "I'm sure. I haven't had a chance to call her, you know. It's been crazy."

"I know. We read the paper." He paused. "I'm sorry. I, er, I know . . . I haven't been there for you in a long time, but I want you to know that I'm here for you if you need legal counsel."

What if I need emotional counsel? Brett heard his mother in the background saying, "Give me the phone."

She said, "I feel so bad. If we had taken Quinn this wouldn't have happened." She sobbed.

"Don't say that, Mom. Dad's health is important right now, and you didn't know this was going to happen."

"Have they found Quinn yet? How's Ali?" Her voice sounded shrill.

"No, they haven't found Quinn. Ali's condition hasn't changed. I'm on my way to the station. I'll let you know as soon as I know something."

"Your father meant what he said. He wants to be there for you."

Why? So he can say "I told you so"? So, he can rub it in my face—that I threw my life away by not finishing my law degree? Would his dad remind him that being a cop didn't pay the bills, that his life was a mess because of the poor choices he'd made? "Thanks, Mom. That means a lot to me." He had to say that because that's what she wanted him to say.

He heard his call-waiting beep and glanced at his screen. It was Clay. "Mom, I have to go. I'll call you when I know more. I'm on my way to the station right now."

"Okay." Her crying quieted.

He switched the call over. "Did you find her?"

"Where are you?"

"Almost at the station, why?" Brett held his breath. "Have they found her?"

"No."

Brett exhaled, the air rushing out of him, draining him of hope. He smacked his fist into the seat.

"We need to hold a press conference. People are calling in, asking if they can be a part of a search party to find her. The phones are ringing off the hook. You need to address this, tell people how they can help."

"Okay, thanks."

"You also need to let this perp know you're Quinn's father. If he knows and thinks you're an offender, you seriously could be his next target. You need to make an appeal so he realizes you won't harm her. Do you think we can get Sarah to address what happened so panic doesn't run rampant in our foster homes too?"

"I think she'll do that."

"They'd better do it. CPS's butt is on the line right now. They were negligent. Someone needs to be accountable."

"Has Peggy given a statement as to how this happened?"

"She said they didn't know Stookey had a son who was a sex offender. She'd been a prominent teacher in our school system for a long time and had a stellar home study. No one knew about her son. He moved away years ago."

Brett's call-waiting beeped again. "Clay, the hospital is calling. I'll be at the office in five minutes."

"Okay, we'll schedule the press conference for eight thirty, in an hour. Oh, one more thing, I've been thinking about the perp. There's no ransom letter. I doubt there will be. He doesn't want money. He never has. He wants to harm sex offenders. Make them live without their wand. I really don't think he'll harm Quinn."

"I hope you're right."

Brett switched calls. "This is Reed."

"Have they found Quinn yet?" Ali's mother didn't bother to say hello. She must have used Ali's hospital room phone, which was why the hospital's number had appeared on his screen.

"Nothing yet. How's Ali?"

"She's still in a coma."

"Nothing's changed?" Brett heard beeping monitors in the background.

Mrs. Greer said, "Some guy came by to visit her. Said she killed his fiancée and he's going to sue her for everything she has. Said Ali took away his entire future." She sniffled. "I told him he needed to talk to you. That you were responsible, not Ali."

Brett rolled his eyes. Of course she would say that. She really believed that if he hadn't divorced Ali, she'd be here safe right now. *Give me a break.*

"I gave him your name and phone number."

"How nice of you."

Brett disconnected the call and pulled into the station parking lot. Almost every single spot was taken with patrol cars from all over the state. A lump formed in his throat. All these officers were here to help find Quinn. Never had he seen a force this large in his little town.

#

When Brett entered the precinct, fellow officers greeted him, squeezing his shoulder and patting him on the back. Several others welcomed him with a nod and a smile. Max's tail wagged as officers approached and acknowledged him too.

Clay rubbed Max's ears. "Where did you find him?"

Brett explained as he took a seat at his desk. "I can't help but wonder if Mark dropped him off. It's sketchy how Max returned home when Mark's car was parked out front."

Max lay on the floor beside him, resting his head on his legs, his eyes following Brett's every move, as if waiting for the moment they could go find Quinn.

Brett noticed Clay's dark beard and wrinkled clothes. "You never went home last night, did you?"

Clay shook his head. "Officer Riggs followed Mark to a geo-site around midnight."

"What?" Brett bolted out of his seat. "Is he our guy?"

Clay waved his hand. "Not sure. Riggs brought him in for questioning, but he claimed he was only out trying to find the latest prize. He said he didn't even know Quinn was gone, and he'd never heard of geocaching before all this."

"You believe him?" Brett bit his lip.

"We had to let him go for lack of evidence, but Riggs is tracking his moves."

Was Mark their guy? Brett didn't trust him. The guy knew more than he was saying. But why would he have taken Quinn? "Can't we search his home?"

"Riggs did last night. Mark said he didn't have anything to hide, and he let him take a look around." Clay squeezed Brett's shoulder. "There was nothing there. Sorry."

Brett's stomach soured. His hands clenched into fists, and he spoke through gritted teeth. "That guy knows more than he's saying, and I'd like to beat it out of him."

Chief Dunson strolled into the room. His wire-rimmed readers rested on his nose as he peered over the top of them. "Let's all meet in the conference room."

By the time Brett and Clay joined the others, it was standing room only. Every chair was filled. Brett couldn't remember a time when so many officers had been in the conference room at one time.

Chief whistled and everyone hushed. "People in the community are starting to panic. This perp has made them realize we live among sex offenders. That they're living all around us—that their children are surrounded by these pervs. This unsub has brought attention to sex offenders in this community—which is precisely what he wants to do. Now, with Officer Reed's daughter missing, we need to ramp up our efforts to find this guy."

Chief's secretary walked into the room and handed the chief a folder. He took it from her and began. "First, I'll go over the facts based on the forensic evidence. Then, I'll give you the rough profile of who we might be looking for.

"Our first victim's identity is unknown, but he was dead at the time of amputation. The medical examiner estimated he'd been dead about two weeks. The next three victims were sex offenders. The unsub used chloroform on a rag to render them unconscious. Then he injected them with an anesthetic, used a rubber tourniquet to cut off the penis's circulation and used something like a scalpel to amputate. The three victims were sleeping at the time of attack. Two were under the influence of alcohol.

"So, given the above facts, we can draw some conclusions. The unsub is most likely male and either a victim of sexual abuse or lost a loved one to a sex offender. But we can't rule out a female who hates men and who may have been abused."

Someone blurted out. "Or a woman who has penis envy." Men laughed, but the women sat stoic.

Brett thought of Sarah. Suspicious thoughts of her loomed in the cells of his brain. Hadn't she alluded that she didn't trust men, that she'd had a difficult experience with them? And she was also a geocacher. That was crazy thinking, but he'd caught her near one of the sites. Was it possible? No, why would she have taken Quinn? Besides, Sadie's description had sounded more like a guy with clunky shoes. That didn't make sense. He forced his attention back on the chief.

Chief chuckled and took off his glasses. "Dog, cat, and horse hairs have been found near the victims. The third victim had a cat, so our guy may have pets or live on a farm. Since the first victim was deceased, he could work in a funeral home. He may think of himself as a do-gooder—his purpose obviously to rid society of sex offenders.

"He's bold in that he's taking risks by going into the victims' homes. He's childlike in that he's hiding the object for others to find, but he *wants* us to find them. He wants the public to notice. He's smart enough to know to use a tourniquet to stop the bleeding, and he doesn't want his victims to die. He wants to take away their joystick and make them suffer without it."

A few men squirmed in their chairs, sniggering and reaching for their crotches.

The chief continued. "He's left each victim alive in the same place he mutilated them—not performing any additional 'staging' for drama. It's unknown if he lives and works in this county, but there's a good chance he does since all the incidents have taken place in this general area."

Chief displayed a map on the overhead projector and pointed to where each victim lived. Then he identified the geocaching sites where the body parts were found. Several officers moved to one side of the room to see the display. Small red dots signified current registered geo-sites. Chief pointed to these sites. "All these need to be checked and monitored. We're still looking for the last victim's prize."

A few of the officers snickered. Chief cracked a smile too. "If the unsub hasn't hidden the last one yet, he'll be doing it soon. It's possible he could live in this area since most of the activity is near here." Chief drew a circle around where the victims lived and where the body parts had been found. "Our guy is organized in that he's taken the time to locate sex offenders and learn their habits—when they're home and when they're asleep. He's most likely working alone."

Next, the chief put a photo of Quinn on the overhead. "This is Quinn. Officer Brett Reed's daughter." Chief motioned for Brett to stand. As he did, the lump lodged in his throat. He let his tears fall. Seeing Quinn's picture put him over the top. Fellow officers glanced his way with brows creased, giving compassionate nods.

Several said, "We'll find her."

The chief continued, "We haven't found the dead victim's body, but here's what we know: Twelve men in this county died in the last three weeks. The background of five have been researched—three were cremated; two were buried in Lake Hursey's Cemetery on the east side of town. The cemetery manager confirmed that the other two had been buried more than a week ago, and there was no sign of tampering at their grave sites.

"If the perp actually severed the dead guy's piece after he died, the perp could be someone who works in a morgue, having access to dead bodies. But the county coroner said if someone had broken into the morgue, severed the organ, and redressed the deceased, the funeral home staff would know. The embalming fluid would have seeped all over the deceased's clothing. The coroner didn't think it was likely that it could have happened before the burial without someone noticing. Two men on the list have been stored in a mausoleum: one in this county at Hursey Lake Cemetery and one in a neighboring county. Neither of these men were registered sex offenders."

The chief pointed to Officer Hudson as he lifted a paper from his file. "You go to the mausoleum at Hursey Lake and check out this victim. Get a search warrant to open it up." He handed her the paper, glancing at it. Then he paused, did a double-take, and whistled. "I knew this guy. He was an asshole." He closed his eyes, took a deep breath, then reopened them. "This is a happy day."

What was that about?

A few seconds later the chief pointed to another officer. "You check out the one in Steward County." He handed her the respective report.

Officer Hudson stood next to Brett. He looked over her shoulder, reading the information on the paper:

Levi Samuel. Born in 1935, married to Rebecca Wright, who preceded him in death in 1990. Where had Brett heard or seen the name Levi Samuel? Maybe it had been on the list of the deceased he'd studied last night. What did the chief know about him?

Chatter hummed in the room. Chief clapped his hands to regain attention. "One more thing. The other foster child, who claims to have seen the perp, was able to give the forensic artist enough information to come up with this drawing." Chief replaced Quinn's photo with the drawing. The photo on the screen was distorted, as if the perp had worn a mask or a nylon stocking over his face. He looked bald, but it could have been the way the stocking had disguised the person's real face and hair color. The child wasn't certain if the perp was black or white.

But something about the photo looked vaguely familiar to Brett—like he'd seen this person before but couldn't place him. Or her. And he couldn't remember where.

The chief separated the task forces into groups, assigning men and women to cover territories across the county. Some were to interview sex offenders, and others were to check geo-sites.

After they all dispersed, Brett returned to his desk next to Clay's, waiting for the press conference to begin.

Max followed.

Chapter Twenty

After Brett left the chief's office, he returned to his desk and jotted a note to himself. *Research Levi Samuel.* Then he scribbled notes for the press release. He sighed, looking up at Clay, who was standing over him, puffing out his chest as if he was Brett's personal bodyguard. The press had arrived. Brett reached for the large photo of Quinn that sat in a frame on the corner of his desk, and his script, which he glanced at one more time.

Clay peered over Brett's shoulder. "Don't read it. This needs to be heartfelt. Whoever he is needs to see that you're a good guy. He needs to believe everything you say."

Brett nodded. He hooked Max to his leash, took a deep breath, smoothed his shirt, and headed to the front of the station. The sun peeked out from its hidden spot behind a white cloud, casting bright rays over the crowd that had already gathered.

Brett recognized fellow officers, the blond anchorwoman from that morning, his mother, and . . . his father. His father looked off in another direction. Brett stared openly. How long had it been since he'd seen him? Six years? The old man's hair had thinned and grown whiter. He stood a little bent, and his clothes hung on him like he'd lost twenty pounds. His skin pallor had a sickly gray hue to it. Brett had never seen him so gaunt. It stunned him, and he was suddenly overcome with emotion and memories of baseball games, camping trips, and games of chess.

Why weren't he and his mother at the hospital for his chemotherapy? The old man turned, and their eyes locked. His father smiled and nodded, then gave him a thumbs-up, as if saying, "I'm here for you."

A lump rose in Brett's throat. His mother waved and took hold of the old man's arm. Together they stormed through the crowd toward him. By the time they reached his side, the media had gathered. His mother slipped her hand in his, and his father squeezed his large hand over Brett's shoulder. His mother stood to his left, his father to his right. Brett took a deep breath, fighting tears, standing a little taller.

Max wagged his tail at Brett's mother. She stooped to rub his ear, and he sat at her feet.

Before the reporter moved the mic in front of Brett, Sarah approached. She stared at him openly, tears in her eyes. She reminded him of his favorite candy—caramels. The way the sun bounced off her hair, her expression—genuine, caring, and warm. What was it about her that made him pause? A look? An expression in her eyes that lay underneath her independent persona, a glimpse of a hurt little girl? She smiled at him. Openly. He felt his face blush. Quinn had touched her somehow, thawed Sarah's heart in some way. Quinn had the magical ability to make other people feel good about themselves. Maybe it was because she'd had so much practice with Ali.

The camera's red light blinked. Brett shifted his attention to the crowd and peered into the camera. His father's hand still rested on Brett's shoulder. It gave him strength. He took a deep breath and let his eyes scan the crowd from left to right, and then he spoke.

"I'm here today begging all of you to help me find Quinn, my daughter. This is what she looks like." He held up her photo. "The last time she was seen she was wearing jeans and a bright-pink top. She has brown curly hair the color of a chocolate bar, and a pale complexion, but it's her blue eyes that stand out. They're as light as her hair is dark."

He cleared his throat, and the wad of tears lodged there. "She's five years old." He stared into the camera. "If you have her, please return her to me. She hasn't done anything wrong. She needs to be with me, her father. If, for some reason, you think she's in harm's way, you're wrong. Child Protective Services placed Quinn in a foster home while she was in her mother's care, not mine. I'm a good father."

He took a breath and licked his lips. "The CPS's job is to investigate every case, and until they knew Quinn was safe, they placed her in a temporary foster home. That foster mother's son is a sex offender. The state didn't know this. His mother and he did not share the same name or address. Typically, foster homes are safe.

"Please, if you're the one who took Quinn, bring her home. She's not in any danger with me. She's safe. I'm safe. I'm not a sex offender. I'm begging you to bring her home."

One newscaster in a navy suit with a red tie said, "Is it true that your ex-wife has a drinking problem?"

Brett nodded. "Yes, she struggles with depression, and sometimes she doesn't use the best coping tools."

"Is it true that she was sexually abused as a child?"

Brett's jaw twitched, and his whole body tensed. "I don't understand how that has anything to do with getting Quinn back."

"Are there any suspects?" someone else asked.

Clay stepped forward and identified himself. "Not for now, but we have one person of interest." He placed his hand on Brett's arm. "If you see anything suspicious, please call the police department. The suspect may have changed Quinn's hair color or disguised her so she's unrecognizable."

Brett's father stepped forward. "I'm Quinn's grandfather, Mason Reed. We're offering a ten-thousand-dollar reward for anyone who comes forward with the information that leads to his arrest."

Brett turned to his father, his mouth agape. His mother wrapped her arm around Brett's waist. He'd forgotten how good it was to have the support of both parents. But was this a show? Was his father only pretending to care so he could make his legal firm look good?

Sarah stepped forward. "Excuse me, but I want to speak on behalf of Hursey Lake's Child Protective Services."

The camera crew shifted their positions, and a mic was placed in front of her.

She introduced herself, and as she spoke, her eyes never left

Brett's. "Unfortunately, as humans we make mistakes, but Quinn's foster mother had an impeccable record. Obviously, if we had known her son was a sex offender, we never would have placed Quinn in her care. Officer Reed is a loving and caring father who would never harm his daughter." Sarah paused, her eyes misting. "I spoke to Quinn before she was temporarily placed in foster care. She had nothing but good things to say about her dad, and as soon as she's found I'm confident the judge will allow him permanent custody, especially after he reads CPS's report."

Days of fear, exhaustion, and pent-up worry poured off Brett's shoulders. *We'll find you, Quinn. You're coming home!*

A man with dark sunglasses, dressed in black, stepped forward. "Your wife is a murderer. She killed my fiancée—the woman who should have been the mother of my children. Your wife took away all my hopes and dreams. If you knew she was a substance abuser, how could you have let her drive?" The man's voice broke, becoming shaky. "Why didn't . . . you take away her keys?" He threw a fist into the air. The crowd hushed. People stared at the man and then back at Brett.

The man scowled at Brett. "I hate you, and I hope . . . your wife . . ." He leaned on a man who must have been his friend. The friend ushered him away from the crowd.

As he did, the crowd came to life. Questions were thrown at Brett from every direction.

"Will your wife be arrested?"

"Is it true she'll be a vegetable for the rest of her life?"

"Are you afraid of a lawsuit?"

Brett stared across the crowd at the back of his accuser's head. His ears buzzed, and his legs felt like rubber. He wanted to say something, but what? What words would compensate for his loss? Had it been his fault? Should he have taken the keys from Ali? He'd tried. Should he have tried harder? He'd known she was out of control. How could he have let his wife get behind the wheel of a car knowing the shape she had been in?

Lost in his own thoughts, he hadn't seen his father step in front of the camera. "There will be no more questions. From this point on all questions need to be directed toward me, Officer Reed's attorney, Mason Reed."

His dad was going to represent him? Brett had sworn he'd

never ask his father for help, but he hadn't. His father had offered even though everything he'd predicted had come true. Brett had ruined his life. One bad decision had dominoed into a lifetime of problems.

Was his father offering to help so his firm would look good? It didn't matter. Regardless of his father's intentions, Brett was grateful for his support. He turned to his father, his eyes stinging from the salt of his tears. "Thank you."

His father's bottom lip curled, and his eyes watered. He reached for Brett and embraced him, heaving in a sob and answering Brett's questions when he said, "I've missed you, Son."

Brett's chest heaved. A sob escaped. "I've missed you too." The scent of the old man's shaving cream flooded Brett's senses with childhood memories of make-believe, of when his father had lathered shaving foam onto his face for a pretend shave. They'd laughed and smeared cream all over the bathroom.

Brett hugged his father in return, feeling the cancer's curse in how frail he'd become, the beefy part of his body gone.

When his father finally let go, Brett's body lost all strength, wanting to collapse. Clay slid a strong arm under Brett, whispering in his ear. "Lean against me, man, until we get in the office. You can do it. Just walk away. Use my weight."

Brett sucked in air and puffed out his chest, willing strength to fill him. "I can walk."

Clay released his arm as they moved toward the precinct. His parents followed with Max.

Sarah came to his side, sliding her arm through his. She whispered in his ear. "You are not responsible for Ali's actions, or her happiness. Ever. You did not kill that man's fiancée. You will get Quinn back too. I promise."

The warmth of her breath near his ear and her kind words, the words he needed to hear, made him pause and turn to her. The sun shone behind her head, encircling her golden hair like a halo. He itched to run his fingers through the curls and feel their silkiness. He swallowed the lump in his throat. He had to stay strong. "Thank you." How could he have ever been suspicious of her?

#

I stood in the kitchen, rocking side to side in rhythm to the ticking wall clock, licking my lips and drying them, licking my lips and drying them.

Get a grip. Keep it together.

I couldn't. I didn't know what to do. The man on TV, the cop, wanted his daughter back. Should I return her?

My head shook back and forth. No. Her father was bad. I had to save her. They took her away from him. I had to keep her away from him. Her father was a liar. They were all liars. Liars, liars, pants on fire.

Father said he loved me. Then he stroked me. It burned and left a scar.

I stomped my foot. I have to protect her. Now was my chance to show that I could. But how do I make her my friend?

Feed her. Maybe she'll come out if she's hungry.

But what if she doesn't like me?

I'll make her macaroni and cheese. Then she'll be my friend.

In the kitchen, I clicked the radio on and boiled the water, staring into the pot as bubbles grew larger, the heat forming sweat on the front of my neck.

After I added the noodles, drained them, and scooped butter into the pot, I ripped open the packet of cheese and dumped the powder into the noodles. I set a place at the table for her, neatly placing the silverware on the right side of the plate.

I squeezed my eyes and tapped on the bathroom door. "Come out and eat. I made mac and cheese." I used my little-boy voice. "I want to be your friend. Please."

Nothing.

She hates me. Everyone hates me.

My phone rang. I'd left it on the fireplace hearth. Dashing across the room, I reached for it. It was the office. I hadn't gone into work. *Oh, no!* I'd forgotten to call. I'd never done that before. "Yes?"

"You sick today?" Doc Spear asked.

"Sorry, I am. I forgot to call. I'll b-b-be there tomorrow though. I'll work extra to m-m-make up for today."

Doc paused. "You feeling okay?"

"I am feeling good."

After disconnecting the phone, I returned to the bathroom and knocked on the door again. "If you come out, you can see your daddy."

The doorknob jiggled. "Are you lying?"

"I'm not. He was on TV."

She opened the door, but not all the way. "When?"

"A little bit ago, but they will probably show it again. Come to the kitchen. I'll turn the TV on in there."

Go to the kitchen. She will follow. You can do this now. Be brave. Daddy is gone.

#

Brett sat at his desk at the precinct, exhausted and raw but wanting to do something to contribute to Quinn's search. He stared at the note he'd left himself at his desk to research Levi Samuel. Why had the chief said Samuel was an asshole?

The officers had cleared the office to go to their respective posts. His parents had gone to the hospital for Dad's treatment, but his mother had begged him to come to the house in an hour for lunch. He'd promised he would.

The door to the precinct opened, and Chief entered carrying a coffee and a bag—probably a scone from the coffee shop.

Brett glanced up at him and lifted his hand. "Chief, can I talk to you a minute?"

"Sure." He waved him toward his office as he continued down the hallway.

Brett picked up his notes and stood, but he had to wait a second for the room to quit spinning before he could continue down the hallway. His fatigue made him dizzy.

"Sit down, Reed. How are you holding up?"

Brett shrugged.

Chief opened the bag with the scone and took a bite. He sipped the coffee, wincing like it was too hot.

"I appreciate everything the force is doing."

Chief shook his head. "This never should have happened. I should have intervened when CPS placed Quinn in a foster home, but my hands were tied. Policies are policies to them." He swung a hand into his fist. "It's easy to look back now and think I should have done things differently."

"It's not your fault." Brett paused and shifted in his seat. "You've lived in this county your whole life, right?"

Chief nodded.

"How did you know Levi Samuel?"

The chief's face turned red. "The asshole." He squirmed and his chair squeaked. "We go way back." He looked out the window as if lost in thought, then turned back to Brett.

"What do you know about him? He wasn't a registered sex offender, but did he have any enemies?" Brett blinked his burning eyes, focusing on staying alert, sleep wanting to take over.

"He killed his wife, but I couldn't prove it. Most people liked him. I'm the only one who had a grudge against him that I know of. At one point, when I was much younger, I wanted to kill the guy."

Brett had never heard the chief talk about anyone this way, and if the chief disliked the guy, he must have been a dirtbag.

"I was the one who found Rebecca, his wife."

He said her name with the tenderness of a lover.

"I was the first one there after she fell down the stairs. After she died. She was even more beautiful in death."

Brett forgot about feeling tired.

"Her old man didn't deserve her." He balled the scone bag into a tiny ball, smashing it with ferocity, and flung it into his wastebasket.

"How do you know he killed her?"

"We couldn't find evidence to nail his ass, but I hated her old man and the way he treated her. I wanted to lock him up for life. And those kids. I'll never forget the way they stood over their mother, the pain in their eyes. And the fear." He took a sip of his coffee. "Her old man hated me too."

"Why?"

"Because I was in love with his wife, and he knew it."

Brett's mouth gaped open. The bad-ass chief in love?

The chief stood, sauntered to the door, and gave it a kick with his foot. Not a hard one—just with enough force to close it.

He continued. "Rebecca and I grew up around here. Our parents were close friends, and everyone thought we'd be together one day. But when we left for separate colleges, we dated other people. I didn't want to tie her down. I thought she wanted to date a bit, but she later told me she only dated other guys because she thought that's what I wanted.

"We kept in touch in college, and then one day, just before Thanksgiving, in our senior year, she called and asked me to meet her. She said she really needed to talk to me."

The chief paused and stared out the window again as if going back in time.

Brett rarely saw the chief's personal side. He couldn't picture the chief with a woman. He'd never been married and worked 24/7.

"I'll never forget that day or the way she looked. She wore a royal-blue blouse and a yellow scarf around her neck. Her strawberry-colored hair bounced on her shoulders. She was always so full of life. We met at Charlie's Restaurant because I insisted. It had been her favorite place to eat when we dated.

"When she walked into the restaurant she glowed, but something looked different. Something in her eyes had changed. No one else would have noticed, but I did.

"When we embraced, I didn't think she was going to let me go, and I didn't care. I didn't want her to. I held her so close I could smell the coconut scent of her shampoo. She felt perfect in my arms. I thought, this is the woman I want to marry. Why have I been dating all those other girls?

"But when she pulled away, and I saw the tears in her eyes, I knew. Something was wrong.

"She told me. The SOB had raped her. She was pregnant. Her parents were pushing her to marry him. They thought it was the best thing for the child. I asked her what *she* thought was the best thing. She said she didn't know. What did I think? I said, 'Don't throw your life away on someone who raped you.'

"She said, 'But maybe I led him on.'"

The chief shook his head before he continued. "I said, 'No! If you said *no*, he should have listened. He was wrong. Don't marry him. Marry me instead. I'll take care of you and the baby. You know that.'

"She cried harder then and took my hand and thanked me. But she said he'd never go for it. She knew he wouldn't want me raising *his* child. They'd talked about me before. He hated me before he'd ever met me. Besides, she said, it would never work. If she lived with me and his child, she'd have to live with the constant memory that she'd been unfaithful to me.

"But I said, 'You weren't unfaithful to me. He raped you. Don't you see? There's a difference. If he raped you, then he'll hit you too.'

"She turned away then, hid her face. I said, 'He's hit you, hasn't he?' She couldn't look at me so I knew the answer. I flew in a rage. I wanted to kill him. I told her, 'Don't go back to him. I'll talk to him.' I thought it would be easier on her if I told him to back off."

The chief returned to his chair and sighed. "She made me promise I wouldn't confront him.

"Then one day I dressed up in nice trousers and a button-down shirt and went to talk to her parents. I begged them to let her marry me instead. I wanted them to help her see the danger in what she was going to do. But they were weak. They said it was her decision. They didn't want to decide for her. It was her life. They didn't want to influence her decision and live to regret it. There was nothing I could do. So they got married."

The chief swiveled his chair toward the corner of his desk and opened a drawer. He pulled out a small photo frame. Inside was a photo of a woman, but it was too far away and too small for Brett to see. He waited while the chief continued.

He stared at the photo. "After she married him I'd see her in town, at church, at the fair—when we least expected it. She'd smile at me, and I'd have to keep walking because it enraged me to see her with that SOB. She tried to hide the bruises, but it didn't take X-ray vision to see them. At one point her mother came to me saying they should have listened to me that day. They knew she was unhappy.

"About six months before she died, we started secretly seeing one another. But I think he found out. That's when he knocked her down the stairs—after he drugged her. The coroner ruled her death an accident due to overdose. He said she'd fallen down the stairs as a result of taking too many sleeping pills. She never took sleeping pills. The SOB staged the whole thing. She'd told me she was going to the attorney's the next day to sign the divorce papers, that her parents had agreed. The jerk must have found out." He clenched and unclenched his fists and finally turned, meeting Brett's eyes.

"I never knew. I'm sorry." How sad. Brett saw a totally different side to the chief—a romantic one. Why did tragedy so often follow love?

The room grew silent except for the phones ringing on the other side of the door.

The chief sighed. "I could never prove what he'd done to her." He pressed his fingers into his eyes. "When I spotted his name on the deceased list, it was a jolt. He'd finally died and gotten away with all the rotten things he'd done in his life." He shook his head and added, "Who knows how messed up his kids must be. They must be relieved the guy's dead too."

Chapter Twenty-One

Sarah cancelled her appointments for the day. She couldn't concentrate, and she didn't want to go to her office and see the sofa where Quinn had sat, swinging her legs and playing with the dolls.

Racked with guilt, she'd begged Clay to let her be a part of the search team since she knew the ins and out of geocaching, but he said the best thing to do was stay home. They didn't want civilians getting in the way.

She turned on the television and watched the news coverage of the press release. It gave her the opportunity to stare at Brett and observe him openly. A sigh escaped from her lips. Why did he cause her heart to flutter?

His bloodshot eyes drooped as he begged the community to help find Quinn. Every time he spoke of her, his eyes lit up like bolts of lightning.

How would Sarah feel if he looked at her that way? She'd never had that. Ever. Is that what attracted her to him? Maybe it was that and the way he wasn't afraid to show his emotions. Maybe it was because she saw the love he was capable of giving.

He fought for Quinn, showing his true character. She'd seen Brett through Quinn's eyes too, and the love she had for him, but seeing his pain now on TV made her ache for him.

She wished her father would have loved her that way. The bastard. It was better if she didn't think about him. For years, thinking about him as dead had helped her cope.

As she watched Brett on the television, she noticed how his blue uniform made his eyes appear a deeper shade. How one of his curls fell onto his forehead. She wanted to reach up and sweep it off his brow. She shuddered. What would it feel like to touch him? To be touched by him?

His dog stared up at him like he was the sun and the moon, another sign of Brett's loyalty and a measure of his character. Dogs seemed to know when their masters were kind.

Would she ever find a man like him? She turned the TV off and checked her watch. If she kept busy it would help pass the time, keep her thoughts from straying.

Maybe she'd go riding. Enjoying the farm's scenery and the warm sunshine of a summer day would do her good.

As she headed into the barn, her cell phone rang. She pulled it out of her pocket and glanced at the screen. Her heartbeat quickened. Brett's name appeared. She answered.

"Are you any good at profiling people?" His voice cracked.

The poor guy. She heard the tiredness in his voice. "You don't believe in saying hello, do you?"

He didn't respond right away. "I mean, you see all types, right? I need someone who can help me find this guy."

"I think I could help, maybe reveal something you haven't thought about." She could hear phones ringing and people talking in the background. He must be at the precinct. When he didn't say anything, she added, "I'm home right now. I took the day off. I wanted to help in some way, but Clay said to stay out of the way. I could meet you at the station, or my office, if you'd prefer. Would that work?"

"Actually, I need to get out of here, and no offense, but I don't want to go to your office. Uh, the last time I was there Quinn was too. I don't think I could handle that. Do you mind if I come to your home instead?"

"Okay, sure." She gave him her address. He started to say something, but he paused, or was he getting another call? Maybe he was simply writing down the address. "Brett?"

"Uh, thank you for saying what you said today. It meant a lot. I needed to hear someone say the accident wasn't my fault. Even though I know it wasn't, it still felt good to hear someone say the words." He cleared his throat.

"You're welcome. I meant what I said."

"I'm headed to my parents' home for lunch, then I'll be over. It'll probably be a few hours before I'm there." He paused. "If . . . that's okay, that is."

"No problem. I'll probably be in the barn, so park around back."

After Sarah disconnected her phone, she continued her trek to the barn. Beauty's head hung out of her stall window, and she whinnied as Sarah approached.

"I've missed you too." Sarah continued into the barn and headed to the tack room. She reached for the halter and went to Beauty's stall. After she moved the horse to the cross ties, she reached for the brush caddy and placed it off to the side. As she slipped her hand in the curry comb, she thought of Quinn. Would she ever get the chance to ride Beauty? She hoped so. Sarah pictured her on top of the horse, with Brett watching, and she smiled.

What would it be like to have a child and lose her? She couldn't imagine. While growing up, she'd always been overly protective of her little brother—as best she could. And when she thought their father was harming him, she was incensed. She'd probably be the same way with her own child.

Would she have a family someday? Was that too farfetched to imagine? She longed for a husband like Brett who would love her the way he loved Quinn. Was she crazy for thinking about Brett? Yes. She barely knew him. But she couldn't help wondering if marriage was a possibility for her. She was definitely softening to the idea.

Beauty whinnied as if she approved.

#

Brett sat at his office desk after most of the staff had gone to lunch and stared at the address Sarah had given him. It was Levi Samuel's address. How could that be? Was Sarah's father the same man the chief loathed, the man who'd killed his wife, the man who died two weeks ago and was buried in the mausoleum?

Why hadn't Sarah told him her father died recently? Was her father a part of her past she didn't want to talk about because he'd abused her too? What had she said about him?

Shoot, he didn't really know much about her, did he?

He did know that Sarah's last name wasn't Samuel. Had she been married before? Maybe she still was. His heart somersaulted. He didn't want to believe that. And besides, he'd never seen a ring on her finger.

His mind whirled with crazy thoughts. What if Levi was the man missing his piece? Was Sarah the whacker? No, he couldn't wrap his mind around that thought, because then she'd have kidnapped Quinn and that was preposterous. But maybe, just maybe, she knew something that could help him find Quinn.

He gazed at his watch, realizing it was time to meet his parents for lunch. He stood to go, waiting for the vertigo to subside, before leaving the precinct. Max stood and followed him to the car, then hopped into the back seat.

Brett headed north toward his old neighborhood, the one he'd grown up in. It had been six years since he'd traveled those roads. He turned down Oak Blvd., one block from his house, remembering the first time he'd driven down the street with his father. Brett had been fifteen—before he'd gotten his driver's permit. His father had tossed him the keys to his Lincoln and said, "Let's go."

Brett had felt a surge of power, confidence, and pride that his father thought he was ready and capable of driving a car. He sighed.

Now, more than fifteen years later, the streets looked strange, older, worn, and dirty.

He parked the car at the curb in front of the house. The house looked older than he'd remembered too. He climbed out of the car and opened the back door for Max, who bounded up the sidewalk, sniffed a few bushes, did his doggie thing, and headed for the front door like he knew who lived there. The manicured lawn looked smaller, and the concrete stairs and porch darker.

Nothing ever lasted.

The front door screen was open. His mom's typical classical music blared from the radio. The scent of bacon, fresh coffee, and his mother's sweet rolls seeped out of the house. She'd probably been up all night making the rolls, kneading them and waiting for them to rise. Whenever she couldn't sleep, she baked. Had she and

Dad skipped his chemo on account of him?

She greeted him and Max at the door. "Come in, come in."

He hugged her, staying in her arms a little longer than usual, loving how warm and safe she felt.

She wiped her tears with the bottom of her apron. "Any word on Quinn yet?"

Brett held his tears in. "Nothing. Life can't get much worse, can it?"

She held his hand and led him into the house. Had the foyer always been so dark and small? When he was a boy, it used to feel as large as an amusement park. He glanced at the little closet under the stairs as they passed it, remembering how he'd spent days there playing with his miniature dinosaurs, pretending he was in a cave or a forest, or sometimes a jungle.

His father entered from his study off the kitchen. Brett locked eyes with his, waiting to assess his father's actions. The man smiled, approaching Brett without any hesitation, and wrapped his arms around him in a tight hug. "I'm glad you're here."

Brett said, "Me too." He bit his lip, working at keeping his composure. "Didn't you go for chemo today?"

His father shook his head. "We needed to be here for you." Max's tail swished across the floor. His father bent to rub the dog around his ears.

Brett said, "Thanks."

His mother took Brett's hand again and led him to the kitchen. "Come and sit down. You need to eat." Her eyes were damp again.

A bright-yellow kitchen welcomed him. "You changed the color in here. It's bright, cheerful. I need that right now." He sank into *his* chair—the one he'd always sat in growing up, between his mother and his father. After his mom placed the food on the table, she reached for his hand and bowed her head. His father reached over for his other hand.

As always, his mother led the prayer. "Dear Lord, bless this food and our family. We pray that Quinn will be found soon, unharmed. We pray that Ali will live and find her way. Love her as you always have. Please give Brett the strength to cope and stay strong in his faith to know that you are by his side. Amen."

At first they ate in awkward silence. Where should he start a conversation when he hadn't been home for more than five years?

"The whole department is working 24/7 to find this guy. We're getting leads, getting closer. I think she's safe." He blew at the hair in his eyes. "Our perp seems to have a vendetta against sex offenders, not little girls. Even though we don't think he's a stable guy, I'm hopeful he's not . . . harming . . . her." He swallowed a lump in his throat.

His father said, "We have to keep the faith and believe that to be the truth. He cleared his throat and reached over to Brett's hand, squeezing it. "Look, I meant what I said at the press conference this morning. They're going to find Quinn, and I'll represent you on her case. According to CPS you have an appointment on Tuesday with the judge. I'm going to make sure you get full custody."

A tear rolled down Brett's cheek.

His father continued. "Don't worry about that guy who's threatening to sue you, either. He doesn't have a case. You aren't married to Ali and had no control over her driving under the influence. The guy can't prove negligence on your part."

Was his father supporting him now because Brett had divorced Ali? Why couldn't he have been more supportive back then—when Brett had decided to marry her? Would his love always be conditional—on *his* terms?

Brett closed his eyes and willed the negative thoughts away. What did it matter now? He didn't want to think about anything but Quinn. It consumed too much energy. He nodded toward his father. "Thanks. I appreciate your help."

Brett lowered his gaze to his plate, squeezing the tears from his eyes, and concentrated on eating.

The food tasted delicious, but he had to force himself to eat. It didn't seem right that he should eat when Quinn wasn't with him. He took small bites, knowing his mother would be crushed if he didn't sample everything. The rolls melted in his mouth. Quinn would love them. She'd never been to this house, but she would someday.

A lump formed in his throat again. It stuck there every time he thought about her.

His phone vibrated. He clicked it off his belt loop and glanced at the screen. A blocked number. Maybe it was a lead. He answered, "Officer Reed here."

Distant breathing rasped into the phone. Brett said, "Hello?"

"Daddy?" Her voice was a whisper.

Brett shot out of his seat. The chair tumbled backward, falling onto the floor with a clatter, just missing Max, who scurried out of the way. "Quinn? Where are you?"

Brett's parents froze, watching and listening.

"I don't know. I'm scared." Her voice quivered.

"Daddy's looking for you. Can you tell me where you are, or who has you?"

"He's sleeping. He told me he'll take care of me, that you're a bad man." Her voice was barely audible.

"No, I'm not a bad man. I love you, Quinn. I'll find you. Who is the man?"

"I don't know. He wants to play games."

"What does he look like?" Brett's adrenaline raced.

"Scarwy, I'm scawed." She had trouble pronouncing her r's.

"Look out the window. What do you see?"

There was a pause.

"Twees, weeds, and gwass."

"How did you get there? In a car?"

"A twuck."

"What color is it?"

"Blue."

"Do you know the man's name?"

No answer.

"Quinn, are you shaking your head? You need to tell me yes or no because I can't see you nod."

"No."

"Has he hurt you?" He held his breath.

"No."

Brett exhaled. He gripped the edge of the table, his shoulders slacking. "The first chance you get, run out the door and go for help."

There was a commotion in the background like knocking, or maybe Quinn dropped the phone. "Quinn?"

The phone went dead.

Brett shouted, "Quinn?"

His mother had come to his side. She held his arm as tight as a rubber band.

He stared at his phone, wishing he could make it ring again.

"No!" He pounded his fist on the table. The plates and silverware clanked. "I can't stay here. I need to go back to the precinct." He turned.

His mother followed him toward the front door. "Can't you call her back? Hit Redial?"

"It doesn't work that way. The number was blocked."

She hustled alongside him, patting his back. "She's alive and she's smart. You'll find her."

His father followed them too, with Max behind him. "Where was she?"

"I don't know. She said in the middle of trees and a field. I'll call Clay, and get a tracer put on my phone. Maybe she'll call again."

His father opened the closet door and reached for his sweater. "I'm going with you. I want to help."

They stood in the foyer. "I appreciate it, Dad, but the best way you can help is if you stay here and pray for Quinn."

His father's shoulders slumped. "Okay, but if you change your mind, I'm here for you." He reached over and squeezed Brett's arm.

"Thanks, Dad." Brett held his father's eyes with his own. "That means a lot." He gripped his old man's arm, and as he turned to go he saw more tears in his mother's eyes. They were probably because of Quinn, but no doubt also because his father had asked to help. Tragedy had a way of bringing family together.

Chapter Twenty-Two

Dark clouds hung low in the sky as Brett headed south in his cruiser back to the station. Was a storm brewing? He hoped not. Storms scared Quinn, and who would be there to hold her hand? Max panted in the backseat, looking outside as if trying to find Quinn. Brett turned back to the dog. "I know, buddy. You're usually the one hanging out with her in weather like this, aren't you?"

The air felt as heavy as his thoughts. Perspiration trickled down his back. He called Clay and told him about Quinn's call and asked to have a tracer put on his cell.

Clay said, "I'll get right on it. That's good news, man. See, this guy isn't going to hurt her. We'll find him. I can't believe Quinn knew how to punch in your number. My nine-year-old couldn't do that."

"I showed her how to do it from the home phone, but I never explained the area code thing, so she must be in this calling zone." Brett put his signal on and turned the corner. "She also said the guy had a blue truck."

"We're tracing all blue trucks in this county, but that's a huge number."

"Any other leads?"

"A few reports from people claiming they saw her, but when we checked them out, they were dead ends. Sorry, man. But Mark's here."

"Why?"

"He says he needs to talk to you. Only you. I was just going to call you—"

"Really? That's great." Brett's heart fisted. Maybe this was the breakthrough they needed. "I'll be there in five minutes."

"Perfect." Clay's cell phone rang in the background. He asked Brett to hold while he took the other call. "How's my little man? Are you going to basketball practice today?"

He must be talking to his son. Brett interrupted, "Hey, Clay, I'll talk to you when I get there." He flipped on his cruiser's flashing lights and sped to the precinct.

What did Mark have to say? Could he be the whacker? No, Quinn knew Mark. She would have said he had her. But maybe Mark was involved somehow or knew who was. Brett shook his head, trying to shake the dull sleeplessness out of his confused brain.

#

Brett found Mark sitting alone with his arms folded in the interrogation room, his face red and his eyes watering like he'd been crying. Clay waited outside the door, observing through the window.

Brett pulled a chair out and placed it in front of Mark, then straddled it. "How's it going?"

Mark stared off to the side and crossed his legs at the ankles. His voice quivered. "Any word about where Quinn is?"

Brett shook his head. "No. Nothing." He leaned toward Mark. "Why, do you know where she is?"

Mark turned and met Brett's eyes. "How would I know? You think I took her?" His face turned red. "I love Quinn. I'd never hurt her."

Brett cleared his throat. "Why are you here then?"

He chewed his bottom lip. "To tell you what happened the other day with Ali." Mark paused. "I screwed up, okay?" He took a deep breath. "Ali needed money. She begged me. Told me she owed someone, and if she didn't get it she was worried about Quinn." He ran his fingers along his bald head. "I shouldn't have gone to the house. I wanted to catch the asshole who was threatening her. She begged me not to tell you. She was afraid if you knew she was using again, she'd lose Quinn for good."

"Why was she worried about Quinn?"

"Because she didn't want the druggies to see her, for fear they'd hurt her, or something. I think that's why she locked her in the room—to protect her."

Mark stood and walked across the room, pacing. "Ali said she wanted to get clean. Stay clean. I went to the house and waited in the bushes for the dude to show. I was only trying to help her."

Tears fell down Marks face. "I should have called the police, but Ali didn't want you to know." He wiped his hands on his slacks.

Brett recognized Mark's guilty look. He'd seen it before. Mark had been trying to save Ali her whole life, to make up for the times when he hadn't been home to stop the abuse, to save his little sister.

Mark returned to his seat, across from Brett. "When the asshole showed for the money, I jumped out of the bushes with a bat and threatened him. Told him I was going to call the cops if he didn't leave my sister alone."

"What did he look like?"

Mark shut his eyes. "Skinny with tattoos on his arms. Rotting teeth, reddish hair, maybe in his twenties. He looked like one of those guys in meth commercials." He put his head in his hands and rubbed his face. "The dog started barking just inside the house. Ali was worried about me, so she opened the door, told the scumbag to leave. Max got out, baring his teeth, snapping at the guy. I told Ali to stay inside with the dog, but she didn't listen. The dude said he'd break every bone in Ali's body if he didn't get his money. I swung the bat at his legs. The kid ran and Max chased him, barking. Ali went crazy, crying and moaning. After I calmed her down, I got in my truck and looked for the dog, but he was gone." He exhaled loudly. "I'm sorry."

Brett looked away and shook his head, inhaling deeply. Then he turned back and glared at Mark. "So, you didn't bring Max home the other night?"

"No, I swear. I didn't have the dog."

Brett searched his eyes. He seemed sincere, but he didn't know what to believe. "Why were you parked outside my house then?"

"I wanted to see if the drug dude was going to return."

Through clenched teeth Brett said, "Quinn might have been safe right now if it hadn't been for you. Trying to save Ali didn't work, did it?" He pounded the table. "You should have called me."

Mark hung his head. "I know that now. I'm sorry." His voice was just above a whisper.

Brett rubbed his gritty eyes. "Did you know this guy you confronted, or his name?"

"No, never saw him before."

"Did Ali mention where she knew him from? Work?"

Mark shook his head.

"Why come clean now?"

"Look, I love my sister. I know how much Quinn means to her. I didn't want to ruin things for her, you know?"

"No, I don't know. What about protecting Quinn? Did you ever stop to think how Ali was putting Quinn in danger? Did you *ever* take time to think about that?" Brett stood and paced.

The door opened and Clay walked in, carrying a stack of binders. "We need you to look through some photos, see if you can identify this guy."

Mark hesitated, chewing his bottom lip. "Sure. You don't think this guy has Quinn, do you?"

Brett stopped pacing. "No, I doubt it. He doesn't seem the type to whack jacks or steal little girls." He turned to Mark one last time. "You better be telling the whole truth or your ass is fried."

"I am. I never wanted this to happen. I had no idea Ali was so addicted." Tears filled his eyes again. "I should have stayed with her after Max chased the druggie away, but I was late for work, and I had a meeting to go to, and I couldn't lose my job. I should have gone back to take care of Quinn."

Brett said, "Yes, you should have." He turned to go but hesitated, realizing Mark was probably sincere. "Look, Ali got herself into this predicament. It wasn't your job to take care of her."

Clay set the photos in front of Mark and pulled up a chair for himself.

Mark rubbed his hands together, twisting them in a nervous manner. "There's something else."

Brett paused with his hand on the door.

Mark said, "I knew Ali was impaired before she got behind the wheel, before her accident. She stopped to see me at the bank." His voice cracked. "I should have taken . . . her keys away." He pressed his fingers into his eyes as the tears dripped.

What a messed-up family. Brett said, "She would never have given them to you. Ali is the only one responsible for her actions." Where had Brett heard that before? Sarah? Yes, she'd told him the same thing.

Mark wiped his face with the crook of his arm and took a deep breath.

Clay opened the first book of photos and slid it in front of Mark.

Brett left the room disappointed they weren't any closer to finding their guy.

#

Brett sat in his cruiser heading to Sarah's. Max panted again in the backseat. *Where are you, Baby Quinn? Lots of people are looking for you.*

Clay had promised to keep a couple of officers staked out at his house and Ali's just in case Quinn found her way home on her own, or in case the perp had a change of heart. Brett doubted it would happen, but prayed it would.

The clouds had disappeared, and the threat of a thunderstorm seemed over. The sun had begun its descent, but it would be a while before darkness fell. He didn't want to think about Quinn being with a madman another night.

Before he left the station, he'd checked in with the chief to see if there were any new leads. None. A few of the officers guarding cache units had called in with zero findings. One officer found another Snickers wrapper near a cache, but that was all.

He drove his fist into the steering wheel and swore under his breath. After unclipping his cell phone from his belt buckle, he called Sarah.

She answered on the second ring. "Hello."

"Sorry, I'm running late. I had to stop by the office, but I'm on my way."

"No problem. I'm in the barn."

As Brett drove to her house, he rehearsed the questions he'd ask her. Yes, he wanted her help in profiling the perp, but he wanted to know more about her father too. What had their relationship been like? Certainly Officer Hudson would know soon if Mr. Samuel's body had been tampered with. He shuddered.

Brett drove the cruiser up a long and steep rock driveway. Oak and pine trees waved their branches, welcoming him. Max's tongue hung out of his mouth, and his tail wagged. Brett double-checked the address on the GPS.

This was where she lived? He surveyed the surroundings, the estate-sized home and property. He never imagined her living in a place this large, although he hadn't thought much about where she lived until now, but she seemed so unassuming. She must have inherited this home. He doubted she could afford it on her salary. The driveway climbed toward a large two-story stone home with an iron fence. Sprawling green pastures and a barn surrounded the back side of the property. Wire fencing hugged the boundaries. A black horse grazed in a nearby field next to a red barn.

That must be the horse Quinn wanted to ride. He continued around to the barn, his tires crunching on the gravel, and parked next to a white Ford F-150.

Sarah appeared outside the barn's entrance. She wore a plaid ruffled shirt, jeans, and cowboy boots. Wisps of her long blond hair fell from her ponytail and blew across her face. She smiled and waved.

He hitched in a breath. The way the sunlight fell onto her blond streaks made her hair seem to glow. His fingers trembled like a schoolboy's on his first date. He scolded himself for being attracted to the same woman who'd told him Quinn would be safe. A part of him wanted to scream at her again, but another part wanted to run to her, hold her, and breathe in her softness.

He shut off the car and set his sunglasses on the dashboard, then climbed out of the sedan. "This is quite a place you have here."

"Thanks." She ambled toward him. "It's been in my mother's family for a century. I'm sentimental about it. The house looks larger than it is. The upstairs is closed off. I live on the main floor." She continued walking toward his car, squinting in the sun, her hands in her back pockets. "How are you holding up?"

"As well as can be expected, I guess." He walked around to the passenger side door. "Is it okay if I let Max out?"

"Certainly! I can't believe you found him!" A smile stretched across her face, flashing her white teeth as her eyes turned to Max in the backseat.

Brett let the dog out, who padded over to Sarah as if he'd known her his whole life. His tail swooshed back and forth in the dirt, causing dust to fly. Sarah laughed and knelt in front of the dog, taking his head in her hands and rubbing his ears. "Hi, boy," she said, squeezing her eyes shut as he licked her face. "You're welcome here anytime. We're used to having animals around." She messed up his hair and stroked his back.

"He showed up last night. I'm taking it as a sign of hope, but I'm not letting him out of my sight, either."

"I don't blame you." The horse whinnied from the pasture and moved closer to the gate. Sarah said, "That's Beauty. Do you ride?"

"Never have. It's not that I haven't wanted to try. I've never had the opportunity, but I don't think today would be the day to start."

"I agree. Come into the house." She led him up the driveway through a side door and into a kitchen.

At the time he'd called Sarah to talk about the perp's profile, meeting her at her home seemed like the right thing to do, but now that he was here it felt too personal. He'd needed someone to talk to, and she seemed sincere about helping him, so how could he resist? But now he needed to ask her questions about her father too. And sleep deprivation prevented him from thinking clearly.

The house smelled of beef and gravy. "Wow, it smells good in here."

"Crock pots are handy for that kind of thing. They make your house smell good for days. Can I get you a bowl? It's stew." She sat on a chair, pulled her leather boots off, and set them on a rug next to the door.

He bent over to unlace his shoes, but she told him not to worry, to leave them on, so he stomped his feet on the rug. "I don't want to impose, and I'm not sure I have much of an appetite."

"No imposition. This is the least I can do." She paused and tilted her head, her serious expression confirming her sincerity. "I always make extra. And you need to eat." She nodded toward his waist. "You're thin."

His ears burned. No woman, except for his mother, had noticed or taken the time to comment on his physique in a long time—at least not that he'd known about.

She pulled out a chair for him to sit on and poured him a glass of tea. Then she set spoons and napkins on the table.

He watched as she glided across the room, so at ease in her home and in the kitchen, her confidence showing in the way she held her head and squared her shoulders.

What was he doing thinking about her and watching her? This was police business. He needed to suppress his thoughts about how attractive she was and talk to her about Quinn.

"Quinn called me."

Sarah stopped and spun around to look at him. "What?"

Brett explained all he knew. He told her about the description of where she was and the perp's blue truck.

Sarah covered her mouth with her hand. Her eyes misted. "This is good news. She's alive, and—"

"She was scared." Brett shook his head. "I can't think about it." He took a deep breath, looking up at her. "It's better if I stay focused on my questions and not let myself go there—you know, think about if she's safe."

Sarah nodded. "I understand. Ask me anything."

"Didn't you say you grew up around here?"

"Yep." She motioned to her surroundings. "This was the house I grew up in." She scooped the stew into two bowls and set them on the table.

"Do you know anyone with the last name Samuel?" He watched her reaction.

"Why?" She filled a bowl with shredded cheese.

"Police business. That's all."

"Did he do something wrong?"

"No, nothing like that, but he died recently, and I'm trying to find out a little about him."

She sat in the chair across from him at the table. "Don't wait for me. Dig in." She hesitated. "Levi Samuel was my father." She stared out the window.

He reached for his spoon without taking his eyes off her. "I'm sorry."

She waved her hand and chortled. "Don't be. I loathed the man. If he were still alive, I wouldn't be in this house right now. I guess you could say we didn't see eye to eye. He's been *dead* to me ever since I left for college."

"Why?"

She gazed out the window. "I spent years trying to forget him, and I'd rather not start remembering him now, so if you don't mind I'd rather not talk about him." She smiled. "Did you want to ask me specific profile questions about your perp?" Her tone had lightened.

He nodded. Obviously, she didn't want to talk about her father, but he needed to press her. "Can I ask you one question about your father?"

"Like?" She wouldn't meet his eyes.

"Why is your last name different from his?"

"I don't know what this has to do with Quinn, but I changed my name years ago so I wouldn't be reminded of him every time I signed my name." She passed Brett a plate of crackers. "Does that help?"

He smiled and nodded even though he wanted to ask her more. It was obvious she was very defensive about him, but because he didn't know for sure if her father was the first victim he wouldn't press her. Yet. Maybe Officer Hudson would call him soon and he'd know for certain one way or another.

"Tell me what you know so far."

Brett reached for a few crackers and set them on his plate. He blew on the stew, took a bite, and wiped his mouth with his napkin. "This is really good."

"Thanks."

"You work with children who live in troubled homes, and I think our guy had a messed-up youth. He seems to have something against sex offenders, which makes us think he himself could have been abused. The perp severs the sex offender's man-part after he tourniquets them so they won't bleed to death—which tells us he doesn't want to kill them. The first victim was a dead man, but the others he kept alive. He wants them to live without their—"

When Brett looked up, Sarah had lost all color in her cheeks. She stared at him, her mouth agape. "Oh, I get it now. You think my father could have been the first victim—that someone cut his—"

"I have to look at every possibility."

"But who would do that to my father?" She licked her lips, seemingly nervous.

"What about your brother? Didn't I meet him at your office?"

"Dean?" She laughed and crossed her arms. "No way. He

wouldn't hurt a flea."

"Do you have any other siblings?"

"No, there's just the two of us. Has someone verified that our father's body has been tampered with?"

"No, not yet, but—"

"Then let's move on. I'm sure he'll have all his body parts."

Brett furrowed his brow. "Okay, I'm sorry I upset you."

"I'm not upset."

"Okay." But she was. Brett could tell. He explained about the chloroform and the ketamine. "I think he might work in a morgue, or a medical place, or with animals—somewhere he might have access to drugs."

Sarah pushed her bowl aside and crossed her arms again. "How do you know it's a man? I know more women who are man-haters than men."

Had her demeanor suddenly changed? Was she acting defensively? "Quinn said a man had her hostage, and he liked to play games." He carefully watched her expression.

She raised her eyebrows. "Really? I counsel women every day who are angry about how men have abused them emotionally, physically, and spiritually, but Quinn would know."

Brett's skin prickled at Sarah's sudden cold demeanor. He narrowed his eyes and continued. "The perp seems methodical, almost neurotically clean about what he does. He isn't staging any of the victims, and he plays games with their penises by planting them in geo-sites."

"Oh, so that's what you found in the site yesterday?"

He nodded. "What does that tell us about our guy?"

She seemed to be thinking. "Typically the more organized, methodical, control-freak types are firstborns, unless—"

"Unless what?"

"The family dynamics in one family differ from another. There are many variables. Sometimes the firstborn and second-born children have reversed roles and the second-born is more organized and methodical, so we can't assume your perp's birth order with certainty."

Was this the situation with her and Dean? Was he the methodical one? Ali and Mark seemed to fit the traditional scenario. Mark was the firstborn and definitely the more organized of the two, but he guessed either one didn't really mean anything.

Sarah continued. "If one of the siblings has a disability, the other might compensate for that too. Add abuse to the scenario, and the dynamics can change too. So again, it's tough to know the birth order of your guy." Sarah stared out the window.

What was she thinking?

She continued, still looking out. "As far as where this perp might live? Based on what you've told me he might be a recluse. Someone who lives alone, maybe a social deviate. Someone who doesn't have a lot of friends."

Brett finished drinking his tea. "Obviously he's a geocacher too. You've been geocaching for a while. Do you know anyone who might fit this profile?"

She stared into her bowl of soup. "Not offhand, but I'll think about it. It's possible he might be a muggle."

"What's that?"

"It's a geocaching term for someone who doesn't know much about geocaching. Someone who sits near the cache site, preventing the hiker from searching the area. They're people who get in the way."

"But if he's depositing peckers in cache sites, he knows more about geocaching than I did. I didn't even know what geocaching was until the Boy Scouts brought the first one in. He'd have to understand the concept anyway."

Sarah rose and rinsed their dishes in the sink. "There are muggles who know nothing about geocaching, and then there are muggles who don't really play the game; they just steal the flag."

Brett rubbed his eyes. "The flag?"

"The prizes inside." Sarah returned to her seat.

"What do you call those who deposit, er, *things* instead of take them?"

"I have no idea. Mugglers?" She laughed.

Brett tried to rub the sandpaper sensation out of his eyes. "Do you know anyone in Hursey Lake who fits this 'firstborn or second-born, abused, recluse' profile?"

Sarah laughed and took a sip of tea. "There could be two dozen kids or adults in Hursey Lake who might hold a grudge against sex offenders. Do you have any idea how many children are abused in this county?"

"No, I don't."

She crossed her arms and sat back in her chair. "More than you know, and honestly, I wouldn't blame some of them if they'd done this."

Brett shook his head. "Really? Would you?"

There. He'd said it. He held his breath.

Her eyes seemed to search his. "Do you mean could *I* have done something like this? Is that what you're really asking?"

Chapter Twenty-Three

Sarah's heart fluttered like a bat's wings trapped in an airless bag. Did Brett really believe she could be the perp? She whispered, "Is that what you think? That I could maim these men and kidnap your daughter?"

His face turned crimson, and he shook his head. "I'm sorry. No, I don't believe that, because we know it's a man, but I don't really know much about you."

She nodded. "You're right about that. You don't."

"There are things about you that I . . . don't understand," Brett stammered. "All I know is that your relationship with your father was less than perfect, based on what you told me, which wasn't very much. You also geocache—which fits the profile of our guy."

Tears brimmed her eyes. She reached into her jeans pocket, pulled out a wadded tissue, and dabbed at her eyes. "I've spent the last ten years trying to forget what happened between my father and me. He abused me emotionally and sexually. He was an evil man. A control freak. But I vowed I'd overcome the pain. I left his home when I was eighteen, and spent years studying psychology, getting my counseling degree so I could help others. I changed my name, determined to rid my veins of his poison. I'm a nurturer. Not a psychopath."

Brett reached for her hand. "I'm sorry. I believe you. It must have been difficult."

"It was. I don't like to talk about him." She saw sincerity in his furrowed brows and felt the warmth of his fingers on hers. "You have no idea." She blotted at her face with the tissue.

He squeezed her hand. "I never intended to hurt your feelings or insinuate you were involved in this. My reasoning is clouded with worry and exhaustion. Of course, I can't imagine you taking Quinn or hurting anyone. I noticed your compassion for children the day I met you. It's a gift, commendable. Quinn took to you right away."

"Thank you." She smiled. His eyes were bloodshot and drooped at the corners. He looked exhausted. She shouldn't have acted so sensitive. Maybe she'd done that because she thought he liked her, was attracted to her. Maybe it was because she felt guilty for putting Quinn in harm's way. Whatever the reason, she needed to get over it and help him find his daughter.

She moved to the chair near the door, suddenly embarrassed for her outburst, and tried to regain her composure. "I need to go feed the animals. Make yourself at home. I'll be right back." She slipped on her boots and left him sitting at the kitchen table by himself.

When she returned twenty minutes later, the dishes were washed, and Brett had fallen asleep with his head on the table. She didn't have the heart to wake him. He probably hadn't slept for days. It wasn't going to hurt anything to let him sleep a few hours. Maybe she should take him into the guest bedroom. She nudged his shoulder. "Brett?"

Nothing.

She poked his arm again. "Brett, why don't you sleep in a bed? Here, come with me." Max stuck his nose near Brett's face and snorted.

He didn't move.

Sarah put his arm around her shoulder. It was as limp as a dead cat. "Come on, can you get up?"

"Hmm? Where are we going?" His eyes remained shut and his words groggy.

"I'm taking you to the guest room. Can you walk?"

"Are you coming onto me?" He stood and stumbled a little.

"Don't be silly. You're exhausted. Lean on me, and I'll get you to a room."

He shook his head. "I have to stay awake for Quinn."

She prodded him on. "A few hours won't hurt. There's nothing you can do. The entire police force is out looking for her."

He didn't argue. His dead weight pressed into her shoulders, and his holster jabbed her hip. He smelled of fabric softener and hair gel. Max followed. A few times she thought she was going to fall down with Brett sprawled on top of her, but they made it. She sat him on the edge of the bed and let his head fall back onto the pillow. He lifted his legs with her help. One by one she untied his shoes, took them off, and set them on the floor.

He mumbled something like, "Don't let me sleep too long. Have to find Quinn."

She covered him with the blanket. Max hopped up on the bed and curled up next to Brett. The dog sighed, dropping his head onto his paws and shut his eyes.

#

The guest room hadn't been slept in for over twenty years—at least, not that Sarah knew of. It used to be hers when she was a little girl, which was probably why she had no interest in sleeping in there now. She returned to the kitchen and glanced at her watch. It was only eight p.m.

She paced, remembering Brett's earlier questions about her father and the perp's profile.

Her brother fit it perfectly. What if he had something to do with severing man parts? He was a recluse, had been abused as a child, and worked in a veterinarian office, but he'd never hurt anyone before. He'd always been timid and into working with animals. And he was a little guy, socially inept, not bold enough to do what Brett said the guy was doing. But still, he fit the personality profile. He knew about geocaching because she always talked with him about her finds.

She dismissed the whole idea and shook the thought from her mind. He'd never be able to do something so morbid, and he hated change or leaving his comfort zone, places he knew well.

She went out into the living room and stared at the television. She turned it on, looking for a distraction. A local newscaster appeared. "Our latest story is one of love, a wedding proposal, and another geocaching incident here in Hursey Lake." Sarah's heart raced. Had they found new evidence?

"Police are advising all geocachers to stop their hunts here in Stark County until further notice. This afternoon Nikki Scheurer and Justin Wright found another severed body part, apparently hacked from the latest victim, when they went on their hike. After they found the cache box, but before they opened it, Justin proposed to his girlfriend, Nikki, pretending someone had left the ring in the box."

The camera moved to a young long-haired redheaded girl with perfect teeth. She giggled. "I was shocked. It was both the best day and the worst day of my life." She dramatically placed her hand on her chest. "I don't think we'll ever geocache again." She gazed at her fiancé with dreamy eyes.

The newscaster spoke to the guy. "Did she say 'yes' before you found the body part?"

Justin laughed and stared at the mic. He looked a little older than the girl. His dark hair shagged down around his ears, and when he smiled his cheeks folded into deep dimples. They made a cute pair. "Yes." He turned to look at his fiancée and reached for her hand. They looked at each other with a glow of adoration. She'd seen that look before and how quickly it could fade.

Sarah watched the rest of the news and saw a rerun of Brett's press conference and his plea for Quinn. She paced, thinking of Dean and wondering if she should take a walk to his house. She hadn't talked to him much since their father had died, and the day he came to clean her windows she'd been busy with Brett and Quinn. She'd have to invite him over tomorrow for dinner.

She went to her bedroom, down the hall from the one Brett slept in. It was her mother's former room, the preserved one that no one had slept in since she'd died—at least not while her father was alive.

After their mother had died, but while their father was still living, Sarah and Dean were forbidden to go in there. But now that her father was gone and she'd inherited the house, she allowed herself to move back in. At first, she'd been tentative about moving back into the house. She hadn't lived there or spoken to her father in more than ten years. But once his funeral was over and she mustered the courage to go to the house, she began to sense her mother's presence, craving the goodness.

Initially, moving back in had been creepy because remnants of her father had been everywhere, but with help she'd managed to remove every bit of his things. She dumped them into a heap outside, made a fire pit, and burned them, watching and reveling in the smoldering of his belongings and every painful memory he'd caused her. But even with his stuff gone, she still couldn't sleep in her old room. The only safe place she could rest without nightmares was in her mother's old room.

She changed into a T-shirt and baggy shorts and climbed in bed with her Kindle, hoping to read, but finding she couldn't focus. She turned out the light and tried to sleep, but she tossed and turned. Just knowing there was a man in the house unnerved her.

When she finally fell asleep, she dreamed she was a child again. That she and her brother were playing tag outside near the barn, and their mother was calling to them, standing in the front yard with a kite in her hand. She played out some of the string, and the kite's rainbow colors sailed back and forth in the wind. She said, "Come, I'll teach you how to fly a kite."

Sarah and Dean giggled and ran to her, running against the wind. But the wind's force pushed Sarah back and made her run harder to gain distance. She gulped air and lost her breath. The more she ran toward her mother, the farther the wind pushed her back. She yelled, "I'm coming, Mama." But the wind took the sound of her words away. Her mama kept waving for them to come.

Dean held Sarah's hand. Little brother, Dean. His tiny arms and legs just like thin tree branches. He was always small for his age and sickly. She tightened her grip on his hand, certain the wind would blow him away from her if she didn't. "Hold tight, little brother. We'll get there."

But the more they tried, the farther they fell back, until finally Sarah couldn't see her mother anymore. She'd disappeared. The wind died, and their father loomed above them. His yellow teeth, his bent nose, and the scar on his forehead stared back at them. When she heard his deranged, boisterous laugh she screamed, which made him laugh all the more.

Sarah bolted upright in bed, her heart racing. Perspiration crawled down her neck like ants marching up a tree. Why had the old man suddenly appeared in her dreams here in her mother's room? It was like he was taunting her, saying, "You can't escape me." Oh, how she hated him.

She glanced at the clock—it was a little after eleven.. She'd only been asleep a few hours. She went to the bathroom, got a drink of water, and tiptoed down the hallway to check on Brett. She peeked in the room and heard Brett snoring softly. Max lifted his head and perked his ears. She whispered, "It's okay, boy. Go back to sleep," and pulled his door shut.

As she made her way down the hallway, she heard a noise in the kitchen. She froze and listened. Was it her imagination? Then she heard it again. But this time she heard him say her name like he used to when they were children. "S-s-sarah?" It was Dean.

It wasn't unusual for him to stop in at the house when he was hungry or bored. His cabin was about a half mile on the other side of the hill. But typically he didn't stop at the house this late. Maybe he was looking for a late-night snack.

He used to stutter when he was frightened, or when something was troubling him, but over the years he'd improved. Why was he stuttering now?

She went into the kitchen. He stood with his back to her washing his hands, his backpack slung over his shoulder.

"What are you doing here?"

Dean swiveled around. "Y-y-you scared me." He wore his shiny boots—the ones he kept polished till they shone—his pressed jeans, and a long-sleeved shirt. He stared at the ceiling and then the refrigerator. Eye contact had always been difficult for him, but typically he was better with her than with others.

"You okay?" Sarah put her hand on her hip. "Or are you here to eat more of the apple pie?"

"I was out t-t-taking a walk and got h-h-hungry, then I saw the car." He pointed outside, twisting the bottom of his shirt.

"Oh, sorry. Yeah, that's Officer Reed's car. I'm okay. He's the man whose daughter is missing."

"W-w-why is he here?"

"For my help, but he fell asleep. He hasn't slept in days. I'm letting him sleep for a few hours."

"He is b-b-bad. Didn't he h-h-hurt his daughter?"

"No. He's a good man."

He shrugged. "I h-h-heard he hurt her."

"Where did you hear that?"

He stared down the hall toward the bedrooms. "Around town."

"Well, they're rumors. That's all they are. He's a good father."

"I saw him at your office that d-d-day I was cleaning your windows." He opened the fridge and took a swig of milk from the carton. "Why did they take his daughter away from h-h-him?"

She took a glass out of the cupboard and handed it to him. "It's too complicated, and it's not professional for me to speak about his case." Sarah took the milk carton from Dean and filled his glass. "I was in bed, so maybe we could talk more tomorrow?"

"Do y-y-you like him?"

Little protective Dean. Always looking out for her. "I like him, yes, and I care about his daughter. I don't want anything to happen to her. The man who took her is crazy. I hope he gives her back unharmed."

Dean crossed the room to the door, but hesitated, rocking from side to side. "C-c-crazy?" He paused. "You s-s-sleeping in the bed with him?"

"No!" Sarah chuckled and crossed her arms.

"You don't need me?"

"No, thank you. I'll be fine. You go home and get some rest." She waited for him to finish his glass of milk.

He wiped his milk mustache with the back of his hand and placed his glass in the sink.

She put her hand on his arm and drew him into an embrace. He stiffened as usual. "Everything is fine with me, protective one. There's no need to worry."

#

Five minutes after Dean had left, Sarah still sat at the kitchen desk in front of her laptop worried about him. He'd seemed off. An uneasy feeling edged in her mind, prodding and invading all other thoughts. She tried reading her e-mail, but couldn't concentrate. How long had Dean been in a funk? What had triggered his stuttering? There were too many similarities between Dean and the vigilante. Had there been guilt in her brother's eyes? Was he hiding something?

Beauty whinnied from the barn again, startling her. Sarah rose to look out the window toward the barn. A light was on. Dean must have gone in to get something and forgotten to turn it off. Or was he still out there?

She pulled on her boots, grabbed a sweater and a flashlight off the hook, and headed out. She'd never seen Dean so possessed about protecting her. Was there something more troubling him? Maybe their father's death had triggered his weird behavior. If she didn't find him in the barn maybe she'd take a walk to his cabin.

Darn, it was so dark and it smelled like rain. No moon out tonight. She flicked on the flashlight and shone it on the gravel in the driveway until she reached the barn, then headed straight to Beauty's stall. The horse nickered and came to her, jutting her head toward the rail.

Sarah rubbed her cheek. "You okay, girl?"

Beauty smacked her lips. Nothing looked amiss.

She walked across the barn to where she stored the hay bales and saw something out of the corner of her eye—a backpack. Dean's backpack, lying behind the feed bin. Why had he left it there?

"Dean?" She turned in circles listening and waiting, but there was no sign of him. The bag had been across his shoulder at the house. Why would he have left it there? He'd need it for work tomorrow. It was what he packed his lunch in every day. Why had he been carrying it? She'd have to ask him.

She stooped to retrieve the bag and hiked it over her shoulder, shocked at how heavy it was. It clattered like metal against metal and must have weighed fifteen pounds. What the heck did he have in there?

She stopped, set it on the ground, unclasped the buckle, and dumped its contents. Thin rubber tubes, plastic gloves, a vial of medicine, large surgical scissors, several needles and long scalpels, and a box of baggies spilled out in front of her. Her hand moved to her open mouth, covering a silent scream. Her fingers trembled.

Oh, no! She stood, backing away from the contents, stunned. Her mouth gaped. *Dean, oh, Dean, what have you done?*

That's when it hit her. If Dean was the guy maiming sex offenders, then he had Quinn too. *No! Why, Dean, why?* Her whole body shook.

She sprinted out the barn the same way she'd entered, then paused in the damp air. The wind whipped her hair across her face. It had started to rain. She glanced up at the house and saw Brett's silhouette at the desk in the kitchen. He must have awoken.

What should she do? She cried, torn. If she told Brett, would he understand? No, he wouldn't. He'd be enraged. He'd lose it, and if Quinn was at the cabin he'd probably shoot first and ask questions later. Dealing with Dean took experience, a counselor's tactics. She had to go alone. She'd talk sense into her brother and bring Quinn back to Brett. *If* Quinn was there. She had to be there. Dean would listen to her.

She headed around the side of the barn and tromped up the hill, through the cornfields, toward the guesthouse, the wind swallowing her breath and the rain spitting on her face. "I'm coming, Quinn."

But dread filled her. What if he'd taken Quinn someplace else? Why would he do this? Now he'd have to go to jail for life. There was no way out.

Oh, Dean, I can't protect you this time.

Chapter Twenty-Four

Brett woke to Max's low growl. "Huh?" His eyes fluttered open. Where was he? Why was he lying in a bed with all his clothes on? He shot up, flinging the blanket off and swinging his legs over the side. He set his feet, still in socks, on the floor and scanned the room.

Frilly hats with long ribbons hung on the wall he faced. A white eyelet bedspread and monogrammed shams with the initials SSS adorned the bed. A lit clock on the nightstand read 11:45 p.m. An antique white desk sat in the corner, opposite a chest of drawers.

Everything came flooding back. Ali, Quinn, Sarah. He was in Sarah's home. How could he have fallen asleep? His heart raced. He listened. Max stood on the bed, tilting his head and watching the closed door.

Brett reached over and rubbed the dog's ears. "What is it, boy? You hear something?" Brett unclipped his cell phone and pressed the button on the bottom to light it, but nothing happened. It was dead? No! How long had it been dead? He'd forgotten to charge it. He hit the palm of his hand to his head. How could he have been so stupid?

How many calls had he missed? What if Quinn had tried to reach him?

He leaned over and shoved his feet into his shoes, not bothering to tie them. Max leaped off the bed and shook from head to tail.

In two wide strides Brett opened the door and tiptoed down the hall. Which way was out? He couldn't remember. His sense of direction sucked. A soft light came from a room across the hall. He peered inside and saw an empty bed in a green-painted room. The bedclothes were thrown back as if someone had slept there but gotten up. Sarah?

He turned toward the other hallway, hoping it led to the kitchen, but stopped when he noticed a painting on the wall: a picture of a woman who strongly resembled Sarah. Was it her mother? She had the same deep-set eyes as Sarah's, but they weren't as large. Her smile drew him in like the *Mona Lisa*, watching him, following him, and tempting him to stay with her. No wonder the chief had been so enamored with her.

Something about this woman's drooping eyes made her seem lonely, as if she were trapped inside herself. He'd seen the same look on Sarah's face—the one that made him want to know her better, learn her secret. His eyes dropped to the bottom of the painting where her hand rested, next to the artist's signature: Sarah S. Samuel. Sarah was also an artist?

Where was she? "Sarah?"

No answer. Max padded by his side.

He went to the kitchen. She wasn't there either, but her computer whirred from her desk, and he spotted her iPhone charger. Thank God! He plugged his phone in and looked out the window. A light shone from the barn. She must have gone out. He'd give his phone two minutes to charge, listen to his messages, then leave.

Wait, why hadn't he heard his phone ding with messages? He picked it up and realized it had shut off, so he turned it on again. Within seconds it beeped from messages and a text. He sank into the chair, hurrying to see them. Had Quinn called?

Max sighed and curled up under the desk.

One text was from Clay: *They found another cache treasure. Need to talk to you. Call me.*

Three missed calls! He moved to the voice mail screen. Were they from Quinn? It didn't look like it. None were blocked numbers. He recognized Clay's number, his parents', and his ex-mother-in-law's. He clicked on his father's message first. "If you need anything let us know. We're praying for Quinn and Ali." Ali? Wow, his father had come a long way.

The next message was from Ali's mother. "Where should they send Ali's body? Was she an organ donor?"

What? Ali had died? The room spun. Ali was gone? No! His ears rang and he felt numb. Why did she have to die? He pounded his fist on the desk and dropped his head into his hands, tears spilling.

Max jumped and whined and poked his nose in Brett's face, licking his master's tears as if he could take away Brett's pain.

"Why? Why did this have to happen?" he shouted, choking at the lump in his throat.

Max whined and cocked his head to the side.

As much as Brett had loathed Ali's issues, she was the only mother Quinn had known. Quinn loved her mother. How was he going to explain this to her? *If* he ever found her. Tears fell. He knew Ali's condition had been critical, but still—he hadn't expected this. Everything was spiraling out of control.

He tried to catch his breath, knowing he had to find Quinn. He had to hold on to hope, get a grip and try to keep it together. *Quinn, where are you?* He pressed the button to play Clay's message, the screen blurry from his tears.

Max returned to his snooze position under the desk.

Clay said, "Man, where are you? We're trying to pull this case together. Are you okay? We got another tip from a few geocachers. They saw a guy in a blue truck, an older model, maybe a 1995 Toyota, just tonight, carrying a backpack and leaving the geo-site, the one that contained the last prize. They remembered parts of the plate number. We're looking them up right now. Did you know that Sarah's father died three weeks ago? Levi Samuel. Officer Hudson had his coffin opened. He's the dead guy who's missing his dick."

What? Brett's stomach twirled. His heart raced. Nausea burned his throat. He felt like vomiting. His attention shot out through the window to where he thought Sarah had gone. He'd been right to assume Dean was involved. Did that mean Sarah was involved too?

Something moved behind him, and then out of the corner of his eye. Max growled. Brett reached for his gun, his heart racing, but just as he turned to see who approached, someone hit him over the head. Pain shot down to his spine like an electric bolt. He moaned and fell, his face smacking against the tiled floor.

No! Not now. I need to find Quinn. Blackness enveloped him as he thought about Sarah, how wrong he'd been to trust her, and what a fool he'd been. Now he'd never find Quinn in time.

Chapter Twenty-Five

Sarah sprinted up the hill toward the guesthouse, through the cornfields, the rain matting the hair against her face. Why had Dean snapped? When had he gone off the deep end? Little brother Dean. She should have realized something wasn't right with him. It was her job to notice behavioral problems. She was trained to see these things, to see people who were emotionally and mentally unstable. But she didn't understand. Why now? Their father was finally gone. Why would Dean be struggling now?

More questions than answers rushed through her mind. She smelled logs burning in his fireplace—pine and earthy—before she turned the corner and actually saw the smoke billowing from the cabin's chimney. Why would he want heat in the summer? At least it wasn't coming from the house. Her heart raced, keeping rhythm with her breathing. She swallowed to moisten her throat.

As she darted into the clearing and approached the house, she noticed the front door wide open. Heat from the fireplace charged her as she entered. She shook the rain off her face and shoulders. Right away she saw the change in the room. Just like him, his house was a wreck too. Typically Dean kept everything in order, but now the living room furniture had been moved around with two chairs upturned, magazines and papers were scattered across the floor, the drapes were drawn closed, and the television blared. Dean never kept the TV on loud. He didn't like loud noises.

When was the last time she'd visited him? She couldn't remember. It should have been more often, more recent. She crossed the room and turned the television off.

"Dean? Quinn?"

Nothing.

Frantic, she spun in circles afraid to turn her back, unsure of what to expect, unsure of where Dean had gone. "Dean?" she cried.

She opened the drapes a few feet, enough to check behind them and confirm that Quinn wasn't hiding there.

The rain hurled against the roof of the house. An ember crackled.

Sarah inched toward the kitchen. Piles of dirty dishes littered the table and the countertop. Dried macaroni and cheese sat in a pan on the stove. She clasped her hand over her mouth, quieting her gasp. Dean never left the kitchen dirty. He was obsessive about cleanliness.

"Quinn, it's me, Dr. Sarah. You can come out now." She ran back to the living room, frantic. "Dean?" Where had he gone?

Thunder crackled and Sarah jumped, her hands trembling. Lightning lit up the trees outside the window and Dean appeared in the doorway, anger and mud splashed across his face, a wooden bat in his hand.

Sarah screamed.

Dean leaned over as if trying to catch his breath, like he'd been running.

She froze. Her heart pounded and dread filled her. Had he hurt Quinn? "What's the bat for, Dean?" Her voice quivered.

He looked at the bat like he hadn't realized it was in his hand and dropped it on the porch like a burning stick. He twisted the bottom of his shirt and shrugged. He wouldn't meet her eyes. His eyeballs spiraled in two opposite directions, giving her the feeling that his brain chemistry was seriously out of whack.

She trembled. This was a different Dean. *Please, God, let Quinn be okay.* "You had Quinn here, didn't you?"

Still on the porch, he nodded and took off his shoes. "She's in the bathroom. She wouldn't come out. I gave her a pillow."

Sarah concentrated on keeping her voice steady, almost aloof-sounding. Meanwhile, her hands quaked. "No, I looked in there. She's not in the house, Dean." Hopefully she wasn't far. She'd find her. She had to.

Panic and disbelief filled Dean's eyes. He ran back to the bathroom. "Quinn?" Then he charged back into the living room to where Sarah stood in the open doorway. "Did you hide her?"

"No. I haven't seen her. You didn't hurt her, did you?"

Dean shook his head. "I took care of her. I'm protecting her."

"Why did you light a fire?"

He shrugged. "You always liked them. You said Mama did too, that they made her feel safe."

"How thoughtful of you." They'd never built one in the summer, and why was he thinking of their mother? "You were trying to keep Quinn safe?"

Dean smiled and nodded, puffing out his chest in a proud manner.

"That's the Dean I know." She took a step toward him and reached to gently touch his arm, but he flicked it off with such force that she stumbled. Her heart beat faster. "Dean!"

He hung his head and moved it in circles.

"What was that for?" He'd never been aggressive toward her. Ever.

He shrugged and stared at the ground, his head chin to chest. "Don't touch me."

He was loaded like a gun! She lowered her voice. "I'll help you find Quinn, okay?"

His eyes finally met hers, and he smiled again.

She exhaled. "She's probably outside. I'll go look. You wait here in case she returns. Sometimes girls like to talk to girls." She needed to hurry, find Quinn, and get back to Brett.

He wrinkled his brow and frowned as if he was confused. His eyes darted right, then left—in a crazed way. He shook his head and threw his shoulder into her, knocking her off balance, and toward the wall. "No! I need to come too. I n-n-need to take care of her, protect her." He held his arms out, blocking the front door.

Sarah stumbled, gripping a nearby chair. She righted herself, the hair on her arms rising, her limbs going weak. She swallowed. Wind blew in from the open door, fraying her nerves. *Stay calm.* "What are you trying to protect her from?"

"Her father."

She inched her way toward Dean again. "Her father didn't harm her. He loves her."

He shook his head. "No, her father hurt her. He's bad like Father."

She searched his eyes. If only she could get him to look at her, connect with her. She softened her voice. "Our father is dead. He can't hurt anyone anymore. Quinn's dad is a nice man. He's not like Father. He won't hurt her. He loves her."

Dean's eyes narrowed, and he looked away.

"Do you understand?"

He nodded and slid down to the floor, his shoulders slumping and his head on his chest. "Father told me I was a yellow-bellied chicken, afraid of my shadow." He pouted. "I wanted to take care of you. I wanted to protect you, but I was too small. Too scared. He was right."

"Protect me from what?" What was he talking about? There wasn't time to waste, but she needed to calm him, convince him to hurry.

"From him. I saw you in the room, in his bed with him, crying."

Sarah paused and squatted on the floor next to him. "What do you mean?"

"When he told you to lie with him. He told you lies. He told me those lies too. He said Mama would want you to do stuff, but she didn't, did she? I wanted to warn you, but I couldn't. I was afraid." His body swayed from side to side.

Her head spun. The room was so hot. Too hot. She didn't want to think about Dean watching her with *him*. Or Dean lying with *him*. She shuddered. Poor Dean. He must have been traumatized, and yet he'd never said anything. She shook her head wishing she could make the vision disappear. "Father was a bad man."

He nodded. "Nobody believed me."

"What do you mean?"

"I told people. About him. They laughed at me. You were gone. At school." Tears streamed down his face.

Her heart wept for him. She took his hand. This time he didn't flick it away. Her tears fell too. "I'm sorry. You must have felt so alone." Rage glared its red face, and her insides boiled. What had happened to her was one thing, but that it had happened to her brother was worse. "I remember. He hurt you, didn't he?"

Dean nodded.

"I believe you. I'm sorry."

He hung his head low.

She wanted to scream that such an innocent child should never have had to endure what he had. But she couldn't fix him now. Maybe never. He needed years of therapy. How had she missed the signs? She thought he'd improved, that he'd moved on.

She wiped her face, trying to move on for Quinn's sake. They'd have to take care of Dean later. Somehow she needed to steer him back toward Quinn, finding Quinn, and taking her to Brett. Soon. There wasn't much time. But how could she get him to move on now?

"What Father did wasn't your fault. And you're right. Mama wouldn't have approved. What Father did was wrong." Her voice shook.

He swung his head back and forth, and his bottom lip quivered. "I didn't do anything to s-s-stop him. I stood outside the d-d-door and heard you crying, but I couldn't help you. I wanted to save you, but I was scared. Too scared. I hated him for what he did to you . . . and M-m-mama. Why couldn't he have l-l-left you alone?" His voice softened. "Why couldn't he have left me alone?"

Sarah squeezed his hand. "It wasn't your fault. He was a mean man. Shhh. I'm okay now but Quinn isn't. We need to find her." She reached up and stroked his hair, but he seemed lost.

"I couldn't s-s-say no. He was right. I was a w-w-wuss. He laughed at me. He told me I'd never be anything." His hands curled into tight fists.

"He was wrong, Dean. You're really brave, and you're somebody. Doc Spear and all the animals at the clinic love you. You're important. Father should never have said those things, or done those things. I'm sorry." Tears fell down her face.

His hands relaxed and he laughed. "You're right. I am somebody. He said I would always be a little boy, a w-w-wuss, but look at me now." He puffed out his chest and lifted his chin. "He was wrong. I'm doing the right thing, aren't I, Sarah—slicing off those guys' dicks? Those bastards will never be able to hurt another child. Ever. I saw to that. D-d-didn't I? Father was wrong about me. I am brave. People are talking. They're scared. Especially those perverts."

"No, Dean. What you did was wrong. Those men were bad, but maiming them wasn't the right thing to do. Taking Quinn was wrong too. She's not yours. We have to find her and return her to her father."

He shook his head. "I needed to p-p-protect her." He twisted the bottom of his shirt, the crazed look in his eyes returning.

A surge of worry and protective love filled her. She saw in his eyes that he needed to believe he'd done the right thing, that things would work out okay, but she knew in her heart how unlikely it was. Nothing she could say would make him understand. She exhaled and patted his hand, knowing she had to hurry. They had to find Quinn. "I know you thought you were doing the right thing." She stroked his arm. "Everything is going to be okay. Let's go find Quinn. Do you know where she might be?" Sarah waited, studying his expression.

He shrugged. "I don't know. M-m-maybe outside."

"Let's go." She stood, praying Brett would understand that her brother wasn't a monster, that he'd been a victim. But she doubted Brett would care what Dean had been through. He was in trouble. Big trouble.

Dean stood and blocked her path.

"Let me pass so I can find Quinn." She waited.

"Only if I can go too."

"Okay, but you have to promise to obey."

He stepped aside and put on his boots again.

When he finished, she retrieved the flashlight she'd left on the steps and searched Dean's eyes. Although they still roamed, they caught hers for a brief moment—long enough for her to think they were calmer. She descended the steps, keeping Dean in her peripheral view as he followed.

The rain had almost stopped. She shone the light on the ground, first right, then left, and noticed two little footprints in the garden near the rose bushes heading toward the brush in the woods. Relief poured threw her. "She went this way." Poor thing. She must be so scared.

Sarah cupped her hands around her mouth and shouted. "Quinn, you can come out now. I won't hurt you. It's Dr. Sarah. Remember me?"

The only answer came from thunder in the distance and the howling of the wind blowing through the trees. Rain dripped off the leaves. The night was black.

They entered the woods and weaved in and out of the path. Dean hung close behind. Sarah watched for Quinn's footprints along the trail knocking limb branches out of her way, ignoring the sting when they clawed her bare arms. The path snaked along the edge of the creek.

She stopped to listen. Had she heard something? A whimper? It sounded like it was coming from somewhere straight ahead. "Quinn? It's Dr. Sarah. I'm here to help you. Can you follow my voice, come to me?"

The noise stopped.

Dean wrung his hands. "Quinn, it's okay. Your father isn't here. Don't be sad." He cupped his hands around his mouth. "Are you hurt, Quinn? I can help you. I w-w-will listen."

A child cried, Quinn's cry.

Sarah turned to her brother. "Shh, don't say anything. We don't want to frighten her."

Dean's shoulders slumped.

Sarah continued on the path, proceeding toward the sound, uncertain of where it was coming from. She ducked behind trees, pushing branches and weeds out of her way. "Where are you?"

The crying stopped when Sarah came to a fork on the trail. An old fallen tree stump blocked their path. Small footprints ceased just before it, like Quinn had jumped up onto the stump and over.

The air grew quiet—as if Quinn knew they were close and was trying to hold back her tears. "Dr. Sarah is here, Quinn. No one is going to hurt you. Everything's okay. Your father is at my house. I'm going to take you to him."

Dean said, "No!"

Sarah turned to Dean and put her index finger over her lips. "Shh." She advanced through the wet grass and peered behind the large tree stump. There, curled up with her knees tucked under her chin, sat Quinn, her hands, face, and knees streaked with mud. Her bottom lip fluttered, and her body shivered probably chilled from the rain. She held her left ankle and winced.

Tears of relief burst through Sarah. She sighed and stooped, meeting Quinn's eyes. "I won't let anyone hurt you. Okay?"

Quinn nodded and reached for Sarah, encircling her arms around Sarah's neck as if she'd never let go. Sarah reached under Quinn's knees and arms, lifting her to her chest. Quinn wrapped her legs around Sarah's waist.

Sarah closed her eyes and held her tight, basking in the warmth of her embrace, a sense of maternal protectiveness washing over her. When she made her way into the clearing, Dean smiled and jumped up and down like a child. "You found her. Let me carry her. I'm stronger than you." He shoved his arms under Quinn, jerking her toward him.

Quinn screamed.

Sarah drew Quinn closer. "No, Dean. I have her now. She's not too heavy."

He grabbed for her again. "No, I want to help."

Quinn said, "No. I want . . . Sarah." Her shoulders shook in short hiccups.

Sarah softened her voice and faced Dean. "I know you're stronger than me, and you're super at helping, but let me hold her. She's frightened right now. Why don't you show us how to get back to the cabin? I'm not sure I can find my way." If she made him feel helpful it would distract him, but for how long, she didn't know.

Dean smiled and raced ahead of them, waving his arms for them to follow.

Sarah couldn't keep patronizing him. She had to find a way to break him out of his funk or something would push him over the edge. A shiver trickled down the small of her back. It wouldn't be long before Brett, or the authorities, found him. She couldn't bear the thought of them taking him away in handcuffs or an ambulance.

She needed to get Dean back to the house and talk him into turning himself in. But how was she going to do that?

Chapter Twenty-Six

Brett woke with a start to pain searing through his head and Max's incessant face-licking. Brett's fingers shot up to a spot above his ear and felt a sticky gash. He groaned. His heart thumped. He stared at his bloody fingers, dazed, rising to a sitting position. The room spun. What had happened? Where was he?

He was on the floor in a yellow kitchen. Whose kitchen? At first he didn't recognize anything in the room, then everything came flooding back.

He was in Sarah's kitchen. She'd fixed him a bowl of stew.

Quinn! He had to find Quinn.

He shot up off the floor, but dizziness made him blind, and he fell back to the floor. Sitting, he closed his eyes for a brief moment and concentrated on remembering everything that had happened before he was hit.

He'd been listening to his e-mail messages when someone hit him over the head. Had it been Sarah? Why? Where was she now? He listened but only heard the humming of the refrigerator and the crickets chirping outside.

His phone lay on the floor a foot away. He picked it up, remembering his messages—Ali had died, and Sarah's father, Levi Samuel, was missing his penis. Everything was spinning out of control.

I need to call Clay. Looking at his cell phone screen, he tried to find Clay's number but the contacts blurred. *Damn, he couldn't see!* He shoved the phone in its belt case and reached for the gun in his holster, unsnapped the thumb break, and drew the weapon.

Now he was pissed. Mad at himself for falling for Sarah, for believing he could trust her, for believing she cared about him. She'd been in cahoots with her brother the whole time. She must have staged the whole thing from the beginning. And he hadn't seen it!

Leaning against the chair, he hoisted himself up to a sitting position, his mind spinning as he remembered when he'd first met Sarah, when she'd been assigned to his case. Had she taken the case because she thought he was an offender? Was she working with her brother to obliterate all pervs in the county? She was in the perfect position to know who the offenders were. She admitted she was Moore's counselor.

Oh, she was a good actor! He held his head.

He'd been such a fool. Why hadn't he gone with his instincts? With the facts? No, he'd gone and gotten all attracted to her. Oh, she was good. She was really good!

Obviously, he couldn't pick women.

Slowly, he stood, his anger propelling him. He leaned on the refrigerator until the vertigo subsided, his gun drawn.

Max stood beside him, looking up to Brett as if waiting to see what he would do next. If someone was in the house, wouldn't Max be barking? Rain pattered on the windows.

A light outside caught his attention. He felt like a sitting duck standing in a brightly lit kitchen. Anyone looking in could see him. He flicked the kitchen lights off. Darkness filled the room. The light from the barn trickled out, blurred by the rain.

He walked gingerly toward the door, every step causing pain in his head, and turned to Max. "You stay here, boy. I'll be back."

The dog cocked his head as Brett went out. Rain pelted his face. Stumbling to the barn, his heart beat double-time. His brain sluggishly muddled through possibilities.

Certain things didn't add up, like why would Sarah take Quinn? Had that been a mix-up? One that Sarah hadn't counted on? Maybe her brother had found Quinn and took her even though that hadn't been the arrangement. Had her interest in him and Quinn been a total front?

His mind argued back and forth. No. He couldn't believe that. She'd wanted to help him find Quinn. Then he thought, *She fits the profile—an avid geocacher, a vendetta against sex offenders*. Brett's mind argued more. But if Sarah had wanted him dead she could have easily shot him after she hit him over the head.

Maybe knocking him out gave her time. Maybe she was on her way back to do him in.

Rain pecked against his face, and a breeze kicked up, whipping through the buttons on his shirt. Thunder rumbled in the distance. Sarah's truck sat in the driveway next to his. He leaned against it waiting for his vision to clear.

When it finally did, he sidestepped puddles in the gravel driveway and approached the barn. Quietly, he pushed open the side door, went in, and closed it without a sound. He flattened his back against the wall and listened. The only sound came from the horse's mouth. It sounded as if she was crunching on something.

Brett took small steps to the horse's stall. The horse turned to him for only a few seconds before she turned back to her feed. Sarah must have been there if the horse was eating.

Something lay on the ground farther into the barn, about ten yards in front of him. What was it? He moved closer before he saw that it was a backpack with its contents spilled out. He knelt to examine them, his head feeling as heavy as a bowling ball.

His heart thumped at what he saw. All the whack job tools lay in a heap. He inhaled sharply. The scalpel, medicine vials, rubber tourniquets. Where was Sarah? Why had she run off and left this? Had this been hers, or had she found it and something happened to her?

He flung around gingerly, keeping his back flat against the walls, checking the rest of the barn, kicking in the bathroom door, almost shooting a cat with glowing green eyes in the tack room.

Nothing.

Sarah had said her brother lived on the property up the hill at the guesthouse. Quinn had said there were fields and trees near her. But which way? He was surrounded by both.

He unclipped his cell phone again. *I'd better text Clay*. Brett knew if he called his partner, he would make him wait for backup, but he couldn't. Not now. Clay would be there soon anyway, especially since he knew about Samuel's body.

Brett's vision cleared enough for him to punch out a message. *I'm at Sarah's. Found the whacker's tools. On my way to her brother's house on the property.*

After tucking his phone away, he raced to the barn's entrance, then stepped outside, looking left then right. Turning to his right with his back hugging the wooded barn's siding, he waited until his eyes adjusted to the darkness. The moon hid behind the clouds. He holstered his gun, reached around to the other side of his belt, and unclipped a flashlight. It wasn't much, but it would have to do. He shone his light to the ground, seeing footprints in the mud. Small prints. Sarah's footprints. Adrenaline fueled the thumping of his heart, and he forgot all about his head injury.

He followed the prints, taking two steps for every one of Sarah's, jogging as the rain pelted his face and the wind continued to whistle through the cornfields along the worn path. He ignored the pounding in his head that seemed to accelerate with his heartbeat. He had to find Quinn.

Brett pressed forward, thinking of her, praying he wasn't too late. He shimmied along the path between the rows of the knee-high cornfield, hoping the guesthouse would be on the other side, the side he couldn't see from Sarah's house. She'd said it was on the grounds, so it had to be close. He squinted and waved his flashlight ahead, but all he could see was a green carpet of cornstalk leaves. He pointed it to the ground, following footprints.

After twenty yards, his shoes and uniform were drenched. Droplets trickled down his face. His head spun, his vision blurred, and he nearly slipped on the wet earth, but he wouldn't slow. Quinn's sweet face filled his thoughts, riveting him forward at a pressing pace.

The rain cooled the summer heat and stirred up the mud, creating a dirt odor. But as he neared the woods, he smelled the familiar winter scent of logs burning—one of Quinn's favorite things to do on a cold day. But why would someone build a fire on a hot summer day?

He stopped and leaned over to catch his breath, silently swearing for not staying in better shape. His chest burned from the exertion.

A wave of vertigo suddenly filled him. He swayed and held his head, squeezing his eyes shut and waiting for it to pass. When it did, he wiped the rain out of his eyes with his sleeve and plowed ahead through the rows of corn.

Finally the stalks ended, and he saw a modest home and an old model blue truck. *The* truck. His hand rested on his gun. He crept toward the house, ducking low. His head pounded. The house and the truck looked deserted.

He crouched near one of the truck's tires, listening, then released the holster's safety snap and removed his gun.

He still heard no voices.

He sidled to the front porch to where a wooden bat rested against the house. Was that what had hit him? He withdrew his weapon and peered in through the window. Lit table lamps allowed him to see inside, but the halfway-drawn drapes gave him only a limited view. He edged his body across the outside of the house, hugging the stone with his back, listening again.

Nothing.

He turned the knob, cracking open the door. Hot air billowed out. The only sound came from the rain. He kept his weapon drawn and inched his way inside, closing the door behind him. Muddy footprints smeared the floor. A fire had burned to almost ash.

He searched the home, finding only a blanket and pillow on the bathroom floor as evidence of Quinn's presence. Lifting the blanket to his nose, he thought he could smell her. Tears threatened to spill, but he choked them back. There was no time to get emotional now. His vision blurred. He gripped the sink until the dizziness subsided, closing his eyes until he felt steadier.

He let himself out the front door and circled the home, keeping his back against the house, and found footprints. Voices came from the trees. He ducked around the corner and hid.

Sarah said, "We're almost there. We'll put ice on it, and it'll feel better in no time."

Quinn cried in her raspy, hoarse voice—the one she had when she was the most upset. "I want my"—she hiccupped—"daddy."

Brett jetted out from the corner of the house, rage spreading through every nerve cell. He was right. Sarah and Dean were working together.

"Freeze!"

Sarah held Quinn. Dean followed behind. Brett wanted to run to Quinn, to take her in his arms and never let her go, but the cop in him waited. He scuttled toward the three of them and pointed the gun at Dean and then Sarah. "Put her down. Let go of her slowly. Move away from her."

Dean put his hands in the air like a bad guy in a cop show.

Sarah spoke first. "Brett, let's get her in the house and get her foot elevated. She's injured her foot."

"Do you think I'm crazy? Get away from her."

Dean dropped his hands and shouted, "She's not c-c-crazy. She's my s-s-sister. Don't talk to her like that." Spit drooled down his chin.

Sarah's forehead creased, and she licked her lips. "Brett, let me handle this so no one gets hurt." She motioned to her brother, her jaw twitching. "Dean is not himself right now." Then she did a double take at Brett and said, "Your head is bleeding. What happened?"

"Don't pretend not to know." Brett waved the gun. "I trusted you once, but not again. I'm not going to fall for your acting. For all I know you're the one who hit me. Set Quinn on the ground and move away. I'm not leaving here without her." Anger foamed like breaking waves inside him.

She shook her head. "I didn't hit you." She turned to Dean. "Did you hit him?"

Dean hung his head.

"Are you crazy?" she said to her brother. She turned to Brett. "I can't believe you think I'm a part of this. Brett, be reasonable. I'm sorry. I had no idea Dean hit you or he was involved. Not until fifteen minutes ago—when I found the backpack in the barn. I wasn't positive he had Quinn until just before you got here."

"How am I supposed to believe you? Why didn't you come tell me?" Seeing her sad eyes begging him to believe her made him dizzier. "Don't mess with my mind." He waved the gun. "Put her down!"

"I didn't stop to tell you because I wasn't sure, and I didn't think you'd understand. It's not the way it seems."

"And how does it *seem*?"

Sarah nodded to her brother. "He's upset. Our father . . ." She shook her head. "He did . . . things. Said things to Dean that he shouldn't have. Dean is not going to harm Quinn."

"Look, if that's the case, then set her down and walk away." He motioned toward Dean. "Take him into the house and call the police."

Sarah's eyes filled with tears. Dean's face lit up like the end of a cigar, and his nostrils flared. His breathing turned to panting.

Quinn whimpered, still in Sarah's arms.

Brett aimed his pistol into the air. "Now, before I shoot!"

Quinn screamed.

Dean gripped Quinn's arm in an effort to take her from Sarah. "No! Quinn is my f-f-friend. She wants to stay with me, right, Quinn?" He hugged her to him.

Quinn's eyes bulged, and she reached her hand out to Brett. "Daddy!"

Sarah spun, turning her back to Dean and causing him to lose his grip on Quinn. "Dean, do what Officer Reed says. He's a good man. A good father. Quinn loves him."

"Listen to your sister." Brett took another step toward Sarah and Quinn, who whimpered and turned her head from Brett to Dean. Dizziness swam in his head.

Sarah set Quinn on the grass and nodded for Brett to take her. She then ran toward Dean and placed her arm around his waist. "Everything is going to be okay. Shh, let me help. Let's go inside."

"You said I'm c-c-crazy. I'm not crazy."

Sarah said, "No, you're not crazy. I'm sorry I said that."

Brett swayed. Quinn's form blurred. He couldn't stand. His knees buckled. He needed to scoop Quinn into his arms, but he was seeing double.

Suddenly, Dean broke free from Sarah's embrace and bulldozed into Brett, headfirst, knocking him to the ground. The gun fell out of Brett's hand as he fell back, limp and overcome with vertigo. He couldn't move. The yard spun. But he caught a glimpse of metal.

Dean had snatched the gun.

Quinn, still lying in the grass, screamed and crawled toward her father.

Brett's vision faded to nothing.

Chapter Twenty-Seven

Sarah shrieked. Her heart fluttered. "No!"

She ran to Brett, throwing herself on the ground, covering him and wrapping her arms around Quinn. She turned to her brother, keeping her voice soft. "Dean, look at me. Don't shoot." She held out her hand. "Give me the gun. You don't want to hurt anyone. You're a good person. A brave man. But brave men know when to give up."

Quinn hiccupped a sob and choked her arms tighter around Brett's neck. "Daddy, wake up."

Sarah's chest tightened, her heart feeling like it would explode. How could she make Dean understand? There was no way out for him, but fear gripped her. Certainly he wasn't capable of shooting them?

Dean's body collapsed onto the ground ten yards away. The rain had turned to drizzle. He shook his head, and his bottom lip turned down. He held the gun limp in his lap, muttering disjointed words Sarah couldn't understand. Something like, "No one believed . . . I tried to tell . . . they s-s-said if I told I'd be sent away." Sarah crawled toward him and searched for peace in his eyes.

The crazed look was gone, but in its place was a blank stare, as if he was detached, disassociating with reality.

She had to reach him and searched for his eyes. "Dean, none of this was your fault. Dad was a bad man. But he's gone. Give me the gun." She touched his leg.

Tears ran down his cheeks, and then it was as if a lightbulb switched on, clicking him back to the present. He waved the gun at Brett. "He's just like Father. He's going to hurt her." He said the words with less force now, like he was tired. "I-I-I have to protect Quinn."

"No, Dean. Officer Reed is a good man. Not all men are bad like Dad."

He met her eyes, his brows creased as if he was confused. "But I saw him at your office that day I was washing your windows." He pointed to Brett. "I thought that's why you t-t-took Quinn away from him. I thought he was b-b-bad."

Sarah placed her hand on his shoulder. "I understand why you thought that, but it's not true. He's a good father." Rain trickled down her face. She wiped it with the back of her hand. "Dad's gone now, Dean. Let it go." She kept her eyes on the gun.

Dean laughed and raised the gun. At first he chuckled, but then his laugh grew to a loud, boisterous, booming sound, sending chills down Sarah's neck. "Do you want to know what I did to him?" He laughed again. "I whacked off his dick."

Sarah gagged, fighting nausea. Poor Dean. How had she not seen how distraught he'd been? She glued her eyes on the gun, contemplating how she could confiscate it.

"Now he won't be able to use it in hell either." Dean laughed again, a menacing, hideous sound.

Sarah glanced back toward Quinn, whose sobbing had turned to hysteria. Brett wasn't moving. He was probably unconscious. He needed to get to a hospital. Soon! Should she search for his phone? No, there wasn't time. Every move mattered. She didn't want to make any sudden or dramatic shifts. If she did she could set Dean off. She turned to him. "Give me the gun."

Brett moaned.

Dean's eyes widened. He ceased his crying and lifted the gun toward Brett. His hand shook.

Sarah screamed and reached for her brother's arm, struggling to take the gun from him, but she was no match for his strength.

Dean jerked himself from her grasp, his eyes twitching and

ricocheting in opposite directions. "I'm not st-stupid. I know what's going to h-h-happen to me." His voice hung in the air, thick like the humidity. He stood slowly, keeping the gun positioned on Brett.

Brett sat holding his head with Quinn's arms still locked around his neck. He opened his eyes and, upon seeing Dean, put his body in front of Quinn's, shielding her.

Dean, with the gun still pointed at Brett, backed away until he'd turned the corner to the front of the house, until Sarah could no longer see him.

"Dean!" Sarah scrambled to stand.

Brett, suddenly alert, reached out and clamped a hand around Sarah's ankle. "Let him go." With his other hand, he reached into his belt clip for his cell phone, squinting. "Call 911. I can't see."

Sarah shook her head, cried, and kicked at Brett, breaking free from his grasp. "No! Let me go!" But before she could stand and gain her balance, a gunshot rang out, the noise blaring and final.

She screamed. "Dean!"

#

Brett heard the shot but couldn't move. Too weak to get up, he closed his eyes and handed the phone to Quinn. "Call 911. Remember how Daddy showed you?"

Her crying slowed to hiccups, and several seconds later he heard her talking on the phone. "Please help us."

When the dizziness subsided, Quinn still lay beside him patting his face with her tiny fingers and whispering into his ear. "The police are coming, Daddy. Wake up."

She held the phone up to his ear, and an operator's voice sounded like it was coming from a place far in the distance. "Hello?"

Brett told the operator who he was as sirens howled in the distance.

Quinn's bony arms flew tight around his neck, choking him, but he didn't care. She held his shirt in tight fists, trembling, her sobs returning. "Stay awake, Daddy."

"I will." He held the phone. The operator wanted him to stay on the phone until help arrived.

Brett held Quinn, never wanting to let her go. The knot in his throat broke free, and all his pent-up tears flowed. He tasted their saltiness and breathed in Quinn's scent—dirt, mingled with a hint of maple syrup from the pancakes he'd made her days ago. So much had happened since that day. He inhaled deeply, thanking God he'd found his baby alive and safe.

He thought of Ali, and his father, and how short life was and let his tears flow. The lump in his throat broke free, and he remembered his father telling him, *"There's no reason men can't cry."*

The sound of Sarah's wailing from the front yard tore through him. He shouted, "The ambulance is on the way, Sarah. It's coming." He ached for her, wanting to go to her to hold her in her grief, but he couldn't leave Quinn. Finally, Sarah's cries quieted to gentle sobs.

Sirens blared in the distance, the sound growing closer and closer, making Brett's screaming head throb. He hoped Clay was on his way because Brett couldn't move. The rain had stopped, but the smell of burnt gunpowder lingered in the air.

He felt a hand on his arm and opened his eyes again to see flashes of multicolored lights against the trees and Clay and Officer Hudson kneeling beside him.

Clay said, "How you doing, man?"

Brett smiled. "Better now that you're here and my baby is safe. What took you so long?" He motioned to Quinn at his side, and tried to sit.

Clay rested his palm on Brett's chest. "Don't get up. The EMTs are going to lift you into the ambulance."

Several men approached with a gurney. Officer Hudson knelt at Quinn's side. "They're going to take you to the hospital too, to make sure you're okay."

"I hurt my ankle," she said, holding it.

Officer Hudson said, "Oh, I see. It looks ouchy. The doctors will fix it."

Brett said, "Don't let her out of your sight, Hudson."

"I won't. Promise."

As they lifted him to the gurney, Brett asked, "How's Sarah's brother?"

Clay shook his head. "He didn't make it."

Poor Sarah. He squeezed his eyes shut, and the tears pinched out. Oh, how he wished he could take away her pain. He thought of Ali and her death, and Dean—two lost souls, their lives warped by the cruelty of others. Why was there so much pain in the world?

#

An hour later, Brett and Quinn lay side by side in the Hursey Lake Hospital emergency room—the same place Ali had been. At Brett's insistence, the nurses had arranged for Quinn to be in the same room with him. No one could separate them now. Given the circumstances, the staff had accommodated his request.

Clay had promised that Quinn would have a full examination to determine whether she'd been molested. Brett hoped like hell she hadn't been.

He lay prone on the gurney, his head feeling as large as a pumpkin, an IV in his arm. The room smelled of alcohol swabs and disinfectant. A short gray-haired nurse dressed in light-blue scrubs with a name tag Hazel, RN, closed the curtains between their space and the next patient.

"Is my daddy going to be okay?" Quinn asked, sitting on her gurney.

Hazel smiled. "We hope so. He's in the perfect place. We're going to take care of him—get him upstairs into a room—and you can stay with him." She lightly touched Quinn's nose. "What about you? Are you going to be okay?"

Quinn nodded.

"Where does it hurt?" the nurse asked.

Quinn pointed to her ankle. "Right here. I twisted it."

Hazel examined Quinn's ankle, took her temperature, and listened to her heart. "Does anything else hurt?"

Quinn shook her head.

Brett spoke, his voice shaky. "Quinn, we need to know if anyone touched your private parts."

Quinn closed her eyes and shook her head.

Brett asked Hazel to move his gurney closer to Quinn's so he could see her. The nurse wheeled him to where he could meet Quinn's eyes. The vertigo had subsided. "I found Lambie under the bed at Mrs. Stookey's son's home. Do you want to tell me what happened there?"

Quinn bit her lip. "He wanted me to sleep with him, but I didn't want to, so I hid under the bed where he couldn't reach me."

"Did he touch you?"

She shook her head.

"Nurse Hazel is going to examine your private parts, but only because I'm here, and I'm saying it's okay."

Quinn glanced up at the nurse, who smiled. "I'll be quick and it won't hurt, I promise." She plucked a pair of rubber gloves out of a bin on a tray table and pulled them on.

After she examined Quinn, the nurse turned to Brett and smiled, shaking her head. "No bruises or any signs of forced entry."

Brett closed his eyes and sighed. *Thank you, God.*

Quinn shivered. Hazel covered her with a blanket, tucking it under her chin. "The X-ray tech will be here in a few minutes to take a picture of your ankle." She turned to Brett. "The doctor wants to admit you for observation, so as soon as we have a room we'll be transferring you up."

Brett nodded and nudged Hazel's arm. "Is Sarah Grinwald here? The sister of the man who was shot?"

Hazel shook her head. "I haven't seen her."

Poor Sarah. He longed to hold her. She'd suffered so much loss in her life. How do people move on? He wanted to apologize for believing she had been in cahoots with Dean, but he'd had to follow every lead and suspect. Certainly she would understand.

#

The next day, Brett lay in the hospital bed, his father at his side and Quinn in the bed across the room, sleeping. The drapes were drawn to keep the sun out of the room. Nurses chatted in the hallway, lunch trays clinking as the staff distributed them. Brett smelled coffee and baked chicken. His stomach growled. When was the last time he'd eaten?

His father sat in a chair next to his bed, his glasses sitting on the tip of his nose while he read his Kindle. He'd been there all night— since Brett was admitted. He wouldn't leave his side. He told Brett he'd been gone long enough and had a lot of time to make up for.

The nurse cranked Brett's bed up slowly and placed his tray in front of him. His dizziness and double vision had subsided. The pain pills had taken the edge off his throbbing headache. The CAT scans hadn't revealed any internal bleeding or skull fractures. He'd been lucky. He guessed he had a hard head.

An aide brought an extra tray of food for his father. While they ate, his father said, "I was wrong, you know."

"About what?"

"About Ali, you, your life. You did the right thing."

"No, I did the wrong thing. I should have listened to you. Maybe if I'd never married Ali she'd be alive right now, and Quinn would be living with a stable family."

"Ali would have aborted her."

Brett nodded. "Maybe. But maybe not. We'll never know. But look at this mess." Brett waved his arms, pointing at himself and the hospital room.

His father's eyes misted as he skimmed the room and looked back at Brett. "All I see is you and Quinn, and what's not to love about that? I was selfish. I wanted you to myself, in the business, successful. I had so many hopes and dreams for you, but they were *my* dreams. Not yours. I was embarrassed in front of my colleagues because I'd bragged about you for so many years—that you'd be the best attorney in our group." He paused. "I never wanted you to be a cop because I never respected them."

His father exhaled and shook his head. "I do now. I respect you. You're a cop because you love it, and it's what you're good at. You chose it because you wanted to do the right thing—the unselfish thing—for an unborn child. You wanted to give her the best life possible. You took responsibility—which is more than many young people do today."

His father's face seemed to relax as he spoke, as if he'd wanted to tell Brett these words for a long time. "I needed to let you go, to become Brett, but I didn't see that at the time."

"What changed?"

His father took his bifocals off and folded them, then set them on the lunch tray. "Watching you. Getting older. Knowing life is too short."

"Your cancer?"

His father nodded. "Yeah, coming face-to-face with my mortality definitely played a part."

"I'm sorry for what you're going through." Brett reached for his dad's hand. "You're still here though, and so am I, and we're going to make up for lost time. Forget the past. We'll only look forward."

He gave his dad's hand a squeeze. "You're wrong about one thing. I don't like being a cop. Shoot, I hate obeying the rules, especially when people's lives are at stake. And I get lost all the time."

His father smiled.

"I still have dreams of being in the courtroom, and I wouldn't get lost there."

They both laughed.

Chapter Twenty-Eight

Sarah stopped in the hospital's gift shop, the smell of carnations and roses filling the room. She bought a stuffed horse and a box of chocolates, and took the elevator up to the fourth floor, where its doors opened with a *clunk*. She sighed, nervously. She'd hesitated a thousand times before finally mustering the courage to visit Brett and Quinn. She had to know if they were okay, if Brett would talk to her. She couldn't sleep until she knew, and even then it would be difficult. Her eyes were puffy, and they stung from crying. Did he still blame her for her brother's actions? Did he still think she had protected Dean the entire time?

She stood in the doorway of room 404 and heaved in a big breath, licking her lips. Her boots clicked on the tile as she entered. Quinn lay in the dark room in a bed to Sarah's right, sleeping. Brett lay with his head raised on the opposite side of the room with his eyes closed. His father, who sat at Brett's side reading, turned to her. He motioned for her to come in and take his seat.

"No, don't get up. I'll just leave these and go." She motioned to her gifts.

Brett's eyes opened. He smiled. "Hi." He reached for her hand.

His father closed his Kindle case and said, "I'm going to go get a cup of coffee."

After he left the room, Sarah set the chocolates and the stuffed horse on the bedside tray. Brett took her hand. She sat in the chair next to him, her hand trembling in his. "How are you doing?"

Brett nodded. "Better. My headache is almost gone." He squeezed her hand and let it go. "I'm glad you came. How are you?"

She dropped her eyes to her lap. "I needed to know if you hated me, or Dean."

"I don't hate you or your brother."

She met his eyes. "I can't believe he's gone. Forever. Just like that. He was such a kind little boy. He didn't understand. He always wanted to protect me, protect Mom. I should have seen he was troubled." She looked over at Quinn. "I'm sorry he took her."

Brett squeezed her arm. "It's not your fault. It's over. She's safe now. If he hadn't taken her from that pervert's house that night, she might have been assaulted for who knows how long. He saved her."

Her lip quivered. "Really? Moore hadn't harmed her?"

Brett nodded. "The exam confirmed she hadn't been touched. Quinn said she'd hidden under the bed."

Sarah sighed and placed her hand on her heart. "Thank goodness. That makes me feel a little better. Dean would never have harmed her. He wasn't cruel like that. He thought he was protecting her from you—something he was never able to do at home—protect me from Dad." She pressed a tissue into her palm.

"I know. It's okay. You don't have to explain."

She shook her head. "No, I need to get this out. Please?"

He nodded for her to go ahead.

"When Mom was alive I never suspected anything was *wrong* with Dean. It wasn't until Mom died that Father teased him all the time. Dean was slow to talk, and when he finally started talking, he stuttered. I always thought Dean was just a socially blind boy who had no friends.

"But once he began to read, I'd bring him library books about animals. He was shy but hyper-focused on learning about dogs, cats, horses. By the time he was ten, he knew every dog and cat breed, what they looked like, and where they originated. By the time he was seventeen he knew how to neuter and spay them from studying books on the procedures. For a while he was fixated on watching video after video of animal procedures."

She shook her head. "He was fifteen when I left for college. I promised to visit him, but returning home wasn't a high priority. I knew Doc Spear was looking out for him—had practically adopted him. I thought he'd be okay." Her lower lip trembled. She bit it. "I didn't return home for almost six months. That's when I found Dean at the cabin curled in a little ball in the corner, rocking. I think he'd been there for days. Facial hair had grown on his face, and he'd soiled his clothes. I sat on the floor rocking him."

She stared at her hands, unable to meet Brett's eyes. "He latched onto me like a child who'd seen a ghost. When I helped him out of his soiled clothes, I saw his wounds. The marks on his back, the blood in his underwear, the bruises on his buttocks. I screamed, 'Who did this to you?' But I knew. I'd had the same bruises."

Brett exhaled, and with the tip of his finger guided her chin, forcing her to meet his eyes. "I'm so sorry for what you and Dean went through. I can't imagine how difficult your lives were. And I'm sorry he's gone."

"Thank you." She stared into his deep-blue eyes, his sympathy freeing her from her anguish, causing a knot to form in her throat. She blotted her tears with the Kleenex. "I thought he'd learned how to channel his anger by working with animals, caring for them in a positive way. Doc Spear had kept him busy at the clinic." She shook her head. "I should have realized sooner that he'd *lost* it."

He leaned toward her, his voice just above a whisper. "You're not God. How could you have known?"

"I was so busy I hadn't taken the time to see him and talk to him after Dad died. He'd been quiet after the funeral, but I thought it was because he didn't care. He was unemotional, which was normal for him." Tears fell, and she looked over at Quinn again. "He would have done anything for me."

"He loved you. Don't blame yourself." Brett pulled her toward him and wrapped her in his arms, holding her tight.

She hugged him in return, savoring the warmth and strength of his arms, her fingers touching his bare back, the part where his hospital gown had gaped open. She hiccupped a sob, finally releasing her pent-up sorrow.

He reached for a tissue on the table tray and wiped her tears, meeting her eyes. "Quinn had an exam. That pervert Moore never touched her." The palm of his hand rested on her cheek, and his thumb traced her bottom lip. "She's okay."

Sarah's lip quivered from his touch. "Thank God."

#

He wanted to console her, to let her know things would be okay. He wanted to kiss her. Moving his hand away from her cheek, he reached for a strand of hair that had fallen onto her face and brushed it away.

She shuddered, her eyes meeting his.

He drew her closer to him, her breath so close it tickled his nose. Would she let him kiss her? She wasn't backing away. She was close enough that he could see the speck of gold in her brown eyes and the fullness of her lips, and smell the scent of her lavender perfume. Her cheeks flushed. His heartbeat thundered in double-time.

Her closeness stirred sensations in him he hadn't felt in years. The parts of his body where her hands had rested tingled. He touched her bottom lip with his finger. She shuddered again, her lips parted, she closed her eyes, and leaned into him. He pressed his lips to hers, drinking and tasting the tangy morsel of hope she offered him. Maybe they could have a future together.

The tension of the last few weeks melted away. He forgot everything except for the way Sarah felt in his arms, filling them with a void he'd needed to have filled for a long time. She moaned. He held her tighter before slowly releasing her.

They broke apart and stared into each other's eyes, speaking at the same time.

She said, "I better go."

He said, "Can I see you again soon?"

She smiled and suddenly looked shy. "I'll be at your custody hearing on Tuesday."

He smiled. "Let's hope the judge likes me this time."

"She will."

A man's voice sounded from the doorway. "Can I come in?" Chief Dunson.

Sarah turned to him. "Please, come in. I was just leaving."

The chief stopped short when he saw Sarah. A faint gasp escaped from his lips, and the blood seemed to drain from his face.

Brett said, "Sarah Grinwald, this is Chief Dunson. Chief, I

believe you knew Sarah's mother, Rebecca Samuel."

Chief approached Sarah with his hand outstretched. He took her hand in both of his, his eyes not leaving Sarah's. "I knew her as Rebecca Wright. You look like her. Forgive me for staring."

"You knew my mother?"

He smiled, still holding her hand. "I wanted to marry her, but that was a long time ago."

"I don't know what to say," Sarah said. "I never knew."

The chief finally released her hand. "She was one of the best things that ever happened to me."

"Really? I'd love to hear about that sometime. I don't know much about her childhood."

"Oh, I could tell you all kinds of stories." He chuckled. "We went to high school together."

Sarah smiled. "That's amazing. What a small world."

"We'll have lunch sometime." He finally turned to Brett as if remembering why he'd come.

"I'd like that," she said, and turned, waving one last time to Brett.

#

Brett drove his cruiser down Main Street, talking to himself. Quinn sat in the backseat playing the bubble game on his iPad. "I could have sworn the funeral home was here on this corner." He continued driving to the next light. Cox Street. Where was it? Then it dawned on him—the funeral home was at Market and Main.

Sheesh, he could get lost in a bag. At least he was early.

He'd never taken Quinn to a funeral home before, and he hesitated about bringing her now. Would she be too traumatized knowing her mother was in the casket? At least Ali's mother had decided to keep it closed. She wanted family to remember Ali the way she'd looked before the accident. His parents had thought it would be healthy for Quinn to go to the service before the funeral to say her good-byes.

But as he parked the car, he hesitated, reluctant to confront Ali's death. He sighed heavily and turned to the backseat. "You ready?"

Quinn nodded without taking her eyes off the iPad. "Wait, let me pop a few more bubbles first. I'm trying to beat my score."

Brett turned in his seat to watch her, knowing she was putting on a front, trying to act brave. "It's okay to be sad. You can cry today."

She pressed the Off button, looked at him, and tears welled in her eyes. "I'm scared. I don't want to see her."

"That's normal to feel that way." He patted her knee. "Her casket is closed. See a picture of her in your mind. Remember her that way. This is your chance to say good-bye."

"Can I bring Lambie in?"

"Absolutely."

She handed him the iPad and gathered the worn lamb under her arm.

She refused to go anywhere without the stuffed animal. Brett understood. She'd gone through a lot, so if Lambie helped her cope, all the more reason to keep him around. Once upon a time he would have turned red carrying it, but not now. He was all about being Mr. Mom, and he didn't give a rip what he looked like.

He hiked Quinn into his arms. With her ankle wrapped, he carried her everywhere. Part of the reason was he didn't want to let her out of his sight, but the other part was that it was faster to carry her than for her to use the crutches.

He and Quinn were the first to arrive. A billboard at the entrance listed the names of the deceased. Ali's name was there, but so was Dean's. Hursey Lake only had one funeral home, so it made sense that both viewings would be at the same place.

Brett's stomach tumbled at the thought of seeing Sarah again.

Mrs. Greer had arranged a photo board for pictures and mementos of Ali, which sat on the table at the entrance of the viewing room.

Brett held Quinn in front of the collage display of Ali's life. They surveyed pictures of her as a plump infant, taking her first baby steps, learning to ride a bike, on Christmas morning as a teen, and in the delivery room with Quinn.

The same smile lit her face in almost every shot. In her younger photos she showed no restraint, smiling openly, innocence displayed in the dimples of her cheeks. But as she grew, her smile changed and became more guarded. She lost the confident look, and in its place was an angry and insecure Ali. Most people wouldn't have noticed, but Brett had lived with her injured look for a long time. He saw it in the way she held her head and rounded her shoulders. If he closed his eyes, he could hear it in the vagueness of her dialogue too.

He couldn't believe her life was over.

Quinn's eyes filled with tears. "I miss Mommy."

"I know, sweetie." He wiped the tears off her cheeks with the back of his hand. "I know."

He took her to the little room off to the side of the viewing area, the one for families of the deceased, and settled her in a chair, elevating her leg, and handed her the iPad.

His parents arrived and entered the kitchen. His mother held several aluminum foil pans full of lunch meats and potato salad. She placed one in front of Quinn on the table. The room smelled of turkey and Swiss cheese. "You'll be here awhile today; you'll need energy to keep you going."

"Thanks, Mom." Brett kissed her on the cheek.

His father pulled up a chair next to Quinn. "What game are you playing?"

"The bubble game. You have to pop the bubbles before they fall. You count your points."

"Do you think I could learn how to play it?"

Quinn giggled. "Yes. It's not hard. Do you want me to teach you?"

Brett watched as his father pulled up a chair next to Quinn, amazed at how easy it was for his father to talk to her. He wasn't sure why it surprised him, though. After all, his father had played all those board games with him when he was a kid.

Brett's mother slipped her arm around Brett. "Ali's family is here. Are you ready?"

Brett nodded and took a deep breath hoping he'd be able to stay calm in front of Mrs. Greer and Mark. Seeing them without Ali nearby would feel surreal. He coughed to clear the lump in his throat.

#

Two hours later, after most of the visitors were gone, Brett snuck out of Ali's parlor, confident Quinn was okay. She'd taken Ali's death better than he thought she would. When friends and family paid their last respects, they'd hugged Quinn and cried. A dry-eyed Quinn told them she'd see her mother in heaven someday. It was as if she was trying to stay strong for other people.

Brett headed to Dean's viewing area at the end of the building. He stood in the doorway watching Sarah say good-bye to the last of her friends who were paying their respects. There were only about a dozen flower arrangements adorning the room. Brett doubted Dean had had many friends.

He watched Sarah without her knowing. She tucked her long hair behind one ear, exposing her slender face. A high heel dangled from her foot as she shifted from one leg to the other. Standing all day took its toll; his feet ached too. The dark circles under her eyes made him want to scoop her up in his arms and take the pain away. When she turned to him, his heartbeat quickened and his lips went dry. He wished he could take away the sadness in her eyes—the same sorrowful gaze he'd seen in the painting of her mother.

Sometimes life wasn't fair. Obviously her father must have been a demon for Dean to do what he'd done. How could Brett have been so stubborn with his own father, a man who'd never hit him or abused him but had only wanted the best for him?

He wanted to believe that the tragedy would bring him closer to Sarah. Maybe in time it would. They'd suffered a tragedy together. No one could ever take away that connection. He understood what had happened to her better than anyone. And she understood him. He didn't want to dwell on it, but it comforted him to know that they'd always have a connection.

All her guests had finally gone. She leaned against the casket with her hand on top, dropping her foot out of the heel of her shoe again. He made his way toward her, eager to gaze into her eyes, express his condolences again.

He gulped down the thick knot in his throat and approached her, gently placing his hand on the small of her back. She turned to him, her eyes searching his. "Hi."

He took her hand and led her toward him, pulling her into his arms. He drank in the softness of her body, her fragrance—subtle, sensual, and clean.

At first, she tensed.

He locked his eyes onto hers, their mouths inches apart. "I'm really sorry for your loss." He embraced her again and felt her gradually relax until finally she hugged him back, and a sob escaped from somewhere deep inside her.

"Thanks. I'm sorry for yours too." She released her embrace and gazed at Dean's shiny ivory casket. "Abuse sucks, you know? People all over the world suffer from the fallout of horrible, stupid parents." She paused. "Helping women deal with the trauma it causes helps."

Brett took her into his arms again, and this time held her tighter, feeling her body relax. He looked into her eyes. "Quinn wants to see you."

She smiled. "She does?"

Brett nodded. "Absolutely." He smiled. "And your horse too." He reached up behind her back and played with the hair that tumbled there. "She asked if she and Sadie could come to your farm to ride."

She chuckled. "Really? Who's Sadie?"

"The little girl from the foster home. Quinn said her parents died in a fire."

Sarah furrowed her brows. "How tragic."

Their faces were inches apart. "Bring the girls. They can both ride Beauty." She sounded breathless, her voice low and throaty.

He bent his head toward her neck, his arm around her back, pressing her body to his, and feeling the strength and the softness of her small frame. He buried his face into her hair, smelling the coconut fragrance and wishing he could hold her for hours. She felt right in his arms, like she belonged there. Why was it when people were totally broken they seemed to be able to hold each other with so much more passion?

Chapter Twenty-Nine

Sarah trembled as she turned the corner downtown in front of Hursey Lake's courthouse. Was she ready to see Brett again? No, but she'd promised to attend the hearing, and she wanted to, but her nerves were raw. Ever since the kiss she hadn't been able to get Brett out of her mind. It had changed everything. She wanted to pursue a relationship with him, but maybe the kiss hadn't meant the same to him. Had he only been consoling her, or did he want more?

She spotted him holding Quinn's hand outside the justice building. Her stomach fluttered at the sight of him in his dark suit. He looked younger and more handsome than in his uniform. He smiled at her and Quinn waved.

Was she late? She glanced at her watch. No, the hearing didn't start for another ten minutes.

Perspiration lined her brow. She hadn't wanted to leave her house, still numb from Dean's death and all that had happened. She didn't want to show her face around town either, but she wanted to make sure Brett was granted permanent custody of Quinn.

She joined them on the sidewalk. Brett's blue eyes twinkled. He took a step forward as if to embrace her, but hesitated and said, "Thanks for coming." His warm breath tickled her ear, and she smelled the scent of his earthy pine cologne. The sound of cars rushing by and people on the sidewalk reminded her that they were standing in public view, so she took a step back even though she wanted to feel him in her arms and tell him how glad she was to be there. But she couldn't speak. Swallowing, she moistened her dry mouth.

When Quinn took her hand and led her skipping into the building, Sarah relaxed. Kids had a way of seeming to forget so easily. They didn't belabor over events they couldn't change.

Quinn looked up at Sarah, her dark curls bouncing in rhythm to her step. "I'm sorry about your brother."

Sarah's heart fisted. What a sweet child. She squeezed Quinn's hand, thankful for her sympathy and lack of inhibition. "Thanks, Quinn. I miss him." Sarah turned and met Brett's eyes, realizing he'd watched the exchange, and felt her cheeks grow warm.

Quinn said, "I miss my mom too."

Sarah squeezed Quinn's hand. "I'm sorry for your loss too."

The child pouted. "Thanks. I'll see her again in heaven someday."

"You will."

Mr. and Mrs. Reed greeted them inside. Brett introduced her as Dr. Sarah Grinwald, as they'd never officially met. He didn't mention that she'd been the counselor working with CPS on his custody case. But she was certain they knew—they probably remembered her from the press release.

Brett's parents shook Sarah's hand. His mother smiled at her. "Wow, you're a doctor? You seem so young. You must be an intelligent woman." She winked. "I'm happy to meet you."

Sarah smiled. "Happy to meet you too." She was sure his parents knew about Dean. It had been all over the news, but neither mentioned him or what had happened. For that she was grateful.

Mr. Reed turned toward Brett and explained what would happen once they were inside the courtroom. They waited in a gathering space until Brett's case was called.

In the courtroom, Sarah sat between Mrs. Reed and Quinn in the first row directly behind Brett and his father, resting her hands in her lap, holding them together to keep them from shaking. The circular room seemed large with just the five of them there. The judge's seat was positioned in front to the left of the room, elevated two steps from where the rest of them sat. Rows and rows of seats behind Sarah were empty.

When Judge Mary Mason entered, everyone stood. She directed a nod toward Brett and the others in the room, and sat. A court recorder sat to her left, her eyes cast down to her keyboard.

Judge Mason narrated the case to the recorder. Sarah heard bits and pieces. "Brett Reed, daughter Quinn, wife deceased, anger management classes . . ." The sound of the judge's voice droned on. Sarah fell lost in thought.

What would have happened if Dean hadn't taken his life? Would they be in this courtroom at some point fighting for his freedom? She trembled at the thought. He would have had to do time in prison or in an institution. She was certain he wouldn't have lived through either. He'd probably known it too, which was probably why he'd chosen to end his life.

She didn't want to think about Dean and what might have happened. She heard the judge mention her name, Peggy's, CPS, their assessment of Brett as a parent, and their petition to grant him as Quinn's permanent custodial parent.

Judge Mason asked Brett several questions about the size of his home. Brett explained that he'd moved into Ali's house since the rental contract was in his name, and Quinn had been staying with his parents until the custody hearing was over. If he was granted custody, Quinn would move back to her original house and have her own bedroom. The home was larger than his apartment. The judge inquired about the anger management classes, and Brett assured her that he'd finish them. Finally, the judge expressed condolences in the death of Brett's ex-wife. She read the statement of Brett's rights and finally granted him custody.

When the judge pounded her gavel, Sarah snapped back to the present, leaving her memories of Dean behind.

Quinn squealed and squeezed Sarah's hand. The child bolted from her chair and sprang into her father's arms. He lifted her and kissed the top of her head. "You're all mine, baby." He closed his eyes and opened them, settling them on Sarah. He mouthed, "Thank you."

Chapter Thirty

A week later, Brett was standing at his apartment door holding several moving boxes, trying to find his key. He'd come to load up his things. He hadn't been to his apartment since the day Ali was there, before her accident, the day after CPS had done their assessment.

His landlady, Mrs. Rozella, walked toward him, carrying a mop and a bucket, the smell of bleach permeating the air. She set her bucket down. "I haven't seen you for a while, Officer Reed. A few weeks ago a woman was here looking for you. She said she was your wife."

"My wife?" He cocked his head.

She nodded. "She had an envelope in her hand and asked me if I could let her in. She said she'd forgotten to give something to you." Mrs. Rozella's bifocals slipped down to the bottom of her nose. She pushed them up. "I couldn't let her in your apartment on account of the law, and I didn't want to be responsible for no letter—or whatever she had in that envelope. I told her to slide it under the door, so she did. I waited until she drove off, making sure there was no monkey business going on—like her breaking into your place or something. We don't want no trouble here."

"Thanks." His voice quivered. Why had Ali come here?

Mrs. Rozella nodded, picked up her bucket, and continued to the apartment next door.

Brett turned his key in the lock and let himself in, searching the ground for the envelope. Sure enough, it lay inside the threshold of the door, his name scribbled in Ali's handwriting on the top. He leaned the boxes against the wall, retrieved the letter, and shut the door.

He sat on the edge of his bed, the envelope in his hand. The moment felt surreal. Ali was no longer living, yet he held a piece of her in his hands. His heart plummeted. Why hadn't she given him the envelope the day she came to see him? He tore it open and read.

Dear Brett,

At first, I packed to leave. I thought I'd take Quinn with me too. Run away. Start over. But where would I go? I can't escape myself. Who am I kidding?

Instead, I dropped my clothes off at the shelter for abused women. I left Quinn's at my mother's.

There's only one out for me. I know what I must do.

I always wanted to be a good mother and live with a man who would be a father to my child. Something I never had. I thought if I had your love my life would be complete. I'd no longer feel the pain.

I was wrong.

I had everything I ever wanted with you and look at me. I'm a mess. I don't understand why God made me this way—why I can't focus on anything, why I'm sad all the time, why booze or drugs are the only things that can take away the pain. I want silence, no more noise, no more voices in my head.

I'm a failure.

You were right. What kind of mother neglects her child? A bad one. I can't believe I locked Quinn in her room and didn't remember. There's something wrong with me. Everything stresses me out. Other women aren't like me.

I'm freeing you, Brett, so you don't feel trapped anymore. You never deserved me. Do what you've always wanted to do. Go to law school. You'd make a great attorney.

People don't understand what I feel because they can't see the pain on my face. But inside, sometimes in my head, sometimes in my body, it hurts and it doesn't go away. It follows me. I can't escape it. That's why I don't want to wake up some days. The pain is unbearable.

I hope you understand why I'm doing this. Don't blame yourself. You aren't causing me to do this. You have given me so much. Thank you.

Quinn will be better without me too. Maybe you'll fall in love with someone who will be a better mother. I can't do this anymore. I don't have the energy. Take care of Quinn. I know you will. You're a good father.

Please don't grieve for me. I hope you forgive me.

Love, Ali

So the accident had been premeditated? Ali had wanted to die? Brett rubbed his face. What did this change? Nothing. Did it change the way he felt? No.

Maybe he could have talked her out of taking the drugs and crashing the car, but he'd never know. What he did know was that he could never have changed her. He'd tried.

He shook his head, but didn't cry. He had no more tears.

#

Six months later

Beauty, Sarah's horse, trotted in the sandy arena, bucking and prancing for her audience. Quinn and Sadie giggled at the gate, stepping on the first rung of the post and leaning into the corral, wearing hats and scarves. The fresh air of a late winter's day surrounded Sarah's farm, leftover snow melting in the dirt. The grass showed its face, reminding Brett of life and how things thaw, grow, and change.

Sarah smiled at the girls from inside the arena, where she lunged Beauty in circles. "She's almost got the wiggles out of her, girls. Do you want to paint your handprints on her sides today?"

The girls squealed in unison. "Yes!"

Brett, with his elbows on the fence, watched Sarah. The sun winked at them, half hidden behind the clouds, reminding him that somehow, even after the grayest days of winter, or tragedy, the sun rises.

Sarah's farm no longer caused him anxiety over what they'd been through. Since Quinn's custody case, he and Sarah had shared new, happy memories on the farm. They never forgot what had happened, but every day that passed made it easier.

He scanned the farm's golden pastures and knew that in a few months, when spring came, the pastures would turn green again. It reminded him of how his life had been reborn. Good things had come out of the bad, like Sadie's life.

He patted her head. "How's the new baby brother?"

Sadie turned and smiled at him, her jack-o'-lantern smile budding with new teeth. "He cries a lot, but my new mom lets me feed him, and he stops. Mom says he likes me."

Quinn shot Brett a look. "I wish I had a little brother or sister." She winked and motioned toward Sarah.

He chuckled. "Uh, Quinn, *not-so-subtle* Quinn, you don't know what you're wishing for."

Sadie's eyebrows lifted. "He's right. You don't get near as much attention when the baby comes. He takes up a lot of my mom's time."

The girls turned to watch Sarah again, their arms wrapped around each other.

Shortly after the custody hearing, Quinn had wanted to see Sadie. Brett asked Sarah to look into her case. When she confirmed that Sadie's parents had perished in a fire, Brett set out to find her an adoptive family. Sarah knew a young couple from her church who'd been praying for a child. Through Brett's father's connections, they'd made it possible for Sadie to be adopted into their home.

Shortly after the custody hearing, Brett enrolled in training to become a CASA volunteer, a court-appointed person whose sole purpose was to be an advocate for children who didn't have a voice in the system. As a volunteer, he got to meet everyone involved in a child's life, including their family members, teachers, doctors, lawyers, and social workers. He gathered information and made recommendations. One of his goals was to help decent fathers get custody of their children, whereas they might not.

It had taken him a long time to see the good in what had happened. Walking through the muck of despair and making it to the other side had taken its toll on him, but now he saw it, because he'd taken the time to look. He took time to reflect and saw the good as plain as seeing the sun. He only had to open his eyes to see God's brightness, and his heart to feel his warmth and consistency.

Brett saw God's goodness in the smiles of strangers, the music in a bird's song, the joy in a baby's cry, the way Quinn's smile resembled Ali's, and the sorrowful glint in Sarah's eyes.

Sarah winked at him and motioned for the girls to come in the arena. As they played with Beauty and finger-painted her sides, Sarah joined Brett at the fence and locked her hand into his. He smelled the leather from her boots and the mint of her gum as she leaned into him and kissed his cheek. "It's so nice to have them here."

"What about me?" he teased.

She chuckled. "It's nice to have you here too."

He wrapped his arms around her, and she smiled, showing him the warmth swelling inside her. He squeezed her close. "Not half as nice as having you in my arms."

THE END

Michelle Weidenbenner is a full time suspense writer and blogger at Random Writing Rants where she teaches teens and adults how to get published. When she's not writing she's winning ugly on the tennis court.

Her other books include:

Scattered Links
Éclair Goes to Stella's

Message from Michelle

Thanks for investing your time in reading my book. I'd love to hear from you. Follow me on Twitter @MWeidenbenner or on FB at: http://www.facebook.com/randomwritingrants
My email address is: mweidenbennerauthor@gmail.com

If you enjoyed reading CACHE A PREDATOR will you please take a few minutes to leave a review?

"I can't write without a reader. It's precisely like a kiss—you can't do it alone."
— John Cheever

I appreciate all my readers. Thank you.

Suggested Reading
Other Books You Might Enjoy

Over the Edge: A Novel, by Brandilyn Collins
Gone Girl: A Novel by Gillian Flynn
Best Kept Secrets by Sandra Brown
If I Stay by Gayle Forman
Murder Takes Time by Giacomo Giammatteo
Wonder by R. J. Palacio